A
Shoeshine
Kill

Also by Grant Tracey

Neon Kiss

Five Hard Bites

A Fourth Face

Cheap Amusements

Toronto, 1965: Cheap Amusements' Beat

Final Stanzas

Lovers & Strangers

Playing Mac: A Novella in Two Acts,
and Other Stories

Parallel Lines and the Hockey Universe

PRAISE FOR GRANT TRACEY'S FICTION

The Hayden Fuller Mysteries

"Lyrical, hard-edged prose, hard-hitting NHL action and even harder-hitting plots . . . The Hayden Fuller Mysteries deserve a wide readership in both Canada and the U.S."
— Brady Harrison, winner of the High Plains Book Award

"[Grant's novels are] a coaster ride through a rough and tumble Toronto, with a tough ex-Maple Leaf turned PI. Grant Tracey gives a winking tip of his porkpie hat to Spillane, the '60s, and film noir, body checking his readers into romance, unsavory thugs, sullied sex, and great detection. A fun thriller, and thrilling fun."
— Thomas Fox Averill, author of *Secrets of the Tsil Cafe*

"Grant Tracey has somehow managed to combine the gutsiness of Lawrence Block, the hockey acumen of Travis Yost and a deep-down love for his characters that rivals Bernard Malamud's. [His novels are] remarkable and thrilling."
— Mike Antosia, author of *Entrance and Exit*

"Sexploitation, hidden cameras, relaxation therapy in the Tangerine Room, murder, corruption in the NHL, a kingpin to complicate matters—and an ex-Toronto Maple Leaf in a porkpie hat to sort everything out. [It's] a lot of fun."
— Robert Hellenga, author of *The Italian Lover*

"[Grant Tracey's books are] rich in historic Toronto details. And [his writing] is especially atmospheric when it's about the hockey jones that the narrator/detective shares with other characters. Tracey's strong narrative voice gets us through the complex plot and scores heavily. . . ."
— G. W. Clift, author of *Everything I Learned by Age Forty*

The Literary Stories

"With the compelling force of cinema, these stories pull us across geographical and emotional borders into the deepest recesses of the heart. [The style] is fine and moving. . . ."
— Steven Schwartz, author of *Little Raw Souls*

"Tracey's knowledge of music, film, TV shows, plays, and literature infuses [his work] at every turn, much to the reader's delight."
— Susan Jackson Rodgers, author of *Ex-Boyfriend on Aisle 6*

A SHOESHINE KILL

GRANT TRACEY

A HAYDEN FULLER MYSTERY

TWELVE WINTERS
a literary project

*For my mother and father who taught me a love of country
and, more importantly,
a passion for the greatest game of all, hockey*

The author would like to thank editor Michael Bracken and Down & Out Books for publishing a small portion of *A Shoeshine Kill* as "Four on the Floor" in *Groovy Gumshoes: Private Eyes in the Psychedelic Sixties*, and editor Andrew Hook and Head Shot for publishing the Eddie Sands story "A Stretch of Ground" in *Bang!: An Anthology of Modern Noir Fiction*.

The author also thanks the following journals for initially publishing the three additional Eddie Sands stories that close out this collection: *Freedom Fiction Journal* ("This Town Called Winsome"); *Mag Pie* magazine ("A Cap for Tom"); and *The Museum of Americana: A Literary Review* ("Artifacts").

Contents

It was done. It was over.
We accomplished what we started.
And it will never. Be. The same. Again—
—PHIL ESPOSITO
ON TEAM CANADA 72'S VICTORY, 1997

A SHOESHINE KILL

Game One

Monday, September 2, 1972

Johnny Buckets and I stood outside his hotdog stand at Front Street and Union Station, talking hockey.

We all called him Buckets because Johnny wore cargo pants and those damn side pockets were always packed with everything from loose change, gasoline company credit cards, a transistor radio, shot glasses from Niagara Falls, flashlights, and the occasional bottle of beer. It was as if buckets of well water were attached to his thighs. "I don't think the commies will win a single game." He raised a tobacco-stained finger. "Not a one."

The sun was high and I was shielding my eyes. "Beddoes says if the Russians win game one he'll eat his column with a bowl of borscht in front of their embassy."

"We'll kill them. Canadians are the greatest hockey players in the world. We all know that, Fuller, and this is our chance to prove it, our NHL pros versus their so-called amateurs who live on the government dole. Damn, you saw them skate around the rink in their dinky, wafer-thin helmets, and hand-me-downs from a PeeWee club. Amateur hour, man."

"Red Fisher has us winning six games." It was an eight-game series. Four in Canada; four in Moscow. Game one was tonight from Montreal. My dog was loaded with onions, green olives, and mustard. I took a big bite. "I don't like ketchup on a dog," I mumbled.

"Neither do folks in Chicago." Johnny rubbed at his chapped

lower lip. It was the size of a leech. "Still remember that goal you notched against the Blackhawks to win the Cup, 1962."

That was ten years ago. I'm thirty-seven now and have a kid, Connie. "Did you read Robertson's column? He's got the Russians winning six games—six!"

"Why doesn't he move to Russia—goddamn traitor."

"He's a good writer." And he knew his hockey and I couldn't help but wonder if we all were being conned, set up. When the arrows in a narrative point in one direction (Canada will kick their asses) I get a little nervous. Russia had been winning world championships since the early 1950s. "They won the last three Olympics. What did we really know about them? I have an eerie feeling."

"You're a detective, you live in a world of *feelings*." He emphasized the latter word and shook his head with disapproval.

I chuckled mildly. Johnny's whole tirade against "the commies" was based on feelings. "You don't have a crystal ball in those pockets, do you?"

"No. Wouldn't fit." He smiled, eyes widening. His teeth were orange and some were missing. "Call me Nostra fucking Damas," he said.

That cracked me up.

"How's the wife and kid?"

"Good, good."

"Working on anything?"

"Yeah, a young high school kid's meeting me in my office as soon as school gets out." I glanced at my Timex. "About an hour. The shoeshine kill—"

"Christ—the shoeshine kill." He shook his head. "I grew up around that neighborhood. Regent Park." Johnny looked at his shoes.

"Me too—Cabbagetown."

We all had been reading about it for five days: sixteen-year-old-shoeshine boy Orlando Prescott stuffed down a roof duct on Charles Street, cigarette burns tattooing his naked body. The ends of his fingernails were chipped down, dusty pulp of silica from limestone found under his fingers.

One of the dailies said he was sodomized.

Orly was a product of the Regent Park housing district, crowded with other immigrants from the islands and Eastern Europe in little boxes. Orly was troubled, the papers said, and ran with sulky youth gangs. *The Toronto Star* labeled Orly a hustler; traces of cocaine were found in his shine box. *The Globe and Mail* hinted that the kid may have been hustling sexual favors, turning tricks with the homosexual crowd at Yonge and Charles.

I didn't know what to think, but fifteen-year-old Abby Munro needed to talk to me, the newspapers had it all wrong, she insisted. I asked her directly, why me. "Did you like the sound of my name or something?"

"No," she said. "Three reasons: First, you grew up in a similar neighborhood, so you understand what is was to be a kid with my kind of background; second, your revelations about surviving sexual abuse as a child. I read all about it in the pages of *The Star* when I was only ten and it was really brave of you and a broken man is a man who cares; third, you were my favorite hockey player when you played for the Leafs. You never took a shift off."

"I appreciated that," I said and noted how polite she was over the phone—no guile, no phony nuance, just direct and honest. But she was just a kid. How could she afford my rate, forty dollars a day? My wife's a reporter so I could do a little pro-bono work, I guess. Anyway, I'd talk to her.

Orly's death shook me up pretty good. Sixteen. Tortured. Sexually assaulted.

Suddenly, a '69 Valiant barreled toward me, its grill resembling the face of a snarling shark.

"Fuck—!" Johnny screamed as I leaped clear, and the hot

dog cart crumpled and hammered into metal pieces that flashed in the air. The car then crunched a mailbox before stopping abruptly in front of Union Station. A hollow pole of a streetlight covered the car like a bent Q-tip.

"You okay," I shouted in Buckets's direction.

"My fucking cart isn't—"

I ran toward the Valiant, my face peppered with shrapnel scratches, the sun sparkling off the sidewalk in small star points.

The driver staggered in my direction. He was fortyish, a big fella, with dusty blond hair and nowhere eyes. He wore briefs. Nothing else. A perforated snake line cut across his body. He struggled to hold in his guts, and then he fell.

There was no color in his face, and within seconds there were no breaths on his lips either.

"TROUBLE FOLLOWS YOU AROUND, Superstar." My pal Sal Lambertino, Toronto's top cop in his Sloan Wilson grays, rubbed at the picket fencing of a Hemingway beard.

"It sure does." The sun was three o'clock high and a headache was blackening behind my eyes.

"Know this guy?"

I shrugged.

"Put on a bit of weight, haven't you?" He patted my paunch—and smiled in that way men have of good-natured ribbing.

"Yeah, when Stana was pregnant I gained a batch of sympathy pounds. I never took them off. Twenty pounds," I muttered.

"Looks like you might have added even a few more since then." He laughed and smacked my shoulder. "I guess you won't be coming out of retirement once again, any time soon, huh?"

I had played in the NHL from 1957 until I was sent to the minors in 1964 for "moral turpitude." It all ended, the first time, when I helped out a buddy, snapping some photographs that proved his wife was having an affair, and the Leafs and league offices didn't approve. After missing a year I was reinstated and played for the Habs, 65–66, and retired after winning the Cup. I had nothing left to prove.

"Married life—" Sal looked off in the distance, his eyes following bits of a Styrofoam cup blowing up against the lip of a curve.

"What about married life?"

"Nothing, nothing—it's good." He had two kids, a home in Etobicoke. "So many people now they don't even get married, live-in girlfriends."

"I'm old school. I like marriage." My wife wants me to grow my hair out, but I still carried myself with a 1950s–style buzz cut. But with my added weight, I had taken to looking like a banker, wearing suits occasionally to hide my dad body. Today, however, I was in a loose-collared Oxford shirt, Lees, and a red windbreaker.

"You look good, though."

"Yeah, right. Thanks, pal."

"Now, at the risk of repeating myself, what can you tell me about this, Superstar?" His hands were in his pockets. "A case you're working on?"

"I am now," I said.

"Uh-huh." He wiped his mouth with the back of his hand. "The M.E. thinks, with the nearly naked body, a homosexual love spat."

"Hmm."

"Stiletto. Maybe an ice pick. Given the depth, type, and size of the wounds—stiletto blade, most likely."

I nodded, the clouds behind my eyes darkening.

"Can you believe Team Canada didn't select Keon?"

Everyone was talking hockey and the Summit Series. "Clarke had a good year. Top ten in scoring. He's gritty and I'm hearing the Henderson-Clarke-Ellis line was the best in training camp."

"But Dave Keon, man. Dave Keon. Money."

"Clarke had a better year—you can't take everyone."

"You got tickets for Wednesday's game?"

Game two was in Toronto. "I do."

"Can you get me in?"

"Stana knows Milt Dunnell at The Star. She'll get you a couple of tickets."

"Thanks—Level with me, Fuller. This was just a random thing? A coincidence? A guy out of nowhere just rushes his car right at you?"

"He was a dead man driving, Sal. I don't think he was aiming at anyone. Saint Michael's Hospital is close by. So's Wellesley General. Maybe he was trying to get there."

"Damn. With you Superstar, nothing's random."

"I didn't know the guy." I held up my hands. "I swear, Sal—"

"You think this is tied into the Shoeshine Kill?"

"Huh?"

"Homosexual angle to both kills."

"That's even more random than thinking I was the intended target. Or Johnny Buckets here."

Johnny shook his head vigorously. "I don't know the fuck. Look at my goddamn cart—"

"Insurance will cover it." Sal lit a cigarette.

Buckets wandered off, a few feet away, waltzing in a dissonant half-circle, and talking to his stuttering hands.

"Look, Sal, there was no ID in the victim's wallet, and not much in the car, just a cashmere sweater and a zippered-key case with a single key in it. I had handed that evidence over to the police."

"Yeah, and the sweater's not his," Sal said. "The victim was a big man. The sweater was of medium size—dainty. Thus the speculation on the gay angle."

"Maybe it's a woman's sweater."

"A guy in his briefs with a gut wound, intestines spilling out—a queer kill—all the way—I'd bet money on it."

"Maybe." What I didn't tell Sal, the evidence I didn't hand

over: before they arrived, I had found a yellowing business card in the fella's wallet: Hilary "Chip" Hampton, Assistant Professor of English, U of T. He was my wife's favorite prof. Back then.

PROFESSOR HILARY HAMPTON still lived on Walmer Road, as he did when Stana was his student. Often, The Professor held classes in his home, and his wife would make a new batch of brownies, cinnamon rolls, or sugar cookies as treats. She was in the kitchen now, the smell a heavy, cozy blanket. Through their bay window shone the black fencing of Sibelius Park glazed with light rain. A group of kids in knit caps were playing road hockey.

Minutes ago, I had called Abby at Park School from a phone booth, apologizing again and again, saying something had come up, and she'd hear all about it on the evening news, and I needed to cancel our appointment. She wondered if I could meet with her, way early, tomorrow morning, like 7:00–7:15, Tim Hortons, on the corner across from her school? I'm barely out of bed before nine I joked, but yeah, we can do that. She thought Yvan Cournoyer would score two for Canada tonight. Kenny Dryden might get a shutout. "I take it you're a Habs fan," I said and she laughed. "See you tomorrow."

Hilary Hampton wasn't laughing. The dead fella had been identified. It didn't take long. Dental records. J. Douglas Gomery. Forty-seven, a clerk for an insurance company. He was also a former student of Professor Hampton's, 1947–48.

"Talented, talented student. Had so much potential and promise." The Professor's fingers tented together. He reached across the coffee table for his pipe, rubbed the bowl along the edge of his nose, and then lit it. "But—Doug got addicted to what the kids back then called tea, marijuana, and never reached his potential. Wound up working in an office. Insurance." He made a slight face. His eyes were close set and his nose too small for his face. His gray hair was slicked back in a very functional style. He wasn't trying to impress anybody with his looks. His voice on the other hand—his speech patterns and diction had a touch of the Shakespearean, almost like those actors in the 30s and 40s and their Mid-Atlantic accents.

His wife nodded in agreement from the kitchen, forehead creased, flour dotting her face with a small constellation of stars. "His writing was so sloppy. Everything about him was sloppy. He didn't sit, he spilled into the furniture." She laughed. "And his thinking, lazy, sloppy."

"She often reads my student papers, stories," Professor Hampton said by way of apology. Behind him was a glass-doored bookshelf crammed with a mixture of Dickens, Hemingway, Steinbeck, Austen, crime novels by Ngaio Marsh, P. D. James, and Raymond Chandler, and several popular crossover works of nonfiction: David Riesman's *The Lonely Crowd*; Auguste Comte Spectorsky's *The Exurbanites*, and Alfred Kinsey's *Human Sexuality: Female*.

I played with the brim of my porkpie hat, shifting it around in my hands like a steering wheel. "Why would he have your business card in his wallet?"

"I don't know." The edges of The Professor's mouth turned down. He puffed gently. "I really don't." He shrugged absently, shoulders slight, tight, resembling the angled edges of clothing hangers. "I haven't seen him in years."

I didn't tell him I thought it might be a frame, a setup. I wanted to see where the conversation headed.

"They had a falling out." His wife, from the kitchen, wiped daubs of sweat from her chin.

I handed him the card, the embossing worn down.

He looked it over. "This is old," he said. "The address lists my very first office. Same with the phone number. That was the office, the small cramped quarters I worked in before the Serchuk series and tenure. Didn't even have a window." He shrugged at the University's antiquated system of privilege. He puffed, once, twice, and flipped the card to the coffee table. It landed face down, a tea-stain the shape of an oak leaf winking up at me. "This probably dates from when he was taking classes with me, 1948, I believe."

Hampton was an assistant professor back then, now he was a full professor and a Governor General's nominee for teaching.

"Why did he keep it?"

"I don't know—Douglas wasn't particularly sentimental." The Professor puffed some more.

"Serchuk—that's the—?"

"The hockey book, the beginning of the series I wrote. Yes." *A Boy on the Leafs Blueline*, the first in a six-novel run that got him tenure. 1949.

I returned the porkpie to my head and pushed my hands into my upper thighs. "It doesn't make sense, Professor, that he would have that card." *Unless, the decedent was trying to leave behind a clue? Or some other someone wanted the trail to lead here.*

I was playing him a little, because something about The Professor's story was all wrong, or maybe it was Hampton's absent flip of the card to the coffee table that just felt a little too cavalier given the circumstances. I bit my lower lip.

His wife offered me something to drink. No thanks, I said.

She had a habit of buffering things when the mood shifted to a darker melody line. "It certainly was odd," she said. "But then he was odd—he wrote a lot of stories about victims, people being hounded, chased by others, and then—look what happens." She shrugged.

"Honey—" The Professor sounded tired.

"Well. It's true." She had read several of his workshop pieces. "They were like nightmares, in which the protagonist could never get away from what's hounding him."

"Like a mid-sized man in a cashmere sweater?"

"Exactly." She opened the oven door and slid in a tray of cookies, glanced at her watch, twelve minutes she said softly.

"It's odd—my card, my old card being in his wallet." The Professor grimaced, shifted in his oversized leather chair. "The fella had a grudge against me. That's for sure. But I thought that was over years ago."

"Uh-huh—"

"How's Stana?" He smiled. "One of my all-time favorite students. Great student." The smile stretched to his eyes. "I read about your marriage and—child, a girl?"

"Yeah. She's five. Looking forward to watching the game with me tonight."

"A hockey fan?"

"She better be."

The Professor laughed and admitted he was worried. Greenway Publishing, who specialized in distributing books to the public schools, was set to re-release his hockey series, updated and streamlined for a new generation. His concern: if we lose this series to the Russians it might affect sales.

"Huh? How could we lose?"

"They play a different game—and maybe it'll make the game I write about seem dated, old—out of touch. We play a dump and chase style of hockey. The Russians. Well, it's more, dare I say, creative."

"I haven't forgot my original question, professor—the card, the wallet, the grudge—"

He puffed on his pipe and reached for my arm. Squeezed. "And how are you doing?"

Nearly five years ago, I told the story of my abuse at the hands of my father. It was a feature story, written by my wife, that ran three consecutive days in *The Toronto Star* right after I retired from the NHL. My therapist, Dr. Cohen believed in telling my story I would find acceptance and release.

"It took a lot of courage to tell your story," he added.

"You want to tell me yours?" I grinned my trademark lopsided smile.

"She always could write," he said. "Stana, your wife."

"Yes," Mrs. Hampton said.

"So tell me about Douglas—grievance?" I rubbed my eyes. Outside, spits of rain sputtered.

"Well, I don't like to speak ill of the dead—but he became unbalanced, delusional." They had been really close at one time, he reflected. Douglas was Professor Hampton's top graduate student assistant. 1948. Red River. Professor Hampton was working on an article on Howard Hawks. Douglas accompanied Hampton on a trip to interview Hawks in Santa Monica. Doug worked the tape recorder. "Anyway, on the flight to California, Doug asked me to ask a question of Hawks on his behalf: Why did the ethnic characters in his films lack agency and subscribe to comic stereotypes? Dutchy, Frenchy, you know?"

I didn't know, but I nodded.

"I was reluctant to ask Hawks," Hampton said, "but near the end of the interview I did ask and Hawks was furious. He said that all he was doing was helping these actors develop personas they already had—and, well, I think he admired me for having the gumption to go toe-to-toe with him because a tight-on-time twenty-minute interview became forty-five minutes." He puffed through a smile. "But that was Doug. He liked to push, take risks—the kid was too smart. Accelerated through high school. Did his undergrad degree in two-and-a-half years—his mind wasn't fully developed—he took risks."

"And those risks got him killed?"

"Maybe—Doug ran with a dark crowd."

"Dark?"

"Demi-monde. Hustlers, pleasure-seekers—Charles Street. Yonge." More puffs. "He had affairs. Men, women. From 1955–59 he was close to a man, real close."

"He was a poof, a homosexual," his wife said from the kitchen.

"Anyone in a cashmere sweater?"

"In his fiction everyone seemed to wear cashmere." He

laughed. "It was like a metaphor in his work, for decadence and privilege."

I lowered my voice. "The police think it's a sex crime."

"Sex crime? No doubt. From the details you've told me. No clothes. Bare feet. A stiletto, a punctured lung." His fingers tented together once again. "Closeted, of course. He confessed his peculiar affliction to me on the trip. Even made a pass while we shared a hotel room. Can you imagine?"

"So this pass—it led to a falling out?"

"No, no." He held up both hands. "Of course not. We're all adults." He laughed again. It sounded like he was hiccuping.

"When did you last see Doug?"

His wife slathered white frosting and red bursts of sugar dust on the tray of cookies that had been cooling. She brought them to us. She wore a plain 1950s dress, blue with three buttons and some fringe, and her dusky hair was done up in a tight knot. She placed a plate by my side on the coffee table. Her skin was smooth like underwater stones.

"Go ahead—" The Professor encouraged me to eat while he spoke.

I did.

The problem was that Doug suggested that my intellectual property wasn't my own, The Professor said, and in my field that's, well, treason. Terry "Chance" Serchuk, a Ukrainian kid, an immigrant, was inspired by my time spent among the Ukrainians in Winnipeg. "I grew up there. I guess I had talked the series over with Douglas on that trip to see Hawks and Doug, in his delusional mind, got to thinking that he had a hand in the plot trajectory of the first book. It also didn't help that Doug's Ukrainian—his parents changed their last name—so he got to thinking Serchuk was loosely based on him." The Professor shrugged and shifted uncomfortably in his chair. He undid the lowest button of his tweed jacket. "Doug demanded financial compensation, co-author credit. Well, my reputation, and tenure, were at stake. The book was all mine—"

"He hire a lawyer or anything?"

"No. I almost did. But—" He couldn't quite look at me, his eyes wandering through the window, to the park, and shadowy figures chasing a hockey game through streaks of rain. Someone scored. Arms and sticks raised. "Just to get him out of my hair, I signed over my first royalty check to him."

"Why?"

"I don't know." He puffed on his pipe. "I talked a lot about the book on that flight. Maybe he did give me a suggestion or two. It's not always easy to know or remember how our students may inspire our scholarly or creative work."

"Uh-huh." I pushed back my porkpie. "How much was said Royalty Check?"

"The advance? $25,000. I gave him half—well, $15,000."

"Buying off Gomery wasn't smart. And $15,000—well from an outside perspective it suggests a lot of suggestions."

"I know—especially now that Greenway Publishing, seventeen years later, wants to re-launch the series—All six books, can you believe that?" And they were going to let him write some new ones, he said.

"Technically sixteen years later," his wife said. "The sixth book in the series came out in 1956. I think it's the best." A wry smile turned at the corners of her lips.

"Right." The Professor nodded at some kind of private joke between them.

"Greenway? Aren't they a small Christian Press?"

He chuckled. "Don't say it as if it's a dirty word."

I shrugged ironically.

Their publisher and board of chartered members love the messages of those old books, Professor Hampton said. "Every story is a morality play as Chance always does the right thing and makes his teammates better by believing in charity, duty, community. A team of their writers is updating the six books, modernizing the fashions and hockey references, and—" He paused, slightly embarrassed. "They're tossing in more kisses between Chance and Kitsey, his ongoing girlfriend and co-star of the sixth book."

"So the new books are ghost written?"

"Well—" He seemed embarrassed and a little annoyed at my question. "Not exactly," he said. "It's the original plots with anachronisms removed and a few new scenes added. Eighty percent of the books are still my original words and I approve all updates." A team of writers, including a priest, was writing the new scenes. "It's still my work," he insisted.

"Uh-huh." I finished my cookie. "Did Gomery want another *royalty* check?"

"I told you, I haven't heard from him in years."

"I'm going to be frank. I don't believe you, Professor. I think he was in touch with you and—"

"He was—" His wife removed a second tray from the oven, the mittens on her hands resembling small pillows. "Tell him."

The Professor shrugged his coat-hanger shoulders. "All right, all right. About a month ago Douglas had got in touch with me, when the relaunch of the series was first hinted at. He wanted a piece of the royalties, just for the first book, the one he feels he 'co-wrote.' I said, no, and then there were these threats on his life."

"Threats?"

"So *he says*—"

"He's prone to exaggeration," Mrs. Hampton added.

The Professor grimaced. "At times, yes. A writer's flights of fancy, let's say. Somebody slashing his tires or some damn thing." The Professor waved a tired hand. "He claims I was try-ing to hurt him. It wasn't me."

"Somebody in a cashmere sweater?"

"Maybe—"

"Somebody in *his mind*," his wife said. "Hilary was home most evenings." She nibbled on a cookie, shifted in her chrome-accented stool and continued, "Tuesday and Thursday afternoons he teaches downtown, a creative writing workshop for non-traditional students."

"Hmm."

Professor Hampton looked faraway, through the bay window. Fresh bulky shadows, heavy rocks, filled the glass. A hard triple knock. The kind that spelled cop.

It was Sal Lambertino and two constables. Sal's hands were in the pockets of his Burberry coat. The officers stood behind him, arms across their chests in an intimidating command presence pose. Mrs. Hampton let in the unwelcomed trio.

Sal shot me a sour, *what the hell are you doing here* look. He pushed back his fedora.

I shrugged sheepishly and flashed my lopsided grin, the one on my PI license.

Sal, all business, began by listing an address on Bay Street, a two-floor, eight room apartment building near Massey Hall.

Professor Hampton stiffened in his chair and laughed darkly, the hiccups heavy.

"We'd like you to come with us. We have some questions."

"Should I call my solicitor?"

"That might be a good idea. Yes sir."

Solicitor? This prof really was tweedy. He rose with a slight wobble, nodding with his head, telling me our conversation was done. He re-lit his pipe to compose himself. His wife helped him with his overcoat and followed him to the door.

I wasn't able to piece together all that was happening then, but in a couple of hours, once I got home, I would courtesy of Stana and her reporter pipeline. The police had received a tip from Gomery's ex-wife Susan that Doug had visited this apartment at least three times in the past week. The police, following the lead, arrived at the Bay Street address, and the key in the zippered wallet fit the lock. Inside they found a swank hipster pad with lava lamps, bright pop-art colors, and framed Man Ray photographs, including the infamous nude woman with a violin back. Incense burned in three different places and traces of thick, dry blood were found under a corner of carpet near the living room couch. It matched Doug's.

The landlord gave a description of who rented the space, and had been renting it since 1947. One Hal Hilton.

The description fit one Hilary "Chip" Hampton.

WE WERE IN TROUBLE halfway through the first period.

We scored two quick goals and then the Soviets netted a pair, including a short-handed goal with less than three minutes remaining in the period, to tie it up. Team Canada looked gassed and the Soviets were buzzing. McClelland Stuart said that their tic-tac-toe passing demonstrated some real team play while Canada looked like a bunch of individuals that didn't have their timing down.

"He's not wrong," I said. "And a shortie. You can't give up a shortie." I was surprised they weren't saying more about that during the broadcast.

Stana leaned away from the couch, elbows on her knees, chin in her hands. "We look slow."

"I know it. Some coronation." We were supposed to blow them out and prove our supremacy. Instead they were ruining our party.

Connie, leaning against Mommy's hip, a foot up in her lap, mentioned we had scored two goals. "Not to worry, Daddy. It'll be okay."

That cracked me up in a sad way, her idealism, the belief in good things happening. I sighed. Once you have a kid everything changes, everything's for her, and at the same time she gives so much in return. And our house. What a cluttered mess. Before Connie, things were picked up, vacuumed, dusted, but now toys were all over the living room: stuffed bears; Hot Wheels and orange track; Barbies and their shoes scattered like small pebbles; pieces of Tinker Toys and Lincoln Logs under the coffee table; and pencil crayons and coloring books. It was awesome.

Stana tapped our daughter's shoulder and said bedtime.

"Can't I see the second period?"

It was nearly nine o'clock and she had school tomorrow.

"Yeah, Mommy, can't she see the second period?"

Stana gave me her wry, *you're no help* look. It was a quick head shake and eye roll with a touch of a sarcastic crumble to her lips. "Okay, but story time is now, during the intermission— and no delay tactics and drinks of water and slices of cheese requests, young lady."

Connie nodded earnestly. She had hazel eyes, auburn hair, and freckles just like mom. But her nose was all me. Poor kid.

I rushed to the kitchen, got a small plate with olives and cheese, and a glass of apple juice for her, and then while she was noshing I grabbed a couple of Dr. Seuss–type books from her bedroom and speed read through *Hop on Pop* and *A Fish out of Water*. Connie loves when the fish gets so big as to fill the whole house. Cracks her up every time. Her laugh is like canaries in cages. I've never heard anything quite like it.

THINGS IN THE SECOND PERIOD only got worse. The Soviets scored twice and they played the game in ways we never did. Five-man units. If they didn't like what they saw they turned back with the puck and came up the ice all over again. They didn't dump and chase and get on the forecheck. Instead they carried the puck into the zone and passed the puck east-west. "That lateral movement is killing Dryden." I pointed at the TV as if the commentators could hear me. Dryden was a great goalie but he was used to the NHL style of play, standing up to the shooter, making himself big and taking away the angles, but the Soviets' quick lateral movement had him flummoxed. And Awrey and Seiling, one of our defense pairs, looked slow. Kharlamov flew around Awrey and went right in to score. I wiped the edges of my mouth. "Damn, this sucks."

Stana, returning from the bedroom, nodded and squeezed my hand. "It's going to be a long series."

"We're out of shape, but damn, they're fast."

"I can't believe they took Professor Hampton in for questioning." Two lines furrowed between her eyebrows.

I shrugged. "I guess he had some other place, an apartment, some kind of casting couch."

"It's not a casting couch. It's a retreat for writers." She knew all about that couch. She had sat on that couch, in that apartment. When she was his student in the early 60s. Everyone knew about the apartment, and the select few, his most talented writers, formed a separate workshop, meeting there for private sessions. They called themselves the Freedom Writers.

"Freedom writers?" I shook my head. "How do you spell pretentious?"

"Anyway, it was a place to write whatever, to be totally free, to do whatever."

"How often did you go there?"

"A few times." There was an edge to her voice, daring me to ask—

"With him?"

"He wasn't interested in me in that way." She stiffened her shoulders, hands on knees.

"You sound like you regret that."

An absent smile. "He did take other women there."

"So it was a casting couch—"

"He had an open marriage and still does—casting couch. I'm married to a real square."

"Yeah, you are."

She pushed off our living room couch and glided into me, kissing me gently. "I'm glad."

I patted her butt.

"But that doesn't make him a killer."

"The blood under the rug near a radiator matches that of the decedent." I wondered if it could be a workshop kill—some current member—

"I don't know anyone in the current workshop. The ones from my day all graduated."

I wondered if Gomery were a workshopper, back in the day.

She kissed me again. "I don't know—Connie wonders about you, worries that you're sad."

"I'm not sad, I'm just bewildered." Team Canada was letting us all down. I wanted to say I felt angry and betrayed, but that wasn't fair, but that's how I felt. We were supposed to kick their asses and here they were the ones doing a number on us. "They came here to learn." I shook my head. "Bullshit. They came here to embarrass us. Their way of life is better than our way of life."

"Go see Connie." She patted my hip. "You're getting all political."

I headed back to see Connie and tucked her in.

"We'll get them next game, Daddy."

I sat at the edge of her bed. "Who looked the best out there tonight—for Canada?"

She squinched up her race and thought and thought and thought. "Mahovlich."

"Which one, Frank or Pete?"

"Number 27."

"Frank." I had to agree with her. He was in on Canada's first goal and had made some great passes and created several opportunities that we didn't cash in on. I ruffled her hair. "You know your hockey, kiddo."

She smiled proudly.

I kissed her forehead and then sang her a song, her evening song, the one I always sing from *Rio Bravo*, "My Rifle, My Pony and Me." I don't hit all the notes, but she always beams and sings along to the refrain.

THE THIRD PERIOD got the fans kind of quiet in the Montreal Forum. We scored early, mounting a comeback, but then they scored two quick ones, taking the crowd out of it. Isolated close-ups of our Prime Minister showed him looking pensive, jaw set, and his wife Margaret sunken in her seat, sullen, and glum. The crowd even gave the Bronx cheer when Dryden directed a shot off his blocker.

"That's not fair." I felt Kenny had made several big saves, but man—the crowd was turning on our boys. "This is ugly—"

I wondered if Tabasco would help take the sting out of Dick Beddoes's column mixed with borscht that he was about to eat on the steps of the Soviet embassy tomorrow.

Stana laughed. "Are you hungry?"

"I'm always hungry."

She patted my belly and offered to warm up some leftover pizza.

"Sounds good."

The Soviets scored one more goal and at the end we gooned-it up a bit, letting our frustration show as Phil Esposito and others dished out some high cross checks and head punches.

7-3.

Stana shut off the television. No need to hear the postmortem.

The pizza didn't make us feel any better—

We both felt awful, probably the worst we felt in six years of marriage. It was just a game, but it wasn't. Hockey is the thing we Canadians are great at and take tremendous pride in and someone was taking that away from us and robbing us of our identity. Damn, I was getting fucking political.

We stared at the gray glassy screen of the TV for a long time, our ghostly faces slowly disappearing—

Tuesday

ABBY MUNRO WAS WAITING for me outside of Timmy's, 7:15 a.m.

The shadows of Park District School's fencing and narrow third-floor windows could be seen in the faraway curve of the street. Abby's eyes, what I could see of them behind her harlequins, were downcast. Like all of us, she was tired of reading about Orlando Prescott stuffed down a roof duct on Charles Street, cigarette burns tattooing his body.

I offered to get her a coffee, if she were allowed to drink coffee, and she said she was, and I said how about a donut, and she said, she'd like that. Toasted coconut. "Good choice," I mumbled.

We walked up to the counter. Abby was petite, small-chested, but wiry, and she moved with an athlete's fine balance and confidence.

"What the hell happened yesterday," she muttered.

My lip curled under my teeth. "Oh, the game. I'm trying not to think about it—"

"We better make some changes, adjustments—tomorrow."

"We will."

"Hockey's a game for ofays," said another customer, leaning his back into the counter, as if it were his private couch, and he gave Abby the once over. "A nice girl from the islands like you. What do you care about hockey?" He spoke with a Jamaican accent.

"I care."

"It don't make you more Canadian. This is no land of milk and honey for our people, sweetheart." He lowered his Ray-Bans to give us a glimpse of his winning personality.

"I'm not your sweetheart."

It was his turn now to look me over. "Aren't you robbing the cradle there, old man?"

"Go fuck yourself."

He laughed and shook his head smugly. His hair was shaved

at the sides and he wore a ring of a raised fist in his right ear. His jean jacket was faded and when he turned to pay for his donuts, I saw True Suns colors: a circle inside another circle. The outer circle was on fire, burning, darting with dancing sunspots; the inner circle a cool placid blue, like water, and a philosophy of flow, malleability. A strange contradiction like the islands' belief in Eye/I and Eye/I, biblical righteousness, eye for an eye, mixed with seeing each other I to I, equals. I knew all about this because Stana had investigated the rising problem of Toronto's youth gangs and growing violence in a recent article in *The Star*. She also explored their religious and philosophical beliefs.

When he left with his cargo—and it was a lot of cargo, two dozen donuts—all the light in the room brightened.

We sat at a small table. I drank my coffee black, hers was a double double.

"Do you know that guy?"

Abby said nothing.

"He acted like he knew you."

"Troy Saba. Dropped out of Park School a year ago. Leader of this area's branch of the True Suns. He was held back, twice, so he was in my grade. He used to pull the back of my hair in English class. That's why I now wear it short." She shifted, shrugged, and reached into the olive-green knapsack at her feet.

From its recesses she pulled out some curled newspaper clippings.

"So what, he's like seventeen?"

"Yeah." Then: "These stories aren't true," she said, a hand resting absently on her left shoulder, her dulled flannel covering—the man's shirt shadowing a pink blouse—was unbuttoned. She pointed at the clippings, ribboning across the spaces between us. "He was a great kid, listened to CBC news broadcasts to improve his accent. He wanted to become a doctor. Hell, he worked at this uncle's bowling alley, weekends and two weeknights, raising money for university. And he's not—" She adjusted in the hardback chair and pointed at the damn clippings—"gay." The newspaper bits glowed hotter with morning sun. "I should know. I was his girlfriend." When she spoke, each word was brushed lightly with a feather.

"Uh-huh."

She shrugged slight but supple shoulders. She sat comfortably in the chair, feet forward, bouncing, as she leaned into her words, unconcerned with being noticed for her dancer-like beauty. Her hair was the color of crows; skin, caramel with a touch of cinnamon.

She played with the necklace glinting near raised collarbones. The pendant was a crescent moon, jade in a gold inlay; the band: a gold pattern, a double helix.

"He gave you that?"

"Yes," she lied.

I didn't know it then, but I'd discover the truth Saturday, early, early morning, sometime after game three.

"And the black eye too?" A blue-black bruise rose slightly behind the left lens of her harlequins.

"No." She laughed awkwardly, a hand crossing to her mouth, a small bird's wing. She had tiny crowded teeth. "A girl at school had called Orly a fag. And we got into it." She swaggered a shrug and pushed an envelope toward me. The lip was crinkled. One hundred dollars. It was all the money she had. Would I take her case? "I raised the money from babysitting." She also worked Fridays at the local IGA.

"Look—" I pushed the envelope back toward her. "I'll look into it. Keep the money. If I get lucky and get some answers, buy me a cup of coffee, black, and a couple of donuts. Toasted coconut: I like it a lot too."

She thanked me with her eyes.

I nodded and played with a curled end of one of the clippings. "What about all this talk—Orly running with the gangs?"

Her green eyes narrowed. "Never. He hated violence. He believed in social justice but through marches and protests, not guns. He was never a member of the True Suns." The birthmark on the left side of her mouth resembled a Soviet sickle.

"It says here—" I raised the newspaper coils, letting their tails slap against the table, that "he got sent home from school last spring for wearing gang colors—"

"Lies."

"Fitzpatrick got him suspended." Fitzpatrick was my teacher, over twenty years ago. Always flirted with the ladies, hated the boys in his classes. It was as if he felt we were in constant competition with him for the girls' attention. I heard that after his son died in a fiery car accident, Fitzpatrick had become much more resigned, less engaged. But he still got Orly suspended.

She couldn't look at me. The eyes behind her glasses flashing like the tails of tropical fish. "He doesn't like us people from the islands."

I smiled, my lopsided grin. In my day, as a swaggering sixteen-year-old, I figured he didn't like us Jews.

So, who would want the kid dead? What was the motive?

"Orly was a shoeshine boy, but he was like a detective," she said. "Watching, observing from his spot at Danforth Bowl. Listening. Seven girls in the past six years, two from our school, all from the islands, have gone missing. From Regent Park. The cops don't care. The news don't care. Orly did. And he was hearing things, and I think he was finding out things."

"What kinds of things?"

"Things? Well—" She shrugged, the swagger shimmying through her shoulders and arms and down to her fingertips. "Sex slaves. Shipped to Montreal."

Back in 1966 I tangled with such a group, tied into a film production company. Real douche bags. I broke up that ring, but the ringleader, Henri Ducat, walked away from it all. He had a walking stick with a hexagonal glass head. Under the glass: two figures, an old man and a pubescent girl, holding hands. Ducat was an ugly man, a pedophile, and is still a Member of Parliament. "Danforth Bowl. You mentioned them. They involved?"

She rubbed at an edge of the band around her neck, her lips parting slightly. "Maybe even my own uncle, who Orly lived with. Maceo Munro, the uncle. Owns Danforth Bowl. The True Suns can be found there most nights," she said. "I don't know, but I think the True Suns killed him, and it wasn't about drugs."

My jaw was tight, the tips of my ears numb. I pointed at her bruised eye. "And what's that about?"

She hesitated, shifting, straightening the collar of her flannel covering.

And I knew.

Her father.

I DIDN'T LIKE THE VIBE as soon as I stepped into the school. The thickness in the air took me right back to tenth grade, Mr. Fitzpatrick, and the only class I ever got a lowly C in. C- actually. Park District School was a turn-of-the-century building with crowded hallways, scuffed hardwood floors, and the smelly octane of nervous sweat and teen angst. And the wainscotting of white plaster roses along all the halls established a false front of hope and calm stillness. This was no house of solitude, believe me.

My breaths were shallow.

Mr. Fitzpatrick's faded red hair burned dully in his classroom's bright track lighting. The fluorescent lights hummed. His face was narrow and shaped-liked a trowel. His eyes narrowed as he spoke.

He remembered me and actually gave me a compliment, saying back in 1966 I made Béliveau better in the Finals, giving him more space out there to make plays. Béliveau didn't start scoring until Coach Blake put me on his line. My mucking it up in the corners freed up pucks for Le Gros Bill.

"Thanks," I said, hands in pockets.

When I had Mr. Fitzpatrick sadness didn't fill his eyes like they do now. Then, he flirted with the female students, but after his son, a York University star lacrosse player, died in a wall of flames, following flipping and rolling his car, Fitz had changed, his shoulders heavy, eyes sinking, voice full of bits of bitter gravel. An aura of too much coffee and cigarettes drifted about him after that. It was still drifting.

He was grading a stack of student papers, ribbons of ink slicing every which way. He wrote more on their themes than the students did on their theses. Slatted lines of late morning sun cut blocks atop his desk.

I played with the brim of my porkpie hat, as he continued to praise me in a somewhat inadvertent fashion. He was glad to see me "flourish": winning the Cup, marrying a reporter ("and a great writer I might add," he said), and coming to terms with the abusive crimes of my father—that's a lot to overcome.

"I got a daughter now too."

"Yeah, I heard—" He looked off, back of the room, no longer present in the current moment. "Congratulations." He sipped coffee from a chipped ceramic mug. "Keep her close."

"I do."

So many, he said, with a similar pattern of upbringing and struggle, an abusive parent like you had, don't make it. "Look at the kids here. Do they flourish? Not hardly. Most wind up on welfare or prison." He shrugged. "So, congratulations. You made it. A wife. A child. What can I do for you?" He sipped more coffee from the burnt-orange mug the size of one of Hamlet's goblets.

I pulled the newspaper clippings that Abby handed me from my red windbreaker. I pointed out that he, Mr. Fitzpatrick, was the source who said Orly showed up in class sporting gang colors.

"You carrying a gun?" He noticed the side holster on my left hip.

"I got a license to carry."

He frowned. "We don't allow guns in the school."

"I'm law enforcement."

"Not hardly."

The disapproval in his voice had me feeling fifteen again. He always had a way of diminishing boys. I pointed again at the clipping. "Did you or did you not say this?"

"Yeah. I said it. So what?" He planted hands around the sides of his cup and sat up regally. He invited me to sit down. I did.

"I don't know if the kid was trying to impress the chicks or what, but he sat in *that chair*, wearing one of *their* jackets." He pointed at a wonky, akimbo chair near the window, brushing against a radiator.

I muttered something about a sex slave racket and several missing girls, two from Park District School and the Regent Park Projects. All poor. All from the islands.

"Sex slaves?" Mr. Fitzpatrick laughed, his flat hair shaking dully. "Is that what Orly told her? Abby, his *girlfriend*?" He smiled. He wasn't asking me to return it. "Look, I always liked the kid, but he had an overactive imagination. Like you, the kid couldn't string together sentences to make a coherent paragraph. No patterns to the words. No organization."

He sipped more coffee. On the wall behind him, just before a run of blackboards, was a small shelf of books bracketed by two bowling pins. Above the shelving were line illustrations of famous writers: F. Scott Fitzgerald, Edgar Allan Poe, William Shakespeare.

"The kid wrote gangster stories all the time. Remember how I used to give you all Free Writing Fridays? Write whatever you want? Anyway, gangland stuff, Jimmy Cagney, except Cagney's from the Islands and not the Lower East Side, mahn."

"Sounds creative."

"Creative? The stuff was a derivative mess. Fragments. Comma splices. Pronoun trouble. To say nothing of plotting, characterization, and credibility. The kid was no Shakespeare, mahn."

And you're no Albert Schweitzer, pal, I wanted to say, but held my tongue.

"Anyway. You disapprove of my attitude toward these kids."

I said nothing.

"The kid had spunk, I'll give him that," he said, the lip of his coffee cup pressed near his lower teeth. "But he was running with the gangs. The True Suns. Red and blue circles, some kind of island voo-doo juju."

"It's actually biblical," I said. "Stana did a story on them a few months back, so I got insider info. It's great being married to a reporter, a real conversation starter. Eye for an eye, retribution, and the idea of I and I, no me, or you, just equals."

"Like I said, voodoo juju."

I wasn't sure what to make of that remark, but it didn't sit well, *mahn*.

Mr. Fitzpatrick often spotted Orly after school on Parliament Street hanging with "a punk in Cuban heels, white khakis, and Ray-Bans."

"Troy Saba?"

"Yeah. That's the boy. Troy Saba."

Abby knew him too. "He bought two dozen donuts this morning."

"Like I said, a member of the gangs. Two dozen donuts—" He shook his head, eyes slitted. "I got him suspended permanently for a series of knife fights over lunch hour." Unfortunately, the after-hours shoeshine boy was tight with Saba and his crew, ran with them, and wore their colors on his jean jacket. "He was doing drug drops on Danforth Bowl, I imagine for them before some rival gang, or the Outfit, got him. That's how it figures."

Rival gang? Who rivals the True Suns? "Maceo Prescott?" He had mentioned the Danforth Bowl. Maceo ran the Danforth Bowl.

"The owner? No, no, Maceo was a tough kid. But he's gone

straight." Mr. Fitzpatrick took a final, heavy slug of coffee. "Maceo just gave a generous gift to the school to refurbish the grass on our football field and build new basketball courts."

"I guess he's another one who flourished, huh?"

Fitzy said nothing.

"Then who, who's the rival gang?"

"The Red Dragons, a motorcycle club. They got their own drug business and they don't want the True Suns muscling in."

Just then a lean fella, with thinning hair resembling a coat of paint you could still see the primer through, bounced into the room. His eyebrows were translucent, and I'd put him anywhere between 35 and 45. The wrinkles around his eyes and under his neck were distinct. If Noel Coward were casting a play, this fella would be the fading juvenile. The only prop missing: a tennis racket.

C. Thomas Everly. He introduced himself, flipping back what little hair he had and flashing a boyish gleam, a toothpaste smile. He adjusted the bottom button of his blue blazer—it was all angles and displayed the school crest. This guy was a regular United Empire Loyalist. "We still on for bowling?" he asked Fitzpatrick.

Tomorrow, Wednesday, early evening was practice night. Thursdays was league play.

"Yeah. I think I'll be done with grading by then," Fitzy said. "Or, I should say, grading will have done me in." He laughed and shoved the themes to a far corner of his desk. "How come you're never grading papers?"

"Multiple choice."

"Must be fun teaching the sciences."

Everly nodded. "I got no choice," he said. "I got to be up in Barrie on weekends, running Shambles." It was a hamburger joint he owned with a brother-in-law on Highway 400. He smiled at me. "Helps pay for a second car. My wife has a little Datsun—It's better than my car, a 240Z, but I have a hard time sliding into it. Not a lot of legroom—or seat room. My head taps the ceiling." He chuckled, self-consciously.

I laughed.

He glanced at his fingers bending together. "I couldn't help but overhear your conversation, Mr. Fuller," Everly said. "We bowl at Maceo's. And he's a good guy. Paid his dues. Now, Orly was also a good kid, but he didn't have time to mature, to change, like Maceo did. He ran out of time. Drugs killed him. Pushing drugs? Who knows. The police found drugs in his shine box."

I rotated the brim of my porkpie around my hands like a steering wheel, and then placed it back on my head.

"And the sex angle?" His lips pressed together. "Sex slaves? No."

How long was this cat standing outside the door? I was waiting for him to mention Béliveau for chrissakes.

Everly bent at the waist as he spoke, afraid of being the tallest fella in the room, but he was at least 6 feet 6 inches, and no matter how much shrinking gymnastics he did, flexing out his left or right hip to make himself disappear, this fella was going no place.

"I liked the kid," Everly said. "Gave him an 'A' last spring in Biology. Kid had spunk as Frank said. Spunk. Took nothing from nobody." He glided toward the parted venetian blinds and high school students smoking at sidewalk's edge. He appeared distracted by them. He rubbed at the edges of his mouth and shook his head as if refocusing. "Remember last October, Frank?" He nudged Fitzy with his words. The ceramic coffee cup was pushed to a far corner of the desk.

Last October, C. Thomas Everly, Biology, Rita Fogels, Vocal Coach, and Frank Fitzpatrick, English Literature, took a small cohort of vocal (as in singing) students camping in Algonquin Park. Record lows, Everly said. "We thought we'd give the vocal kids a treat, you know? Vocal students don't get the same respect, at least here, as orchestra and band, so we had a three-day getaway. Did I say it was cold? Anyway, we teachers stayed in the heated mess hall, a big 1950s-style admin building, and the kids were in log cabins. No heating. So Orly and Abby and a group of other boys decided to break into the boiler room of the admin building. There's an outside entrance, and it's warm in there. And they would have got away with it, too, if they weren't laughing so damn loud."

Mr. Fitzpatrick picked up the story. "So we trundled them back to their cabins with extra blankets and nobody got suspended or in trouble. Told them at five a.m. they could make their way into the admin building and crash on the floor until breakfast at 7:30." He smiled, the sadness of his eyes briefly lifting. "It *was cold*. And it took spunk. Orly and Abby were the ringleaders. Leaders of the cause." He laughed ironically.

"Mr. Fuller—" Everly now flexed his other hip. "I'm convinced that kid would have fulfilled his dreams. He was talented, special. Would have been a doctor someday. A real credit to his people."

"Uh-huh."

"The kid was smart. And—" He returned to the slatted blinds and kids smoking outside. "Well, he was curious. Like a scientist. A researcher. Orly had these notebooks, composition books really, that he wrote reams of observations in, interviews with people, of a differing lifestyle. Like Dr. Kinsey." He shoved a hand in a pocket of the blazer. The subjects of these notebooks, he said, were people who frequented TomBoys and Dicks, a homosexual bar in the heart of Toronto.

"Looking for patterns, breaks in patterns," Mr. Fitzpatrick said.

I wasn't quite getting all that pattern stuff. "The police have these notebooks?" I pushed back the brim of my porkpie.

"Nobody does," Fitzpatrick said.

Everly nodded solemnly.

Abby might. She might know.

"And I believe that's what got him killed," my former teacher said. "Not drugs. Charles Street." He reached for his faraway mug and tipped it forward, hoping to find a final sip of sludge. "Maybe somebody told Orly something they regretted—"

Charles Street. And Yonge. Professor Hampton had mentioned that area and lifestyle as possibly being behind Gomery's murder too.

"Maybe. But the kid was only sixteen. How the hell did he even get into the joint?"

"Who said he went inside?" Everly shifted hips again. "He hung out outside, maybe. No law against it. Check out Charles Street. That'll lead somewhere."

"Yeah." There were a lot of things I needed to check out. Like, what was so damn interesting to Everly outside that window?

ONCE FREE FROM PARK DISTRICT SCHOOL, I was breathing easily again.

I needed another coffee and a donut to get the taste of the school and the attitudes of Fitzy out of my system.

The streets weren't as crowded as they were hours ago. Tuesdays are always slow in the city and most students were in class.

I walked past a One Hour Martinizing, a coffee-pot place, and a red brick building with keystone arches in its four curved windows.

Orlando Prescott was like light hitting a prism—so many different Orly's: scientist, seeker, a boy searching for his sexual identity, gang member, possible drug pusher/addict. Who was the real Orly?

I had no fucking clue.

I guess we're all a mix of Orly's, there's no single definition of self.

I shoved my hands in my pockets and followed a jet contrail that twisted the powder blue sky.

Outside of Timmy's, another True Sun, in white khakis and

a jean jacket displaying their colors, stood against the donut shop's plate glass window, as if he were holding up the building.

"Read any good books lately?" I said to him as I passed.

Acne dotted his chin and his eyes were different colors. "Funny, real funny."

"Yeah, and I'm real cute too."

"Mr. Fuller—" Abby grabbed me by the right arm.

"What are you doing here? Shouldn't you be in school?"

"I wanted to know what Fitzpatrick said."

We entered and I got another cup of black coffee and shared a donut with Abby. The sun glowed against the shop's window and now there were two True Suns holding up the building. "Tell me the story about the boiler room and the cabins out in Algonquin."

"Oh, he told you about that."

"He did."

"It was really, really cold." Her green eyes brightened telling the story of how Orly cracked the lock using a paper clip or some damn thing. The retreat was supposed to be a celebration but, at times, it was more like a punishment, the damn weather. No insulation in the cabins, and the whole place is condemned now. It was so old. The admin building had a flagpole out front and it didn't fly the Canadian flag but the Red Ensign, Canada's old flag. "Damn it was all wrong, in some ways. The damn building was crumbling, even then. We were afraid if we sang too robustly, the whole thing would collapse down around us. But it was a lot of fun. Even went on a hayride."

I chuckled. "What about these books? Notebooks—"

She nibbled on her half of a chocolate-coconut donut.

"TomBoys and Dicks. Charles Street?"

"Oh that—" She looked away.

"Yes that."

"Orly interviewed people, compiled notes. He was curious about what it meant to be human?"

"Uh-huh." I leaned forward. "Where are these notebooks?"

"I don't know," she mumbled. "The police took everything from the bedroom at his uncle's house. Maceo Prescott, I told you about that. He's the man Orly lived with—" Orly's father had died some time ago, a knifing over in St. James Town.

I had to find those notebooks.

Suddenly a *poppoppop* like a thousand ladyfinger firecrackers going off at once and one of the boys outside jittered and juked against the glass, a large red stain following him down.

People in Timmy's were screaming, ducking under tables, and I shoved Abby down and reached for my snub-nosed .38 and combat crawled toward the front door.

There were two corpses across the sidewalk, brain matter smeared on glass and concrete. A fella on a motorcycle rumbled off in the distance. His back was visible. A dragon, rising on its heavy rear legs, was letting loose a stream of fire. The fire was orange; the dragon, red.

Onlookers gathered and Abby trembled by my side.

"You know these two?"

She glanced at their crumpled distorted shapes. She didn't know their names. "Classmates," she said. "Classmates—"

SAL WAS GETTING REALLY TIRED of bumping into me. He didn't even tease me, or call me Superstar. He just grunted. They chalked outlines of the bodies and carted them to ambulances that rode off silently, a pair of white hearses. Sal huffed on a cigarette, the lines in his face heavy with worry.

I told him about the guy on the motorcycle. These Red Dragons.

He shook his head and pushed back his fedora, blinking in the sun. It was unseasonably warm in Toronto for September. "A bunch of ex-servicemen, World War II veterans. Formed in 1949."

"So, they're not kids." I kicked at a chocolate-bar wrapper

stuck to the cuffs of my pants. It curled like a leaf down the street.

"No, they're not kids."

"Was Orly working for them? Was this payback for Orly's death?"

"There was coke in Orly's shine box and this is a war." He shrugged. "But I don't know."

"You got any files on these guys—their leader?"

"I can get it to you." He flicked his cigarette into the street and it sparked when it hit. "One more time, you were saying you were eating a donut—"

"Sharing. And drinking black coffee and then *poppoppop* like firecrackers."

I told him the story, once again, my meeting with Fitzpatrick and Everly—I left Abby's name out of it (I'm not sure why; maybe I figured she'd seen enough trauma and there was no need for her to have to relive it for the police).

When they had rolled the bodies over, their youth hit me. One of the boys' faces was full of incredulity like, *How could this be happening? I'm just a kid.* The other fella, skinny and barely fourteen, had no face.

I asked about Orly's notebooks.

Sal knew nothing about that. They didn't find much in Orly's bedroom. "You know he was living with his uncle."

"Yeah, Maceo. I heard."

Anyway, he said, all Orly's stuff was in three boxes down in the evidence locker. No notebooks. If I wanted to look the boxes over he could arrange it.

I did want a look.

"Let's finish up here, give me another hour or so," he said, "and I'll sign you in to the Bay Street Station."

"Thanks—I heard the kid was hanging around Charles Street. TomBoys and Dicks—he's sixteen for chrissakes, how's that even possible?"

Sal sighed heavily. "We need to do a better job of monitoring all of Yonge Street, the head shops, the strip joints, the massage parlors, the gay bars." The bright sun blistered the brim of his fedora that shadowed his face. "A permissive society doesn't mean anything goes." He shook his head with disdain. "There's a lot of monitoring we all need to do—"

I didn't quite follow him. It was another one of those cryptic remarks my buddy had been making lately, like his weird tangent on marriage the other day. "It's good, it's good," he had said that day. *Was it?*

Is it?

THE EVIDENCE ROOM was a crowded place that smelled of cigarettes and coffee and sweat. It was a cage with a few metal chairs and hard-top desks and file boxes full of item upon item in Ziploc bags and accompanying notes. A dull light hanging from the ceiling on an extension cord cast a dim glimmer.

The materials in Orly's files were full of books: science fiction by Robert Heinlein; *Grey's Anatomy*; two volumes of Kinsey on *Human Sexuality, Male* (1948) and *Female* (1953); jewelry (chains, an emerald ring with an oak leaf cluster under the glass, a cross, and earrings with raised fists—the same design I saw Troy Saba sporting); an AMF bowling pin with red stripes; a series of photographs including Orly outside the Science Centre, flashing a peace sign, and Orly and Abby at Centre Island grinning atop their carousel horses; and a cashmere sweater, medium-sized. This I kept out of the box. It was a different color than the one I found in the Valiant.

I wondered about the jewelry. Trinkets? From a lover? There's no way a kid could afford all that. No way. These were prizes, tokens of affection.

Sal, a cigarette daubing along his lower lip, suddenly sat next to me. "Find anything?"

I pointed to the sweater.

The lone bulb shook above us, as I nudged it while holding

up the sweater. "Same size as the one in the Valiant. A medium." The light from the hanging bulb cut a sharp arc across us.

"We checked on that," Sal said. "The hairs on that sweater were of African ancestral origins. The hairs inside the one in the car were shorter, male, and definitely white. Just a coincidence—the two sweaters—part of the chaos of any investigation." He slid a manilla folder my way.

Information on the Red Dragons?

Their leader was Lieutenant Tan Mylow, saw action at Dunkirk and D-day. The Dragons saw themselves as a neighborhood watch group, protecting their communities, a force of vigilance. "This is a bunch of shit," I said. There were photographs. A lot of photographs. They all rode Triumphs and had skull rings on their fingers.

"A bunch of assholes." Sal wiped at the corners of his mouth. "But, whatever you saw, the guy on the bike. I don't think he was the shooter."

I followed the trail of smoke off his cigarette—it stretched toward the light above us that was still swinging gently. "Come again?"

"Ballistics says the shooter was across the street, probably on the roof of a red brick building, a former meat locker."

"No. No way," I said. "The sound was not the crack of a high-powered rifle. It was the *poppoppop* of a handgun. And no one would use a handgun from a rooftop."

"Well, this guy did. Thirty-eight caliber bullets and the size and position of the wounds suggest shots from above. I don't think your fella on the motorcycle could have got down from the roof and on his bike and clear from the crime scene that quickly. Highly unlikely."

I popped a Certs. "Well, why was he there?"

"Maybe they're working together, the shooter and him, or maybe he was meeting up with the kids, the True Suns, or maybe he heard that that Timmy's had the best donuts in town, how the fuck do I know?"

"What's eating you, man? You haven't been yourself lately."

He raised one shoulder and smiled briefly. "The Red Dragons were located in Scarborough, near the bluffs. And they wanted to spread their drug business."

"You find out who owns the Valiant?"

"It was stolen from a Mrs. Whitelaw," Sal said.

"Hmm—"

"Did you hear? Beddoes ate his column."

"Really?" I always liked Beddoes. He was irreverent, witty. Great sportswriter. "Good for him. A man of his word—outside the Soviet embassy?"

"Yeah."

I nodded with approval.

"What adjustments are we going to make?" Sal pushed back his fedora. The whites of his eyes were somewhat red.

"We'll find a way to slow them down. Coach Sinden was a bright guy and with John Ferguson as his assistant they'll change it up: more grit, collapse to the middle of the ice, protect the front of the net. "I always thought Fergie was just a goon, but the year I played for Montreal I learned to respect him. He's tough, but knows his hockey—a good tactician."

"Yeah—Awrey looked bad. So did the Hadfield line."

"Agree—"

Sal worried his lower lip. "You ever wonder, Superstar, how we tracked down that swinging apartment with the lava lamps so quickly?"

"Yeah. Susan Gomery called and—"

"That was just the spin we put out there." He looked away. "For the goddamn media. The real answer: Miriam. My wife. A cop's wife. She recognized the key. She'd been there—at the crime scene—hours before."

"Huh?"

"Yeah—" He picked at a piece of lint the size of a grain of rice on his thighs. Miriam Lambertino was taking Professor Hampton's non-trad creative writing workshop. "I don't know, she needed something new, you know? The kids are now fourteen and twelve and she was kind of bored and she had a lot of time on her hands and needed an outlet. So I said, what the fuck, you know, take the class. And I guess, they go there after class. Write and—"

"She's a Freedom Writer?"

"Yeah, yeah. Freedom Writers *Society*. Yeah." He lit another cigarette. "Romantic interludes happen—but not my wife." He pinched his lips, lines bracketing the edges of his mouth. "At least I don't think so. Should I think so?" He took a long slow drag.

"You don't want me looking into that. I don't want to look into that."

"Yeah, yeah." He took another drag. "She doesn't share her writing with me, but when she saw that key—you know, once I get home, I take out my gun and lock it in a box and place the box in a lower desk drawer. Also locked. Well, as I was emptying my pockets she saw the zippered case and the key—her fingerprints are on the case—her fingerprints are all over the apartment—"

"Christ—" She a person of interest?

"No, not yet. A lot of people's fingerprints are in that apartment. A regular Toronto International Airport. The key. It gets passed around."

"Yeah, I heard about that—my wife's been there too. Years ago. So, Gomery was still a part of the workshop or it was a plant—a frame job."

"I guess." He took another short, absent drag. "She was there. Miriam. She saw Gomery two hours before he checked out. Saw him squabble with Kittle, the Greenway publisher. And then Kittle and Miriam left. He brought her home."

How long after she saw Gomery at the apartment was he

dead?

"Like I said, two, three hours."

I whistled, low, slowly.

Sal stubbed his second cigarette. He wasn't really smoking them. They were just something to hold onto.

"Is this Mrs. Whitelaw, the owner of the stolen Valiant, a workshop member, too?"

"She is."

I sighed. "Let's take a look at the apartment. You and me, and Miriam—The once over. Maybe there's something your boys missed."

"Sure, sure. I'll gather up the others, a cast of thousands. Kittle, Whitelaw, Gomery, Hampton—"

"I'm sorry, man." I didn't know what else to say.

"Can you call Stana? I'd like to have her along—I'd feel more, I don't know, secure."

Connie's middle name was Miriam. Sal's wife was my daughter's Godmother. "Sure," I said.

The light was now still. A conical shadow separated the two of us.

"Only thing, one of us just needs to be home by 3:30, that's when Connie's home from kindergarten—Kids from the neighborhood walk her home."

He looked at his watch. It was nearly noon. "Call Stana."

"Will do."

He rubbed at the edges of his mouth. "You know, I found a poem she wrote? Miriam? It was sitting atop our bedroom dresser: 'Everyday, everyday, everyday / I repeat and repeat and repeat.' I don't know, that doesn't sound good does it?"

THE PAD WAS EVERYTHING you expected from a Beat Generation writers retreat: violet walls with orange trim; lava lamps; incense in the corners of each room (along radiators and the edges of kitchen counters) and on the dining and coffee tables;

and a set of bongo drums near the solid-state color television. Framed Frida Kahlo and Man Ray prints along with posters for avant-garde theater showings covered the walls. Man Ray's woman with the violin back appeared to be repelling my gaze with her over the shoulder disapproving nonchalance.

The refrigerator was loaded with Molson's Export and Golden. If you're hungry there were loaves of pumpernickel and rye bread and slabs of brick cheese and Kraft slices. Tucked in Tupperware: a variety of cold cuts.

On the counter a plate piled high with Snickerdoodles dotted in red dust clusters. I gently tugged on Miriam's left arm and gave her my lopsided grin. "Just what is this?"

"Mrs. Hampton. She always brought cookies." Miriam's dark hair swept to the left like a small waterfall. She wore glasses that made her eyes look half their normal size. Her voice was a husky, push of sounds, like she had a slight case of laryngitis. I always found it sexy. Of course, I never told her that.

"She handed me some cookies when I visited, yesterday."

Miriam nodded good naturedly. "She's out of control with the cookie thing," she whispered.

"She came here often?"

"Sometimes."

"Sometimes? Rarely. On occasion, let's say." Stewart Kittle was a big, barrel-chested fella in a green glen plaid suit, blue oxford shirt, and white hair and no-nonsense, laconic expressions that made him look like a live-action version of Race Bannon on *Jonny Quest*. "She loved treating us however—" he emphasized with small waves, like rolling tumbleweed, with his hand.

"What were you and Gomery arguing over?"

"Arguing?" His white-blond eyebrows stitched into a salamander. "Who told you that?"

I looked in the direction of Sal who glanced over at his wife.

Stana coughed gently, the freckles on her face dancing. "Three hours before he died, you two had a conversation, let's say."

Kittle laughed. "Conversation. That's good, that's good. I can tell you're a writer."

"Thanks."

Stana and Miriam shared knowing smiles. *This guy trying to sell us a sports car? Sheesh.*

"He was a bitter man." Kittle shrugged and shambled toward the radiator that was covered with black lacquer boxing. "Things didn't work out for him so he took it out on the rest of us." He pointed at those in the room. Whitelaw had recently published stories in *Chatelaine* and *Redbook* and Kittle was a publisher and Miriam showed real promise. "He was mad at our success."

Mrs. Whitelaw, fifty something, with pince-nez glasses and hair done up in a bun with a jade Zan pin holding it in place, agreed. "He was sloppy. In his writing, his lifestyle—the way he moved through a room."

If I had to bet money on it, I'd say Mrs. Whitelaw's birth certificate would say British Subject and not Canadian. She wore a long mauve dress with pleats and a Peter Pan collar. Gloves that climbed to her elbows were on both hands and she sipped tea from a small china cup buttressed by a tiny plate. "A sloppy, sloppy man, he didn't sit, he slid into chairs."

Seems I had heard this spiel before. Same damn wording. Slipping or sliding into furniture I think Mrs. Hampton had said.

Kittle placed his heavy hands with square blocky fingers on his upper thighs for emphasis. "Gomery's skin color was green with envy and that's the truth—believe it."

I stood in the center of the living room between Kittle and Whitelaw. Somehow, Sal on such short notice had gathered several members of the workshop together. Among the missing: Susan Gomery and Professor Hampton, and his wife.

I nudged back my porkpie and pushed into Kittle's lean with a lean of my own. "This all seems fairly vague, Kittle. Like those guys on the radio, how to talk talk talk and not really say anything."

"I resent that—"

"What had Gomery feeling pissed off?"

"The Serchuk series," Miriam said.

The radiator clanked which I thought rather odd because it was too warm of a day for it to be on. Maybe it was just the pipes in the old building—This place was built in the 1920s.

"The six-book series that got the prof tenure," Stana added.

Miriam nodded. "He wanted respect. He wanted credit. He felt that the first book, in part, was his. It wasn't about money." She sat down on a couch covered with an Aztec-style blanket. Lit a cigarette.

"The guy was crazy." Kittle slid between the two of us. "Absolutely crazy. A conversation with a writer makes you a co-author? Come on, now." His voice slipped into FM easy listening. "Look at his track record." He crowded closer to Miriam and talked to her as much as to the rest of us. "He wanted to grab, to hold onto The Professor's glory because he had none in his life, right Miriam? Douglas wasn't even invited here. He just popped in."

"Yeah. To talk to you, it seems. What's the beef?" I rubbed at the edges of my mouth.

Kittle smiled grandly. "Beef? More like delusions of grandeur. Visions—A nutter."

"He wanted co-author credit?"

"Yes," Miriam said.

"Like I said, a total nutter. You tried the cookies? They're delicious. I had one. Well, actually I had three or four." He patted his stomach that rode a little above his belt.

Mrs. Whitelaw laughed and I sensed some connection between them beyond an admiration for each other's sentences.

"Miriam, can you tell us about the argument?" Stana asked.

"He said he was going to sue Greenway unless they put his name on the book. The first book." She took a drag off her cigarette. "The first book, not the others. Just the first."

"And what did Mr. Kittle do?"

Kittle patted her knee reassuringly, or perhaps with a touch of warning.

Miriam shifted to the far side of the couch. "They got into a scuffle."

"Punches?"

"No, Stana, just a scuffle."

I turned to Kittle. "That sounds like a little more than an argument, pal."

"Or a conversation," chimed in Stana.

"The guy was tiresome. Do you know how many times he called my office to complain—and then he just pops in here unannounced—and pops off at me."

"So, it was just you and Miriam, here?" Sal adjusted the brim of his fedora, with his left hand, and his right, dangled near his side holstered snub-nosed.

Stana shot Sal a look.

"I was here," Mrs. Whitelaw, intervened with a pleasant smile. "And Mrs. Hampton, too." She smiled briefly at Mr. Kittle. "We were having an extra session over a story of mine. The New Yorker asked me to revise and resubmit, and I was in a rush to make the changes they suggested. Anyway." She played with the thin gold chain about her neck. "And then Gomery comes crashing in, in one of his dark moods, and disturbs our sessions. I don't blame Mr. Kittle for being annoyed. We couldn't get any work done with that character here." She shook her head. "I mean, we're all tired of his act."

"Is that how you saw it, Miriam?"

She smiled up at me. "I guess so."

"You guess or—?"

"Yeah, that's how I saw it, more or less."

"So the argument happens and you two leave and then what?" I turned to Mrs. Whitelaw.

"Well, he left—Gomery," Mrs. Whitelaw said. "He was here to see Mr. Kittle and once Mr. Kittle decided to take Mrs. Lambertino home there was no need to stick around."

"What about your car, when was it stolen?"

"I don't like what you're hinting at or suggesting."

"Donna reported it to the police late last week," Kittle said.

"Donna?"

"Mrs. Whitelaw," he quickly added.

She smiled up at the publisher, demurely.

"But what about the blood we found, under the radiator and at the foot of the couch?" Sal, hands in the pockets of his Sloan Wilson grays, followed Mrs. Whitelaw to the kitchen where she topped off her cup of tea.

Upon returning, she paused at the threshold between kitchen and living room to reach into her purse and pull out some tea biscuits. She apologized for the disruption but was hungry. "I can never eat a full meal. So I nibble, eight or nine times a day. And I find Mrs. Hampton's cookies a tad too sweet."

"Oh, I love them, they're delicious," Kittle said. "I don't know how she does it, so I asked her." He leaned forward about to give away top government secrets. "It's the butter. She never uses shortening." He shrugged. "I like cookies. I make a science of them." He laughed at his own joke.

"Speaking of science, pal, the blood on the floor, under the radiator, matches that of the decedent—" Sal pointed with his gray fedora.

"I don't know anything about that." Mrs. Whitelaw wiped away crumbs from her lips. "Gomery left shortly after Mr. Kittle did. Then Emily, that's Mrs. Hampton, and I went to Tony's around the corner for a beer."

"Can you check on that, Sal?"

"Check on it?" Mrs. Whitelaw's chin dropped and her face darkened. "Check on it? I'm not in the habit of lying, young man."

"We'll check on it," Sal said.

"My, my, my, you're all so suspicious," Kittle's voice purred like he was reading the radio's weather report. "Maybe Gomery returned after we all left and somebody else arrived and killed him. It's possible."

Over sixty students over the years had access to this apartment, these rooms. Anyone of them could have had a copy made, Kittle reasoned. The locks have never been changed, as far as I know.

"Maybe so," I muttered. "Maybe so—"

"Take a look around, honey," Sal said to his wife. "See if anything looks suspicious or different, anything. Try to find a misfit detail. Something that just doesn't fit. It might be important."

Miriam nodded, pursed her lips, and wandered away from the couch. I followed.

There were two bedrooms down the hall. One was converted into a writer's nook, floor lamps for all five individual carrels, a center table, and a small refrigerator to stockpile supplies. There were no lava lamps or incense present in this room. The walls were white, the floor hardwood, scuffed and stained, and there was a reading chair and couch against a far wall. Kitty-corner from the reading zone was a wall of books, bestsellers to obscure classics. The second bedroom was straight out of Hugh Hefner: a huge circular bed, mirrors on the ceiling, and a Hi-Fi sound system built into the headboard. On one of the walls, crate-like shelving, a series of boxes upon boxes, full of over a thousand records from jazz to rock to country.

"Anything here?"

No, she mumbled, and then smiled awkwardly. "I never, ever—" She pointed to the bed.

"I didn't say you did."

"But you thought it."

I said nothing.

"Sal wonders—doubts—"

"I'm not so sure—I think he really doesn't want to wonder at all. I offered to—to look into things—and he turned me down," I lied. "He's a little hot about it all, but he wants to protect you and he doesn't want to lose you."

Tears crowded the edges of her eyes.

She opened the cubby holes on the headboard. Found some condoms, cigarettes, and a couple of Erle Stanley Gardner paperbacks.

"Nothing out of the ordinary," she mumbled.

"How about the bathroom—let's check it."

"Sure."

We wandered into it.

The smell of vinyl was overpowering.

From the living room Kittle's voice was climbing the ladder as he told Sal all of his grievances against Douglas Gomery. "The man called my office nine, ten times a day. And when I didn't answer my phone he left rude messages with my secretary—Absolute nutter—"

"Absolutely," Mrs. Whitelaw said.

I wondered if she had a book under contract with Greenway.

Miriam checked the cabinets, above and under the sink, and the additional narrow cabinet over the toilet, nothing odd, she said, and then a hand lightly touched her mouth, and she gasped, the curtain, the shower curtain. She pointed, desperation in her voice. "The old one was a map of the continents. But this one—" see through, featuring tropical fish and three or four orcas, "it's new."

The vinyl smell.

Brand spanking new.

The shower curtains had been switched. Of course. I snapped my fingers. "The old one was used to wrap up the body—maybe it was even used as a mat to place under the body while Gomery was stabbed. And maybe, the killer or killers thought he was dead and then he surprisingly revived in Mrs. Whitelaw's supposedly stolen Valiant. In some way or other Gomery had been incapacitated, drugged. And then knifed. The lab results from the autopsy hadn't come back yet. Maybe another day or so Sal said, but I wonder—"

I touched Miriam gently on the shoulder. "You okay?"

Her face was heavy and downturned. "Yeah—"

"I don't like the looks of this," I said. "And all that stolen car crap. It's too neat."

Kittle's voice was climbing yet another ladder, discussing how annoying and clumsy Gomery's prose style was, and no wonder he never made it. "The guy often separated his subjects from his verbs with a comma, I mean, come on, man."

"There's lots of things I don't like," Miriam said.

WHEN I ARRIVED at Tan Mylow's modest home on MacGowan out in Scarborough he asked if this was an official meeting, Red Dragons business? I said it was and he said to give him a few minutes, he'd be right back, make yourself at home. I was in the rec room, paneled walls, blue carpeting, a wet bar, brown and gold light fixtures that resembled upside down pots for plants, and a snooker table. I practiced a few set shots. Forget about it. Bowling was my game.

Mylow returned, a Scotch in his hands, the cubes clinking and clacking. He was no longer in the powder blue suit with a skinny tie and neatly pressed shirt that he wore at De Havilland Aircraft where he was an engineer. Instead, he now sported fatigues, dragons on the epaulets, black boots, and a black beret with a shield that said "Always Vigilant." He handed me a club soda, three cubes. He knew I didn't drink.

"I do my research." He shrugged proudly and told me to go ahead and keep shooting. He didn't mind.

He was a big man with unnaturally dark hair, dark eyebrows, and eyes the color of coffee grounds.

I tried a bank shot. The ball rimmed out of the pocket. "Look,

I'd like to kibitz and play some pool, but I haven't seen my daughter all day, and I'd like to get home. So, not to be rude but—"

"I hear you got tickets for tomorrow night?"

How did he hear? "Yeah?"

"Lucky sonofabitch. You're a made guy. Connected."

"I wouldn't say that."

"I would. Tickets to *that* game. Christ. That's—" He held up a hand. "You earned it. Nine years in the NHL. Tough guy. You deserve the perks. But some of these other folks that come in on boats. They want to find the quick way to success. Shortcuts." His hands on his hips made his arms look like sideways chevrons. "We protect against that. We connect. To our neighborhoods. To our people."

"Uh-huh." I heard some asshole on one of those call-in radio shows the other day say we ought to bomb the boats and feed the fish. This Mylow fella would be supplying the cannon balls.

"You better be careful with me, us, I'm, we're, connected too—made."

"I don't follow."

"You will. When the time comes." A quirky grin of benign malice flashed across his face. "Canada's going to win tonight, right?" It wasn't really a question. More of a threat. He grabbed a cue stick from the wall.

"I think so."

"You think? They better." He smiled, it had rattlesnake style. No empathy. "I'm a virulent anti-communist." He leaned over the table with his cue and did a two-ball run into the corner pocket. "I assume I'm hitting solids—"

"Yeah, yeah. I sank a striped ball."

On the large walnut desk behind us were framed family photos, grenades, and four or five magazines to load into various handguns and machine guns.

He sank another ball in the far side-pocket.

"Vigilant? So, what, you help old ladies across the street?"

"Don't try to throw me off my game, Mr. Fuller. It's been tried. Doesn't work. My blood pressure never gets above 120. My heart rate, 68." He ran the rest of the table and then the eight. "Rack em up?"

"Fuck, no." I sat in a chair near a portrait of Rommel. "You served in WWII?" I was talking to Mylow, but glancing back at the general behind me.

"Rommel was a great tactician and he stood up to Hitler, stood up to fascism."

"And who are the fascists in your scenario?"

"Now, now.. Be nice. This is my home. I invited you here. You're a guest. Fascists, troublemakers, malcontents. Immigrants who don't want to play by the rules, new people who want things too soon, who don't want to work for it, people who invade and mess up our neighborhoods. We gotta protect ourselves from those who want to find the fast way."

When this guy got going he talked in paragraphs, not sentences. It was like he was a low-fi character in a Eugene O'Neill play. "My parents were new people to this country. Dad was a milkman; Mom a secretary."

"I'm not saying they're all bad. I'm saying those who take shortcuts need to be cut down permanently, if you know what I mean."

"I get the drift."

"And you, your people. Jews right? From Russia?" He made a face. "Russia. Christ. Anyway, you rose above. Good for you."

"Look, I'm not here for a civics lecture."

"Be nice—" He wagged a finger.

"I saw one of your 'club members' outside the shooting, at Timmy's driving away."

A hand swayed like trimming away weeds in a backyard. He placed his cue stick back on the wall rack. "Look anywhere around this area. Scarborough. Regent Park. Even Cabbagetown. You'll find our club members. We're 150 strong."

Holy shit. I had no idea. Para-military?

Some of those last thought bubbles I had spoken out loud. I do that sometimes. No internal censor. The inner monologues and dialogue get all mixed up. A result of too many concussions playing hockey, I guess. "I came to ask about a murder. Orlando Prescott—"

"That wasn't a Red Dragon assignment."

"What about the hit on the two True Suns out front of Tim Horton's?"

"My guy just happened to be there. Our information says he wasn't the shooter."

"Right. Your information. Care to tell me who your guy is?"

"I do not."

"I think you're running drugs. And I think you're in the middle of a drug war."

"Think what you want. Last time I checked, it's still a free country."

"Your guy just happens to be there when all this goes down— he just happens to like the donuts in that part of town?" It was Sal's joke, but why shy away from such damn good material?

"Not bad, not bad. I think I could use you as a copywriter at De Havilland." He looked at his fingers. On one of them was an Iron Cross.

"This drug business of yours? We'll stop you."

"We? Who's we?" He towered over me, eyes burning. "I don't see no cavalry behind you. We?" He laughed. "Look, stick to the Prescott kill. Look into Tomboys and Dicks. I hear a lot goes down there. Things vice should look into, but they got their hands full." Another rattlesnake sneer. "Oh, yeah, in case you haven't guessed, some of my boys work for the police—you want me to top off your drink?"

The rest of the conversation went nowhere. He lectured, opined on the sins of the "mongrelization" of Canada. On my ride home five of his always vigilant boys trailed behind me on their Triumphs. The afternoon sun glinted like sparks of flint off their handlebars. It wasn't really so much of a polite escort as a powerful reminder of just how outnumbered I was.

Stana saw them pull up and turn around in our driveway out in Willowdale. From the kitchen window she absently nodded as two of their riders waved at her before driving off.

I kissed her and hugged Connie.

Susan Gomery called minutes ago. Seems she heard about our big powwow out at the Freedom Writers apartment and she wasn't too happy with what was said.

"How does she know what was said?"

"I don't know, someone in our little group talked." Stana's eyes danced.

"Hmm."

"We got a meeting with her tomorrow. My office at *The Star*. 9:30. Dinner's ready."

She'd made steak and onions with a side dish of sour cream and cucumbers. And a salad—vinegar and olive oil dressing. What Susan Gomery had to share with us, would knock our world sideways, Stana said.

And, goddamn it, it did.

Game Two

Wednesday, September 4, 1972

Stana couldn't believe that her old professor was still the police's prime murder suspect.

We were in her new office at *The Toronto Star*. She had joined their staff six years ago and just got promoted to features editor. She had a daily column and was in charge of the Weekend Sunday supplement, writing human-interest stories. Susan Gomery was due to arrive any minute with a yarn guaranteed to create some serious radioactive fallout. "She's claiming," Stana lowered her voice to a sullen alto pitch, "that the first Chance Serchuk novel was written *solely* by her ex-husband and wants justice on Doug's behalf, wants me to write a story about it, exposing my former professor as a fraud and a thief, and possibly a killer." Stana's lower lip curled under the pencil tapping her chin. "Honestly, in terms of Professor Hampton's legacy, I don't know what's worse, being a killer or a plagiarist." She laughed at her joke, the pencil shaking slightly in her fingers. Stana can have a bit of a dark sense of humor.

"So, we're not just talking suggestions here, conversations between the two, but outright stealing. Gomery wrote the first draft alone—no collaboration," I said.

"Correct."

I slid a Chinese takeout box from Sai Woo's toward her. "So, Susan Gomery clearly suspects that Professor Hampton did her ex in—? Perhaps that explains her absence from the writers' retreat, yesterday."

"Perhaps—but—"

"But what?"

"Chip's no killer."

"Chip now?'

"Don't be a mope." Her pencil stopped tapping. "Let's hear her out."

My box of chicken chow mein had some smoke flavoring added to the mix, making me even hungrier. Stana neatly unfolded the lid to her moo goo gai pan and dropped her pencil on a desk blotter, the size of a small living room rug. Her new desk was freshly wood-stained, mocha red. "The Professor can wither you with words. He doesn't need a damn stiletto." She shook her head, eyes flashing, the freckles on her upper cheeks brightening. "The former lover angle was nonsense. Professor Hampton loved women." A hand rested near the bend between her neck and shoulder. About every other year, he had an affair with a young grad student, Stana said. His wife knew about it too. "It was an open relationship. Hampton was very heterosexual. Very. Gomery—wouldn't interest him. At all."

"*Open relationship.* I bet he messed around and the wife didn't."

Stana couldn't disagree.

"The fact is Doug was killed in Professor Hampton's apartment. The blood matches."

"Yes. We've already been over that. But as you learned, that place was a regular love shack."

"But this charge of authorship backed up with an earlier manuscript, a complete early draft, changes things. That's evidence and a real motive." I dropped my porkpie next to the two Parker pens parked in their brass quivers.

"Like his open marriage the writers' retreat had an open door policy. Who knows how many keys were out there floating about." Stana ate with chopsticks.

My wife's sophisticated. I was digging in with a plastic fork. And fingers. "But why rent the space under an alias?"

"Decorum?"

"Decorum," I mocked and nudged sauce from my chin. "What's so great about this guy? Goddamn libertine."

"He's a brilliant man, made you believe that you were brilliant. I don't think I would have become a reporter if I hadn't taken his classes." She reached for my hand. "Look into the victim's story. Who might want Doug dead? Who might want to *frame* The Professor?"

The sky outside her window was red and the lake glowed as if little fires were dancing on the blue-capped peaks of broken waves.

"Have you read the Serchuk books?"

"I barely have time to read the *Fantastic Four*," I said.

That cracked her up.

She leaned back in her swivel chair. It had padded armrests and the entire office was brightly present with gentle lighting from fixtures that resembled glow-in-the dark Frisbees. She had a file cabinet, a view of Lake Ontario, expensive Parker pens, lithe blond curtains, like long petticoats, that reached the floor's edge, spotless venetian blinds, and a brand-new electric typewriter. *The Star* did it up big when they promoted her. That's for sure.

I was looking for the bowl of candy with the brown M&Ms removed.

"His writing is lyrical, beautiful," she said. "He cares about people. Affairs of the heart. And his books are so kind."

"Art's always bigger than us," I said. "Faulkner was a great writer, but I think I read somewhere that he once told his daughter to leave him alone, no one remembers Shakespeare's daughter. A real piece of work that Faulkner guy. But *The Sound and the Fury*. It's pretty fucking good."

"Note taken," she conceded.

There was an insistent knock on the doorframe that I felt in my shoulders. There stood Susan, a slight woman with dull hair the color of snow that fell a few days ago. On her right wrist was a hexagonal chain attached to a briefcase. Behind her right ear, a cigarette.

She was expecting her first child around Christmas. It took great effort to sit in the padded chair Stana directed her to.

"You're Hayden Fuller—Scored the winning goal in the '62 Finals."

I smiled my lopsided grin.

Her tongue quickly darted across thin lips. "I'll keep this short." She flashed a key, undid the lock around her wrist, and gently placed the briefcase on the desk as if it contained a nuclear isotope. From inside, she pulled up a sheaf of paper, inky blotches spilled across yellowed pages. The title *A Boy on the Leafs Blueline* by J. Douglas Gomery, 8/17/47.

"The J stands for nothing," she said. "Doug just thought the initial lent him an air of class." She laughed. "Forensics has already looked at this. The wood fiber in the paper, the ink from the typewriter ribbon. This was written in 1947. Two years before Hampton's version. The words are different, but the plot is the same. Scene for scene."

"You show this to Hampton?" My lips pressed firmly against my lower teeth.

"Hampton?" Susan Gomery looked away, out at the lake, his upper lip curling back. Her teeth were too big for her mouth. "I told him about it. Several times. But he had no desire to see the pages or meet with me. Doug met with him. Hampton denied everything, of course."

"Of course." We had tried to meet with him recently, a followup to yesterday's confab at the retreat, and he curtly said, he'd only talk to us with his lawyers present, and presently they were golfing.

"I insisted to Douglas that we work through a lawyer—but he

trusted in one-on-one communication, coming to terms, man-to-man. The sap." In the distance the blue waves bounced in the splash of sun with flames of water. Susan shifted in her chair, trying to get comfortable—her back was sore. "Money wasn't what it was about for Doug. 'I don't need any ambulance chasers,' he said. This was all about his reputation. And that's why I'm here. To restore his reputation. He's no druggie, and he wasn't a *peevish* person or all green with envy as I heard Mr. Kittle had said. That company man. That suit. That piece of shit."

"Don't hold back. Tell me what you really think—"

She laughed and pulled a crumpled pack of cigarettes from her black purse, apparently forgetting the one behind her right ear. She offered Stana one, but didn't offer me one.

"How did you know I didn't smoke?"

"I'm observant," she said. "No nicotine stains on your fingers and all the cigarette butts in the ashtray have lipstick on them." She beamed. Stana slid the ashtray between the two of them. She lit Stana's cigarette with a Zippo and then her own. "You see, that's the first lesson Hampton teaches in his workshop, the power of observation—the greatest tool a writer can have." She pushed her small hands against the top of her thighs. "A few years back, I too took Professor Hampton's creative writing class. I too was a member of the Freedom Writers Society. But my writing wasn't worth much beyond mediocrity. Still, I learned a lot. He had this exercise where you had a list of a hundred and twenty adjectives and were instructed to pick three to inhabit your lead character. Three. And there were some weird words on that list, let me tell you. *Churlish. Parsimonious—*" She laughed. "And a favorite of the workshop: *peevish.*" She returned her gaze to the blue, watery flames.

"I've also shown the manuscript to Kittle the publisher—nothing—total denial—Greenway Publishing says Hampton's a great Canadian artist and with the Summit Series and everyone talking hockey this is the time to uplift our artists, not denigrate them."

"Shakespeare's daughter," I mumbled.

"Huh?"

"Private joke. Sorry."

She tilted her head and gave up on trying to follow what my damn aside was all about. "Anyway, is it okay to denigrate my ex? Doug hasn't done drugs in years—and he's no homosexual. I don't know how that rumor started."

"That's not what I heard," I said. "Miriam told me after canvassing the apartment the other day that Doug told her, in a private moment at a wine and cheese party, that from 1955 to 1959 he had a very tempestuous relationship with another man—"

She looked away and chewed her lower lip. "That was a phase—"

"Four to five years?"

"He got shock therapy to help." Her lips quavered as tears sprinkled her cheeks. "It helped—He hasn't slept with a man for over thirteen years—but the therapy also ruined his creativity. He hasn't written anything good in thirteen years."

"What about the sweater we found in the car? Your husband was like what, two hundred and forty pounds? The sweater was a medium—"

"A false narrative?" She butted her cigarette. "A narrative tapping into his bisexual past that is no longer a part of his straight-man present."

Stana jotted down notes.

"My husband may have been sterile, but that didn't mean he didn't like the ladies—"

Stana and I shot each other looks.

"Doug caught the mumps when he was twelve." She patted her stomach. "The child isn't his—and he's, was, okay with that. He knows, knew, how much I want a kid."

Stana flipped through the manuscript's pages, quickly catching some of the rhythms to the prose. "It reads like Chip," she said.

"Or Hilary Hampton reads like Douglas Gomery."

"But there were five other novels after this one," I said.

"I want my husband, my former husband, to get credit for this one."

"I'm surprised by the attitude of Greenway, a so-called Christian Press," Stana said. "What did Dr. King say? The arc of history bends toward justice?" She patted the pages in front of her. "This is some kind of history."

"Stewart Kittle? A suit, that's all he is. No heart. Christ—he's the Tin Man of publishing."

We paused, waiting for her to continue.

She shook her head dismissively, the pink part of her hairline shining under white snow. "Thinks he's a love god. I mean, the fella runs a religious press and then has sex with me to give me what I want, a child, but it's all about what he wanted, to sleep with every woman in the class and then brag about it later."

"He's the father?"

"The child has no father."

"Cool." I held up my hands to apologize.

"Mrs. Whitelaw, he's done her too. But her husband's dead so I guess that's okay," Susan said bitterly.

The Mrs. Whitelaw sex dig sounded like embellishment— more a fancy of fiction than reality.

"I'll look this over," Stana promised, thumbing through pages and pages of the "Gomery" manuscript.

"Three days—I'll give you three days, and if you turn me down, I'll take my story to *The Globe and Mail*."

"Well, we can't have that, can we?" Stana winked playfully.

"You'll learn a lot about the beloved professor by looking at that."

"Some things, I wish I didn't have to learn," Stana said.

—

FRAMED POSTERS OF GREENWAY BOOKS, including a new up-dated cover in bright blue with white piping for *A Boy on the Leafs Blueline* dwarfed the room of color and light, as did the sentimental posterized aphorisms on success, optimism, and Christian love. Stewart Kittle offered Stana and me Perriers. "Best thing for you," he said. "Lay off the coffee and the soda. Drink water."

"I'll take my water from the tap, thanks," I said.

Stana, sitting by my side, chuckled. She wondered if Kittle had a twist of lime on the serving tray propped on his desk. He did.

"Tap water, huh. Old school." He had a high forehead that shone like a thin coat of car wax. His eyes were shaded smears of charcoal in a bright, robust face. Heavy trough lines ran around the sides of his mouth.

"Today's my birthday and look—" He gestured with two out-stretched arms. On the granite table and shelving behind me were platters of desserts: coconut-clustered dates, three kinds of fudge, and lemon and butter tarts. "Everybody brings treats to the office. Especially on birthdays." He shook his head with faux disapproval. "Instead of a smoke break, you get a fat break." He patted his stomach.

"It's quite an assortment," Stana said.

"Mrs. Hampton has yet to give me any cookies." He sighed. "She makes cookies for all us Freedom Writers on our birth-days, wraps them up on colored plates with big bows. I know you heard I'm one of her husband's students."

"We also heard you're the father of Susan's child—"

He sat back, one thin eyebrow raised, his white hair very still. "She told you that?"

"She did." Stana lit a Parliament, blew smoke in a far corner.

"Well, she's better at creating fiction than I thought." He laughed and sipped at his Perrier, the ice cubes clacking. "You can't believe everything she says."

There may be some truth to that—Susan Gomery's crack about Mrs. Whitelaw sleeping around was a little shrill and inauthentic.

"Her absence from the meeting yesterday was noticeable." Stana leaned forward in her chair, eyes narrowing.

"Look, I want to clear all this up once and for all."

"I understand that Hampton is only talking now through lawyers."

"That was my idea." He squeezed his hands together. "The manuscript, the first book, is not and never was a product of Susan's husband's so-called creativity. And she knows. That. God how she knows that." His head shook disparagingly. "She's just trying to cash in—the literary gravy train." His upper lip quivered slightly with anger. His client, his personal mentor, was an honest man. "He never cheated no one."

"Except on his wife," I muttered.

"That's an understanding between them. No need for the media to get a hold of that."

"Yeah, I can only imagine how it might affect the rep of a Christian Press."

Kittle put his glass of Perrier down.

The clock behind us, shaped like a star, stuttered.

"We're all fallen in some way, Mr. Fuller. Or should I call you, Mr. Perfect?"

"I'm not perfect."

"Exactly, he who is without sin cast the first stone?"

"Yeah, yeah. I read that somewhere."

Greenway Publishing was rushing the first three books of the Serchuk series to press, just to show the media and all involved in the case against The Professor of Greenway's undying support. "The book is his. The series is his. And soon it will be a gift to Canada."

The desk he sat behind was marble. The lamps were made of jade. The carpet was midnight blue. The whole room oozed luxury and acquisitiveness.

"And the second book, *Overtime.* Wow," he said, adding that the North York Board of Education was assigning it to all their seventh-grade classes in the district. "Do you know what that means for our sales?" His smile brightened the edges of his eyes. "The first reprinting of that book can pay for, well, just imagine what it can pay for, and *do* for a small press like ours. Moreover, we'll be bringing Canadian content into our schools. Expo forced us to see who and what we are. It was all about nation building. Don't kid yourself." His smile stretched. "And now the Summit Series."

His speech felt rehearsed—like in front or a mirror or some damn thing. The cadence was stentorian, and the accompanying hand gestures, sharp flags raised on each word, were a little too choreographed.

All of that patriotism had me almost puking in my mouth. "Why would Doug make up such a thing?"

"A desire for fame? A need to be seen? I mean, the guy was a loser, his mind drug-addled."

That line again. "Susan feels differently and a forensic study of the paper proves that the original manuscript was written in 1947, two years before Hampton's version came out in 1949."

"So what? How long did it take Milton to write *Paradise Lost*?"

"This is a question of ownership—What if Douglas did write the first book and Hampton aped his style—what if you're wrong?" I pushed back my porkpie. I hadn't touched my Perrier.

"Then I'm wrong. But I'm not." Kittle peeled cellophane off a cigar. He cut the end with a small guillotine gizmo. He struggled lighting it. "Sure, sure, sure. Look, Chip told me something in confidence and I'm telling you in confidence—" He sat forward, the cigar finally catching. Across the room, the clock that looked like a star stuttered straight up the hour, its two hands appearing momentarily stuck.

I'm never very confident with folks who share other folks' confidences.

"Hampton wasn't queer or nothing, Fuller, Stana, but he wanted to know, like a writer, a scientist, what being a homosexual was all about. I know that sounds pretentious but did he tell you about interviewing Howard Hawks? *The Red River* trip?"

"He told Hayden," Stana said.

"J. Douglas Gomery went with him on that trip. And they experimented, Kittle told me one day, while we were playing racquetball. They shared a motel room in Santa Monica. And he and Dougie boy, who was queer, carried on. Lovers. Well, Douglas was serious; Chip was just experimenting. And he felt guilty. Afterward. He felt he had been trifling with Doug's emotions. And maybe he had. Who's to judge? Hampton shared all this with Doug on their return flight home. 'It was all a mistake,' Chip apologized and Doug, feeling jaded, and somewhat *peevish—*"

There was that word again. *Peevish.*

"Stole the original manuscript written on yellow paper." He shifted in his chair. "I'm sure that's the copy Susan showed you."

"It was yellow alright," Stana said.

"Gomery wrote a new cover page with his name on it to wallpaper over The Professor's words and genius. Proof of ownership, my ass."

"I don't know—the typeface matches—title and manuscript pages."

"So, he wrote '*his* authentic title page' on the prof's typewriter—he had access to his office. That's all you got?" He sighed. "You're fishing for red herrings—inconsequential details—"

"Maybe. But the question of ownership remains. You know what Hampton told me in his home?" My fingers tented together. "He said he *discussed the plot* of the book on the flight to Santa Monica. He never said it was completed. He hadn't written it yet when they made that trip together."

"He wrote the first draft *after*." Stana finished my thought.

"Why else would Hampton give Gomery fifteen thousand in severance pay," I said.

"And Susan Gomery insists that her husband was bisexual but is now straight."

"Susan Gomery insists on a lot of things. Like that utter nonsense that I'm the father of her unborn child. Please." He puffed on his cigar. "She leans towards delusions—check her medicine cabinet. Every time she looks in a mirror she says hello to five or six of her friends." He laughed.

I didn't like this fucker.

"You can't trust anything she says. And the severance pay? That was to assuage The Professor's conscience. He can't admit to what really happened now can he?" Kittle shrugged. "Would you admit it? Sleeping with a male student? It could tank the book, the series. So in the version of the story he told you in his home he muddies up the truth."

"How much are you muddying it up now?" Stana tapped her fingers impatiently atop his marble desk. "I don't quite believe you, Mr. Kittle. There's something off, not right, about this workshop group and the stories you all spin. You benefit from his death. So does The Professor. So does the press."

"That's true." He puffed his cigar. "Absolutely true. But it doesn't make us guilty of murder. But, yes, we do benefit from his murder—case closed there, counselor." He let loose another low chuckle. "And to be honest with you this publicity won't help the book. I'm trying to do damage control here and Susan Gomery is out of control." He tapped ashes off his cigar and let it rest at the lip of the ashtray. "And then we have this Summit Series which should help promote the book but could also kill it." He blew air between his lips. "If we don't beat the Russians, maybe the North York Board of Education only uses our book for a year and then drops it quickly because suddenly Serchuk appears incredibly dated, our brand of hockey, the brand Hampton writes about, no longer relevant. I don't want any of the Soviet players murdered or anything, but if a few of them could blow out a knee or get a broken wrist or ankle, that would be really convenient." He laughed again. "Especially that Yakushev or Kharlamov—we, Greenway, would *benefit* from that. Just kidding. Sort of."

"Great, we appreciate that. The honesty part."

I was being ironic.

I don't think he got it.

"Can I continue with my story?"

Stana nodded.

"That copy in yellow was the only one Hilary had. This was the days before Xerox." He shifted in his chair. "You ever hear the story of Edna St. Vincent Millay, *Conversation at Midnight*? A collection of poems. Well, maybe a drama poem? Anyway—" He waved a hand covered with five or six rings. "Nineteen thirty-six. Sanibel Island, Florida. Hotel fire, manuscript lost. She goes home and rewrites the whole thing from memory, and it was published the very next year. That's what happened with The Professor. Dig? He rewrote the whole book, so of course the plot matches. That's what he told me." He pushed some papers to a far corner on his marble-top desk. "And I believe him."

I looked over at the Christian Love poster, and felt a block of ice melting in my stomach. I shook my head. "Hmm? Fifteen thousand is a lot of severance pay, huh? Who wanted to sever Douglas permanently?"

"Probably the guy in blue cashmere—gay love gone wrong— Look, I'm backing The Professor's play on this, his story," Kittle said.

"Right." I rubbed at the edges of my mouth.

But so much about this wasn't right.

"Look into the blue cashmere angle. I bet you'll find some illegal wrangle behind it. Gay love mixed with, what, drug dealing maybe?" He held up open hands as if he were checking for rain. "Just saying."

"Uh-huh," Stana said.

On my way out I grabbed a chunk of fudge and two butter tarts.

"Hey, hey, easy on the butter tarts, pal. I haven't tried them yet," he said. "Save me some."

"LET'S KEEP THIS OFF THE RECORD," Mrs. Whitelaw said. "What I'm about to tell you is true, you can follow up on what I tell you, only don't mention my name."

"Deal," I said.

We were sitting in my office. Thankfully after dropping Stana off at *The Star*'s offices I checked with my answering service and discovered Mrs. Whitelaw wanted to meet with me. It was early afternoon, a warm day for September. She wore a fawn-colored dress with three buttons, white trim, and ruffled sleeves. Her shoulders were straight, knees together, horizontal age lines around both lips as she sipped tea that she had brewed up on my hot plate. She brought the tea bag with her. I only drink coffee, black, or Pepsi, real real cold. And tap water, of course.

"I feel bad about what I said yesterday."

"Go on—"

She dipped the edge of a biscuit, which she also brought with her, into the tea. It darkened slightly and she ate the damp part quickly before it broke away from the rest. She said she felt like she was living in two crowded spaces at once: that of the workshop and the need to please Mr. Kittle and that of her good friend Susan Gomery.

"You're the one that told her about what we said."

"Yes." She nodded firmly. "If the reprinted and updated Serchuk books did well they were going to add some new ones to the line, and Mr. Kittle had promised that I could ghost write one, possibly two, of the new novels."

So I was right. She *did* have a book contract.

"That promise has me excited but I also feel compromised in some terrible ways."

"Such as?" I cleared several papers and bills to the far side of my desk and placed my phone at right angles, squaring it up. I was giving her time to consider how much she wanted to reveal.

"You were right about *peevish*."

"Uh-huh." The sun burned through the slitted blinds creating thin snake lines across my desk.

"The workshop, me, Kittle, the Hamptons, and Miriam, in part, although she's not really a full-fledged member of our group, came up with that spin. *Peevish*—"

"One of 120 adjectives—"

"Right. Miriam's an adjunct member of our group. She's been invited out to the retreat a couple of times. By Stewart. I think he rather fancies her."

"I see." My cheeks were burning and the back of my neck was sore.

"We chose that word to paint Gomery's character. To create a man who is jealous to—" She put aside her biscuit and stared into her tea cup and the blue scrollwork on the edgings of the saucer. "We wanted to discredit him because he was jeopardizing the reputation of The Professor and the re-launch of the series."

"And your crack at books seven and eight—"

She studied the ruffles around her arms. "Yes."

"So did he write the first book?"

"I don't know. The point is he was making enough chaos about the whole thing that we had to counterattack."

"And the cashmere sweater?"

"That I'm not sure about." She looked about my office: two filing cabinets; three chairs; an old wooden desk, a coat rack, a hat rack, a sink, a small fridge, and an Export A calendar of the 1962–63 Toronto Maple Leafs, the best team I ever played for. "You don't put on much of a front."

"You can't if you want to stay in my kind of business."

"I believe you are honest."

"And I believe your meeting with me is well-intentioned."

"Thank you." She sipped more tea. Except for the lines around her lips her skin was extraordinarily smooth. "I think we were trying to ghost light him—or his memory."

"Ghost light?"

"Like that movie with the husband who acts like he doesn't see what the wife sees but what she sees is what he puts in front of her. He's trying to drive her insane—"

"You mean gaslight—"

"Gaslight. Right. Right."

"Like the film with Charles Boyer—"

"I was thinking of the earlier English version. It's much better."

I smiled.

"Susan and I have been friends for ten, eleven years—and—"

"Is the child Kittle's?"

"The child is hers."

They *were* good friends.

"Of course. Let me rephrase the question. Did Kittle father the child?"

"That I'm not at liberty to tell."

"Is that a no?"

"I'm not at liberty—"

"Firm no, soft no?"

"Not at liberty—"

"What about—"

"The gay angle? It's just an angle." She finished her biscuit, wiping at the corners of her mouth with a silk handkerchief. "We came up with that in the workshop too. Well, Kittle did."

"Why?"

"Misdirection."

I told her about the affair J, Douglas had had with a man,

1955–59. He had confessed as much to Miriam.

"That's a long time ago. Susan told me all about that. He wasn't that way these last ten or so years."

"Uh-huh. And your car, it was stolen?"

"Oh, yes." She finished her tea, tilted her head, and pondered the possibilities. "Well, as far as I know. I feel it was stolen, I reported it as stolen, but whether or not a member of the workshop took it from me, well—"

"That brings us back to the night of the killing. Two, three hours before Doug died, presumably in that space, Kittle and Miriam left early. He drove her home. And then you and Emily Hampton went to Tony's for a beer?"

"Or two or three. I'm afraid we got a bit tipsy."

I laughed. "Two or three. And then what?"

She walked me to the subway station and said she'd catch a cab home. "Do you mind if I brew up a second cup of tea?"

"No, no. Not at all."

She searched her purse for a second bag. "During the Great Depression Mother used to park used tea bags on the edge of her saucers. Often she'd get three cups from one bag." She tilted her head and let the memory leave quietly. "I'm glad the days of those frugalities have passed."

"So, you saw Mrs. Hampton get in the cab or did she only suggest she was hailing a cab?"

"Well, I'm not—yes, I remember, it was a Diamond cab. Yes, she got in."

"Hmm."

"So, you really think he was wrapped up in a shower curtain—and then somehow revived once placed in my car?" She found a fresh tea bag.

"I do—I think he was drugged, stabbed, left for dead, and then came to in a rolling Valiant."

"What happened to the people transporting him?"

"They were freaked. Jumped clear."

"And where's the shower curtain? If they were freaked out, I don't think they'd grab the shower curtain while exiting."

"No. I don't think they would, Mrs. Whitelaw. That's a good point—a damn good point—unless they put him in the car sans curtain."

Suddenly the door to my office kicked open.

It was unlocked yet these knuckleheads had to do things the hard way, with style. They hit the door with such force that the frosted glass with my name on it splintered, and bits and pieces crinkled to the floor.

"God damn it, Saba—"

"Blame Chunky here. He doesn't know his own strength."

Mrs. Whitelaw had both hands on her purse.

"Sorry about that." Chunky's high-pitched squeal didn't match his size. He was big, blundering, with hands the size of small sofas.

They both carried .38s.

"Sorry to break up your little tea party, ese." Today Saba wore all white Lee clothing that looked like he grabbed off a rack at the Gap in Buffalo. His buffed and waxed boots had Cuban heels. On his back, the double sun crest, Eye/I. And the .38 in his left hand glistened with shivers of sunlight. "I like revolvers," he muttered. "They don't jam."

The burly fella over Saba's left shoulder sniggered. There was a touch of a hyena to it.

"And speaking of guns, put yours in the desk drawer. Easy, ese, easy—"

I removed my snub-nosed .38 from its side holster and slid it away in the desk.

"Lock the drawer."

I did.

"Leave the key here."

I plunked it on the blotter. "You fellas always wear Ray-Bans?"

"They make us look good," Saba said. "And that's part of being in a gang. Always look good."

"All showboat, pal. Who you trying to impress?"

"You, ese." He waved the gun. "Let's go. The boss wants to see you."

"Maceo?"

"This ain't twenty questions, ese—Move your ass."

"Mrs. Whitelaw, it was a pleasure meeting you." I stood, performed a half-bow, and reached for my porkpie on the hat rack. "All right, Mr. Clean. Lead the way—"

"Mr. Clean? Is that some kind of joke."

"I figured you all had a registered patent on ese. I had to come up with something on the fly."

"Some joke," Chunky echoed. He could only be about fifteen. Acne dotted his chin and forehead. "Mr. Clean—"

Hyenas filled the room.

As the three of us left, I realized that Mrs. Whitelaw was probably going to give a pass on that second cup of tea.

IT WAS THE PERFECT SPOT, across from the bar and the pro shop, and just down from the pinball machines. This was where Orly listened, observed, and shined shoes on weekends and Wednesdays and Thursdays, league nights, Maceo said, his skin the color of cooked lentils, his breath full of cigar ash. He wore a checkered chambray shirt that looked best spread over a breakfast table.

I studied Orly's abandoned chair, imagining him here now, the clatter of pins filling up the lobby, causing our shoulders to shudder. I had a slight headache. I get them a lot—residual fallout from playing a tough brand of hockey.

I dry swallowed some Anacin from the pocket of my red windbreaker.

"The kid's a thief," Maceo muttered. "A gonif, as your people would say."

How did he know I was a Jew? And what did he mean by the

comment?

Maceo escorted me by the arm to his office, in back of the pro shop and cubby holes full of bowling shoes.

For a Wednesday afternoon, Danforth Bowl was busy, the ceiling full of curling cigarette smoke, a gauzy haze of low-slung hammocks.

Around the arcade games, Troy and his boys, all in Ray-Bans, pushed flippers and leaned and lifted their feet and shoulders to the ball's movement in, around, and against bumpers. I didn't know how they could see a damn thing. The interior lights were dull, dim.

In the farthest lane, Fitzpatrick and Everly bowled, splashing pins about. Fitzpatrick bowled a hard ball with a lot of spin, and a quaking explosion upon impact. I never would have known he was that strong. Everly bowled a straight, restrained ball. No action. Between frames, he sipped a tall glass of soda and laughed, his voice full of the spirit of one-upmanship. "I dare you to pick up that 7-10," he pushed. "I dare you. Ten says you can't. Ten bucks."

"I trusted that kid and he stole from me." Maceo pulled me away from the 7–10 drama. He rolled up his sleeves, crinkling the cuffs above the elbows. On the office walls were vintage pin-ups, sexy Elvgren–type knockoffs of women bowling.

One of them was falling because her panties had slipped to her ankles. I wasn't sure what that was about.

Maceo dragged a cart to the edge of his desk. It housed a pair of bulky TV monitors and a square electronic box that was the size of a tank lid. Mark IV Video Recorder, security tapes, he said. Maceo directed my look with his hand to a camera hanging in the nook of the far corner. Its target: the wall safe across the way, behind us. He pressed play.

Grainy images jittered. Fallouts of snow. And then Orly. He opened the wall safe, pulling out policies, folders, bonds, and cash in brick-thick bands.

"Twenty-thousand. The kid took twenty-thousand from me. Me, his uncle. I'm no altekaker. You like that word? I'm well-read." He laughed, a little too pleased with himself. He lit a fresh cigar. "I trusted him with closing the joint up and with the combination to the safe and this is how he shows his gratitude?" A hand rested on his hip as he puffed vigorously. "What would you do?"

"Kill him? What else?"

That cracked him up. "You got a good sense of humor. Of course, all you people do. Mel Brooks, Lenny Bruce, and that new kid, Woody Allen." Another puff, followed by a long slow drag.

"Let's not forget Jackie Gleason," I said.

"He's a kike? Who knew."

I give up.

"Me, kill the kid? I loved him—I even let him drive my car, now and then." He sat down, puffed heavily. "Let him take it to Niagara Falls. What's that 85 miles away? One sixty, one seventy round trip? When he brought the car back I checked the odometer. He took it only 120 miles round trip. It came up short. He insisted he had taken it to Niagara. He didn't. The kid had secrets—Anyway, I didn't know the money was missing until he went missing."

It took two days to find the body.

"You loved the kid. Okay." I shrugged. "I think the True Suns had something to do with Orly's death. If you loved the kid, why do you let punks like the True Suns bowl here?"

"They're okay kids. A little mixed up. I too at seventeen was. Give them a chance."

"Was Orly working for the Red Dragons?"

"Red Dragons—" That irritated Maceo, big time, his lower teeth denting his upper lip. His eyes darkened and the personable smile slipped away from his face.

"Drug war," I said. "Them and the True Suns. I was there

when two of Saba's boys got got. Early morning. Outside of Timmy's near Park District School."

"I heard, I heard. But drugs. That's a big assumption—"

"There was coke in Orly's shine box."

"Coke? The police said a little bit of coke—the kid was an experimenter—how did this all of a sudden become a drug war?"

"The Red Dragons are WWII veterans. I don't see them fighting for turf out front of a Tim Horton's, Maceo. This is a war—and I get the sense you're keeping your cards close to your vest."

"I always liked seven-card stud."

"Right."

He rolled up his right sleeve. An ace of spades and tagline scrawled below it in jagged letters: "Never show your hole card."

"I think Orly was working with the Dragons. The Suns found out. Killed him. The Dragons, angry, reciprocated, killing two Suns in vengeance."

"You really need to write for the movies. There hasn't been a good gangster film since *Bonnie and Clyde*—"

"I prefer *Wanda*."

"Huh?"

"Inide film. Arty. Something a philistine like you wouldn't understand."

He swaggered away my cultural criticisms with a shrug of his shoulders. "Charles Street did Orly in. The gays—that Orly—" He puffed heavily. "He was a little funny. Like Rock Hudson, huh? A regular fegele."

"You read the Yiddish dictionary while sitting on the john?"

He held up both hands, enough, enough. No more kibitzing.

"How about sex slaves? Orly thought you were heading a sex-slave racket?"

"What. That kid. A gasser. Maybe Orly *did* write for the movies. Roger Corman. Sex slaves," he muttered. "What an imagination."

"Cigarette burns were all over his body, Maceo. The kid was

tortured. Humiliated," I said. "Sodomized."

"Sounds like a sex crime," Maceo quickly added. "Charles Street set. Tomboys and Dicks." He rubbed at an itch along an eyebrow's edge. "I'm telling you what goes on there, and all along Yonge Street, a goddamn Sodom and Gomorrah. One early, early morning, Abby, Orly's friend, was leaving a party she had stayed at all night. She wanted to get home before her dad did from his second shift. The girlfriend's place she slept over that night was around Yonge and Bloor. At 5:30, 5:45 a.m. she was heading to the subway station when a couple of fellas in a blue Rambler cat-called and chased her down. She ran back alleys to Church Street and hid behind an appliance store near a Dominion's, hid inside some huge refrigerator boxes, while she heard the two boys shouting, mumbling, their voices like axes. 'Where's that bitch, where is she? I'm going to fuck her up.' Toronto has become murder city, pal. And Yonge Street is the capital. Make no mistake."

"How did Orly even get access to Charles Street? He was just sixteen."

"His teacher, that tall fella, knew a guy who knew a guy, and that guy got the kid access. No names. And if I knew, I'm pretty sure I wouldn't tell you."

"Mr. Everly knew a guy who knew a guy who got the kid access?"

"Yeah, Everly. Thought the kid was special." Maceo rolled his eyes. "Special? Please Orly never struck me as special. Oh, sure he read, but anybody can read. Big deal. The kid had no plan, no future."

Special? Just how special? What about all those trinkets, expensive jewelry, I found among Orly's things. Gifts from Everly? Special?

"I heard he was saving up money to be a doctor," I said.

"People who look like we do don't become doctors. A bus driver maybe." A couple of more puffs and he stubbed his cigar in a tin ashtray. "The kid never did figure that out. A dreamer. That Everly filled the kid with ideas. A real bleeding-heart liberal, that teach. You know, every Halloween he had a UNICEF box on his desk for the kids to drop spare coins in. Christ." He laughed. "Loaned Orly all kinds of books."

"So, Everly was helping Orly find himself?" *And maybe Everly was finding something on the side? Special. The trinkets. The MO of a predator—*

"Yeah, I guess so." Maceo smiled as if posing for a vacation photograph. "I want you to find my money."

"I already got a client," I said.

"Client? A hundred bucks to her name? Abby? That's some client."

How did he know?

"I've been following you, ese. My boy Saba does some errands for me. Keeping tabs on you is one of them." Another vacation smile. One of his front teeth was gold, the other one looked like a Chiclet with the candy gloss rubbed away. "That Abby chick was probably in on it with the kid. In on stealing my money."

"That doesn't seem to fit with a girl who would tell you such a vulnerable story about a near rape."

He shrugged again. "I don't know what to tell you, shamus. Kids trust me. The True Suns trust me." He picked at an eyelash hair of tobacco on his tongue. "Her dad's a white fella, mad because his colored woman ran out on him. Went to get a pack of smokes, and she never came back. Ten years ago, now. He wants to beat the islands out of that girl. Hits her. So, Orly, probably reached into my cookie jar to help. Nest egg. For her. Love, you know. A filial love. Not carnal. That kid didn't swing straight. But you know what? She doesn't have the money. My boys asked her. Worked her over just a little. I'm no saint, okay. You dig? But where's the money? Who took it from the kid? I want it. It's mine."

He leaned back, arms tangled behind his head.

My boys.

And that's when I saw it, the tattoo on the inside of his left wrist, two circles, placid blue, and dancing arrows of red. "You were a True Sun."

"Wayward youth."

Saba said he was the leader, what are you the consigliere?

That cracked him up. "I'm a spiritual advisor." He smiled, a third vacation photograph.

"So what did your *boys* do to that girl?"

"Nothing worse than what her father does." He rubbed a fist against a flat hand. "They were, let's just say, persuasive, ese. Somebody else has the money. Find it." He sat forward, pressing his hands into the sides of his hips. "One large in it, a thousand, if you find the stash."

"Stash?"

"Of cash. Yeah. Stash."

"Make it two thousand." I pushed back my porkpie.

"That's ten per cent."

"Two thousand," I repeated. *I didn't like the guy.*

"Deal," he said.

CHUNKY WAS GIVEN THE TASK of driving me to the nearest subway station.

He wasn't too happy about it, going on and on about how he was always treated like a functionary.

"Functionary?"

That's a word his boss uses all the time, he said, when they're out and about at a restaurant or shopping at Canadian Tire and he doesn't reshelve something. "'They have functionaries to do that,' he says. I'm not a flunky—I'm no functionary—"

"You old enough to drive this heap?"

"I'm sixteen, motherfucker, I can drive."

"I'm glad to see you've graduated from the pinup art of the bowling alley to the punk lingo of Toronto's mean streets."

"Big joke."

We approached a white '66 Ford Galaxie. It needed a wash and rust dotted the rocker panels like mold spores. "Open the door yourself. It's unlocked. I'm no chauffeur."

"Right."

I hopped in back. The red seats burned my hands and I lowered the automatic window once the 427 engine revved to life.

He lowered his window too, elbow resting on the edging of the door and glass.

"No AC, huh?"

He shook his head with displeasure.

I love muscle cars. After my '63 Galaxie was destroyed by a gas station collision in Bannerville, I had a shitbox '65 Falcon for a while and then in 1968 Stana and I bought a '69 Roadrunner. Red, like the dropping curve of the evening sun. It kicks ass. Connie likes to go cruising with me, late at night, windows down and the radio on.

"I guess you guys haven't been able to find any functionaries, huh, to clean up this claptrap."

The floors in the backseat were piled with crumpled chocolate-bar wrappers, rolled-up, half-eaten cookie packages, Coke and Orange Crush empties, and cold, cold, bits of French fries. There was a gray-and-green gym bag riding atop the wave.

"Kill the patter, pal—it's stale."

"Oh, you hurt me." I reached for the gym bag.

Chunky turned around in his seat. "Hey, I didn't say you could look at that—"

Suddenly two low gunshots blew off the back of Chunky's head, grapefruit pulp and pieces of hair and brain matter splattered all over the front passenger window.

Lou Fortunado, muscle for Babe Migano, pushed aside what was left of the corpse and grinned in my direction. His black hair—a little less of it than a few years ago and now spackled with salty gray—still rode in a high pompadour and was soaked in enough pomade to keep a barbershop in supply for a week. "Hey, Superstar. The boss wants to see you—let's bounce."

"What the fuck, Lou—he's just a kid."

"Word is he killed Orly—some kid."

I grabbed the gym bag and followed, my ears clattering with the ghosts of every windchime in the city. Shit, I was sitting a little too close when Lou-Doo pulled the trigger.

Lou glanced at the bag, returning his gun in his shoulder holster. "Underwear you need laundered?"

"Everyone's a comedian."

He reached into his wallet and pinned a business card on the chest of the victim. White Heat, Babe's nightclub on Queen Street. "Maceo will now know who came a calling. Let's go—" He nudged me with blocky fingers toward an alley.

MINUTES LATER WE WERE UPSTAIRS, above a pizza parlor that overlooks the back of Danforth Bowl. Babe himself was moving soundlessly about, like a panther, from camera to camera. He had two of them, and two operators, ready to film things across the way if anything of importance turned up.

Lou stood by one of the camera operators eating a sub sandwich the size of a football. There was nothing green on the sandwich that I could see. Prosciutto and capicola slices leaned from the end like sheets on a clothesline. Every now and then he stopped to comb back his pompadour.

Babe grabbed a metal chair and told me to sit. "Don't worry. I'm not going to hurt you. If I wanted you dead, you'd be dead." He smiled in that subtle don't-give-a-damn way he had. In the lapel of his pin-striped suit was a red carnation. On all his fingers: diamond rings.

I sat, rubbed at the edges of my mouth.

The room was an apartment, the furniture piled across the room, away from the windows. The walls were gray, muting the interior light and making it hard for people outside to see what was going on inside.

I discovered later that Migano was renting it from the owner for a month to get evidence against Maceo and the illegal goings on across the way.

Babe leaned over me, his aftershave a bright, hard splash. "I wasn't too happy about you killing Athol."

I didn't know what to say. It wasn't as if I enjoyed it—

A modest shrug was followed by a gentle pat on my shoulder. "But I suppose you had no choice."

Athol Leighton was married to Babe's niece and had been one of his bodyguards since 1963. A few years back in a case the newspapers tabbed "The Final Portrait" I killed Athol in self-defense with some kind of exploding camera gizmo. "It was him or me—I—"

"I realize that—" Babe held up a hand. "I realize that—but we haven't spoken since that time, have we? What was it two years ago?"

"Yeah."

"Fucking guy," Lou said.

Lou and Athol were tight. I wasn't sure if Lou were talking about me or the late bodyguard.

"And I think of us as colleagues, associates. Not friends, but we travel in some of the same circles."

"We do."

"And I feel bad about the months of silence between us—" He sniffed at his carnation and took a quick drink of scotch from a portable cabriolet that always seemed to make its temporary home wherever he made his. "The man betrayed me, he got what was coming to him." He looked up at the ceiling. "'Goodnight, Sweet Prince.'"

I nodded. There was nothing sweet about Athol.

"I'm going to be frank with you, Mr. Fuller," Babe said. "You know my business. I have a foot in legitimacy, with my nightclubs and film interests, and all that, but I'm also, well, shall we say, an entrepreneur in recreation—a man who brings fun and games to those with means."

"Drugs."

"Don't ruin my mood." He smiled in his off-handed way. "I'm trying to pass the peace pipe here."

"Okay, okay."

"What did Maceo want with you?" He sipped his scotch and offered me a club soda. I asked for a Pepsi. Three cubes.

"I only got Coke. Pepsi, Christ." He shook his head with disapproval.

"Canada Dry? Neat."

"I got that."

I cracked the can, sipped slowly. "Maceo wanted me to find $20,000 that the Shoeshine Kid stole from him."

"The kid had a name."

"Fucking guy," Lou said.

"I'm sorry, you're right," I said. The ginger ale was chilly and hurt some of the fillings in my mouth. "Orly."

"He was working for me—spying on Maceo."

"Wow—" I sat forward in my chair, ready to share notes.

"I'm convinced they killed him, Maceo and the True Suns—"

"Chunky," Lou said. "Fucking guy."

"That's my hunch too. But Maceo keeps pushing the killing off onto Charles Street," I said.

"Of course he does—what a great cover for *his* crimes. Blame it on Toronto's queer community."

"I hear the kid hung out there—"

"He did, but they didn't kill him." He looked out the window, over onto Danforth Bowl. From its backside it was a big block of white brick with high sideways windows and a large loading dock with a corrugated door that rises on a pulley. "Still, no action," he muttered. "Sometimes trucks, 18-wheelers, pull up and unload cargo in boxes, and take away cargo in different boxes. That's the drop, the distributors. I'm trying to capture images, faces."

"And what, turn it over to the RCMP?"

"Yes." He wanted to crush Maceo. "He's a competitor—muscling in on my turf."

"I guessed as much."

"I'm a businessman." He sipped more scotch. "Someday I'll leave this all behind me, but that day has yet to come."

That *someday* I'd been hearing about for some seven years. "Seen anyone we know at the back door—dropping off packages, picking up packages?"

"That schoolteacher, Fitzpatrick. A couple of times in a car. Getting boxes—Small, long boxes."

"Holy shit—I saw Fitzy bowling there. Just minutes ago. He and Everly."

"Regulars, Thursday night league," he said.

"Drugs? Fitzy's mixed up with drugs?"

"I don't think he's acquiring rare copies of *The Complete Works of William Shakespeare*." He lit a cigar. "What's in the bag?"

It was resting at my feet. "It was something lodged in the back seat of the Galaxie that the late great Chunky was driving. And I was curious about it. The late-great Chunky didn't want me poking my nose around inside it."

"Well, let's poke around it now—And I'm sorry about the late-great Chunk." Babe mirrored my sarcasm and disapproval. "But that sixteen-year-old kid already had a couple of notches on his gun. He was also involved in the beating Abby took. I won't shed any tears over that douche. And I hear he sodomized Orly before they burned his body with cigarettes and killed him. Of course, that's just hearsay—don't quote me."

When it came to Babe, hearsay was a lot more than just hearsay—it was damn credible. "Fair enough." I unzipped the bag at my feet. Inside were more chocolate-bar wrappers, a parking pass to hang on a rearview mirror for North York General, and a blue cashmere sweater, medium-size. No stiletto blade. "This mean anything to you?"

"Not really—I'm more of a cardigan guy," he said.

I held up the sweater and explained to Babe the somewhat murky backstory of Douglas Gomery's death, and the vague references to cashmere sweaters that various people had mentioned.

"Gomery?" He snapped his fingers. "That name rings a bell. Gomery, Gomery. He bowled there too, league play. Douglas J., right?"

"J. Douglas, actually, but yeah."

"What does the J stand for?"

"Nothing. He figured the initial gave him class, it sounded more like a writer's name."

"Writer's name? Sounds like the name of a fella in a top hat and a monocle in an eye."

"Was Gomery on Fitzy's team?"

"No, different team."

"Shit." Pieces of this case were starting to line up in strange ways, the two varying investigative threads that I was following (the brutal murder of Orly and the stabbing death of Douglas) were intersecting.

"So what do we make of the sweater?" Babe flecked ash off his cigar.

"I'm not sure. But I don't believe in coincidences. It fits, but how? The right size too. Can you imagine, Gomery's killer has a whole cedar chest full of these things?"

Then Babe downed the rest of his scotch, punched his lips together, and slammed the shot glass down. "I never finished my story about the kid, Orlando. I got derailed by that goddamn gym bag. Anyway, the kid was working for me," he said. "Spying. Maceo's been muscling into my racket. As I already mentioned. My turf in Scarborough. Maceo's trying to undersell me. Moving cocaine. I wanted Orly to find out who was involved and how they were distributing. The kid thought it was in boxes loaded with bowling gear. And so far the dealers: Maceo and the True Suns—"

"And maybe Fitzpatrick—"

"I think he's just a recreational user. Ever since his son's death the guy has fallen apart."

"I don't think he was all that together to begin with."

That cracked Babe up.

I smiled, pleased with myself. *C-*. *Kiss my ass—*

"Maceo was distributing the shit to other bowling alleys, drops, throughout the Greater Toronto Area." He lit a second cigar, puffed a few more times, wisps of smoke trailing around his broad face like snakes. Babe forever reminded me of a young Rod Steiger and his face was always shaved raw and close with a straight-edge. His eyes widened. "And then I lost contact with the kid. He didn't check in." He leaned forward in his leather chair. "I think he found the coke and took some, some for himself, for him and his girl Abby, to get away from all this—poverty, Regent Park—" He smiled warmly. "I don't blame him."

"Shortly before he died," I said, "Orly took a round trip of 120 miles. That makes for 60 or less miles, one way. So—"

"You think he took the drugs somewhere?"

"Or to someone," I said.

"Possibly."

"Fucking guy," Lou said. Half the sandwich was obliterated.

"We'll pull up a map and make a circle and vector out all the possibilities." He shrugged. "At least we can guess the town he buried the goods in."

"And the True Suns figured this all out and had him whacked."

"In all probability."

"And they never recovered the coke and that's why Maceo hired me. He doesn't want me to track down $20,000, that's just a MacGuffin. He wants me to follow the trail and find the goddamn coke."

"Bingo. And I bet it's worth more than $20,000."

"Christ," I mumbled, looking at my shoes. "So, how do the Red Dragons fit in?"

"Think—" He nudged a finger toward my chest, and took another puff off his cigar.

"They work for you?"

"Uh-huh." An absent shrug. "They're my distribution network and they got a little rambunctious over the Orly kill, took matters in their own hands and took out some of the Suns. The True North, glorious and free, my ass."

"So, what do you want from me?"

"I don't want you getting in my way." Babe respected me, he knew I was good at what I did. "But stay on your rails, Superstar. Don't ride my track. Solve the kid's killing, prove that Maceo and his boys did him in, but if you find the coke don't go all boy scouts on me, bring it to me."

"I don't know if I can do that."

His head turned to the side and he flashed an extremely inviting grin. "Come on now. We got a pact. You and I. We got shared secrets—we know about the murders of Lisa Steinmetz and Spinner Terrien, know where the bodies are buried."

The Cheap Amusements case. My silence bought me and Stana guaranteed protection from Babe for life.

"I'm just suggesting you look the other way," he said.

"Any ideas where the kid hid the coke?"

"Maybe TomBoys and Dicks?"

"That's where I was thinking of going next."

"Good."

"You haven't checked it out, Babe?"

"No. TomBoys and Dicks. I got a rep—I can't go in *there*."

"I'll go. After the game, of course." Game two tonight. All of the country would stop what they were doing to watch Canada-Russia.

"We better win." Babe flicked ash off his cigar into an ashtray he held in his left hand.

Babe and Tan Mylow were used to winning, getting what they wanted.

I laughed. "Why does that vaguely sound like a threat?"

He winked at me. "Keep that in mind, Superstar. Keep that in mind—"

ALL OF US IN MAPLE LEAF GARDENS were feeling somewhat schizophrenic.

That feeling oozed all through the first period. We were rooting for Canada, sure, cheering every Canadian scoring chance and big save by Tony O. And our goalie made *four* big saves in that first period, including a side-to-side move that stopped a Kharlamov easy deflection from going in. It was a perfect pass from Maltsev. Tony's lateral movement was something Ken Dryden couldn't master in game one.

But when our boys went after the Soviets with bodychecks and high sticks and trips and the odd punch or two, courtesy of forwards J.P. Parisé, Wayne Cashman, Phil Esposito, and Bobby Clarke, and defenseman Gary Bergman, the crowd booed, booed Canada, and our way of playing the game, rough and skillfully, *heavy hockey* as Coach Farrell used to say.

It was like the fans wanted success for Canada, but they wanted us to play more like the Soviets, quick rushes up ice, spreading around the puck with precision passing, and firing pretty shots on goal as opposed to banging the front of the net for rebounds.

Maybe Stewart Kittle was right to be worried on behalf of Greenway Publishing. The Soviets played a brand of hockey that Canadians admired and perhaps the kind of hockey Professor Hampton wrote about was now dated, and dare I say dying, soon to be dead—

I just shook my head. I needed to walk and get some air. "I think I want an Eskimo Pie," I said. "Can I get you folks anything? Hon?"

Stana wanted popcorn and a Coke. Sal was fine. Miriam wanted a Coke and popcorn too and offered to help with "the bounty."

Stana said she might wander off for a smoke.

Sal said he didn't want to go anywhere. He had been on his feet all day. "So, what do you think?"

"I don't know," I said.

"I like our grit," Sal said. "We're playing more like a team."

"If not for Tony the score should be 2-0 for them."

"Come on, we can talk hockey later—I'm hungry." Miriam grabbed me by the arm. I gathered from her expressive eyebrows that she wanted to talk. The black waterfall of her hair was swept to the right tonight.

"Sure." We made our way to the lobby.

I muttered in the direction of my shoes, yes, the Soviet brand of hockey was different, but not that different. I remember seeing Chicago's Pony Line at the Gardens in the 1940s, the Bentley brothers and Bill Mosienko: they fired the puck around just like the Red Army. Tic-tac-toe. But honestly, the subtle booing in our own building was a bunch of shit. Leaf fans have always loved teams full of grit and hard-working, forechecking determination. That was the Toronto style in the 1940s, and we didn't win five Cups back then without the help of the two-fisted Metz brothers and Bill Ezinicki doing their muck-it-up thing.

"You finished with the lecture?" Miriam smiled good-naturedly, kindness filling her eyes.

"Sorry, I do that sometimes—"

"Talk your thoughts out loud?"

"Yeah."

Her laughter was even huskier than the tissue-paper rustle to her deep voice. "Me too. I'm often talking to myself or imagining future conversations."

We moved into the bracelet of human bodies heading to a

concessions stand. "How are things going?"

"With Sal?"

I smiled gently and soaked in Miriam's bright green eyes. She also wore a fetching pillbox hat that gave her a look that was both retro and mod. "Well, yeah." I looked at my fingers.

"Good. Better—he wants us to do marriage counseling."

"Good, good—"

"Yeah? You think so?"

"It can be good, yeah. I had trouble with intimacy, early on with Stana." I lowered my voice to a whisper. Miriam was a nurse and a friend and I was comfortable talking to her. When she had a miscarriage between the births of her two sons, I stayed up with her and Sal through the night, just listening, being there. Days later I helped them plant a tree in their backyard as a memorial. A remembrance. "I had trouble sustaining during sex. It was all connected to feelings of worthlessness and drowning in black dirt. The desire was there but the overwhelming shame over my body, and naked bodies in general, messed me up, bad. Dr. Jeanette Cohen told me I had to forgive myself, find my worth, and with her love and help, and Stana's love and help, I— Listen to me, going on and on."

"No, no, it's good." Her eyes were encouraging me to remain open.

"So, I confronted the past, and the sexual abuse my father put me through. And somehow in sessions with Dr. Cohen and Stana I overcame all that. I let all that shit go. Is my love life perfect? Hell, no, but we have fun together, inside and outside the bedroom."

"The bedroom has never been our problem." She looked surprised by her own vulnerability. "It's the other stuff. I'm a nurse, he's a cop, and we both carry so much damn trauma. Makes it hard to communicate sometimes, to share our experiences. When I first had kids, the first seven years, I stayed at home, took care of them, raised them because I was told that's what good mothers do. But, I was losing my mind. Bored. I needed work. Now it's good to be back at work, but I also need to be able to talk about my work. Maybe a therapist will help with that." She shrugged. "I don't know. We both need to debrief. Every day. Creative writing became an outlet—but it was kind of narcissistic."

The line in front of us was moving so damn slowly. It was seven minutes before the second period started. "Narcissistic? No. It probably allowed you to express things—let you work out what you needed to."

"It wasn't all that healthy. The workshop. I craved their attention. I was tickled when Professor Hampton or Stewart Kittle invited me to the writers retreat—it was like I needed validation, I needed a community outside my family and my work communities."

"I get that."

We ordered our food. I asked for four hotdogs too. What the hell.

"You were right about Gomery. Secobarbital. There was a high concentration of it in his body at the time of death." Miriam had recently seen the autopsy report.

"Sleeping pills?"

"Yeah."

"That's when they stabbed him and wrapped him up in a shower curtain?"

"Most likely. But who? Who are they?"

"And the cut lines across Gomery's stomach—someone sought to carve out his goddamn intestines."

"Shit—" A feather of fingers touched her lips. "A serial killer?"

"Possibly."

She shuddered.

"But I'm not so sure." I told her about what I discovered just earlier in the day. "Could have been somebody from the True

Suns. Gomery bowled at Danforth Bowl.. They distribute drugs. Maybe he was messed up with that business, maybe one of them got him."

"But how did they know about the apartment? The blood was in the apartment."

"Maybe he'd gone there with someone, a romantic tryst." *Maybe the fella he had an affair with from 1955–1959. Maybe they still got together. On occasion.*

A girl with hair pulled back in a tight ponytail handed us our bounty. "Have a nice day," she said, not really connecting or looking at us.

We made our way back in the direction of our seats in the end blues.

"Where's Connie?""

"With her grandmother. Stana's father died four years ago, two months after retiring from the TTC."

"I always tell Sal, don't wait too long to retire. You can't get time back. He was a cop at eighteen. He'll have a pretty good pension at 55."

"Wow. How old is he now, forty?"

"Forty-two."

"I don't know what I would do without this job," I said. "I need the jobs as much as my clients need me."

She moved closer to me. I could smell her French perfume. "I need to talk to you about something, something weird."

"Sure."

"It involves that sweater. The blue cashmere thing—"

"Uh-huh."

Yesterday she was working a 12-4 shift at North York General. "While I was seeing patients, some fella came to the front desk asking when I got off work. The gal at the front desk, Dana Carr, figured he already knew the answer to the question, there was something about his look, his body language. He wore a blue cashmere sweater and said to Dana, 'Tell Miriam I stopped by," and then he left."

"Was this fella from the Islands?"

I was piecing the sweater, the gym bag, and the parking tag for North York General together.

"No, he was white—Not tall, not short. Just a normal, average-looking white guy. With a big mustache, probably false—"

"Hmm—age?"

"Anywhere from late thirties to early fifties. It's hard to tell with some men."

I'm a hard thirty-seven. I look it.

"Two days ago," she continued, "there was sugar in my gas tank and my car wouldn't start—and when I got off the bus yesterday to walk home I was definitely being followed, two blocks behind a shadowy figure trailed me."

"In cashmere?"

"It was dark, I couldn't tell."

"You told Sal about this?"

"Of course. He thinks it's someone in the writers' group."

We returned to our seats. Everyone nabbed a hotdog. Stana squeezed my hand. "You okay?"

"Yeah, yeah—"

I wiped mustard off Stana's face and kissed her. I'm not usually that impulsive, not in public, but I don't know, I just did it.

THE CROWD WAS FULL of mixed emotions during the second period too, but when Phil scored they went nuts.

I jumped to my feet and threw a punch in the air.

Phil had been tripped up in the Soviet end and was slow getting to his feet. Dogging it. After a scrum at the blue line, the puck bled out to him and he banged it home for our first goal. Leave it to Phil to get a goal like that. Nose for the net that guy.

The rest of the period was fairly even, chances at both ends. It was pretty clear that Kharlamov, the star of game one, was targeted by our boys as he got bumped and roughed up every time he touched the puck. In one post-whistle gathering he and Parisé mixed it up and J.P. tugged off Kharlamov's helmet. The Russkie was none too crazy about that and there was no penalty called on the play. Later in the period, after more bashing and banging, Kharlamov lost it, and bumped an official to complain. Ten-minute misconduct.

The period ended with us up 1-0.

"Phil is money," Sal said.

"He's a thug," Stana said. "Throwing punches. High sticking. He looks like a mad man out there. The Canadian Rasputin."

"He's just desperate to win, Stana," I said. "He's playing good, old-fashioned Canadian hockey."

"I know what Canadian hockey is. I just think there's something to the Russian game we can learn from—there's a finesse to it, nuance."

"*Finesse, nuance.* Yeah, I'll say. They're just as dirty. They're constantly spearing, hooking, slashing, slowing us up."

"I didn't see any of that."

"Because it's away from the puck. That's their brand of finesse and nuance. Play dirty away from the puck."

"I like the way they pass it around."

"You're not rooting for *them* are you?"

"No, of course not." Stana's eyes narrowed. "I'm a Canadian girl. Irish, Irish-Catholic by birth—Irish-Jew by marriage—but their game is so pretty to watch, I like it, the movement."

"Movement? I'm about to have a bowel movement—listening to this."

Stana punched me in the arm. It wasn't gentle.

"My sons," Sal chimed in, "Say their national anthem sounds like a machine, a march for robots."

"Sal—" Miriam punched her husband in the arm, too—it also wasn't gentle. "Hayden, you're a bad influence."

"Fuck the commies," I said.

"Yeah, fuck the commies," Sal said. "Their song *does* sound like a bunch of marching robots." He shrugged unapologetically.

I chuckled.

And Sal sang, "We're just a bunch of ro-bots, we're just a bunch of ro-bots—" to the tune of their anthem. I joined him. No barbershop was going to sign us up anytime soon

The two ladies gave us the stink eye.

Sometimes, men like me and Sal are forever twelve.

WE SCORED EARLY IN THE THIRD PERIOD. Yvan Cournoyer on a pretty, long pass from Brad Park. Cournoyer arced right around the Russian D, cut in on goal and placed the puck through Vladislav Tretiak's legs. The whole Gardens shook. 2-0.

The Soviets scored on a powerplay, Yakushev, and minutes later they were on another powerplay. One of their guys took a real dive to get the call. Anyway, we kept them to the outside and then Pete Mahovlich scored the goal of his life, one he'll never, ever top. It was sensational. Short-handed, he took the puck at center skated to their blue line, deeked their D-man with a fake slapshot and some kind of toe-drag move, worked free, and then deeked Tretiak with inspired backhand, forehand, backhand hoodoo magic, before jamming the puck into the net. 3-1.

And that was pretty much it.

Frank Mahovlich added a fourth goal and Johnny Esaw interviewed the Esposito brothers on air following the game. They were voted by a panel of sportswriters the most-valuable players.

We sat up in the blues, soaking it in.

The crowd was happy, but a weird schism lingered: fans rooting for their country but feeling the brand of Soviet-style hockey was superior to the Canadian dump-and-chase game.

"Shall we get something to drink at Mainly Drew's," Sal said. It was a bar across from the Gardens that I used to hang out at as a player.

Sure, the girls said.

"What's wrong, Superstar? Canada's back, baby!"

"Are we?"

"Big win."

"We scored three goals with Kharlamov sitting in the box for ten minutes. Peter Mahovlich and Cournoyer scored sensational goals. And Tony Esposito stood on his head in the first. We could have easily lost that game," I said. "We got lucky tonight."

"Don't be a downer, man. We won. Come on. I'll buy you a club soda. And maybe we can really live it up big, and I'll get you a tonic water."

Everyone knew I didn't drink and Sal liked to rib me a little. It made me feel like I belonged.

"Okay, but we can't stay long. Mom's taking care of Connie. And we had to get the kid home. School tomorrow."

I gotcha, I gotcha, he said. "One drink—that's all. One drink. God damn, this is our game. Our game! We're back!"

Thursday

TOMBOYS AND DICK'S TAVERN, built in 1862, had a gabled-clock tower, a beacon that rang on special occasions: Oscar Wilde's birthday and the publication of Walt Whitman's *Leaves of Grass*.

I rubbed at the edges of my mouth, pushed back my porkpie, and wandered in.

The bartender smiled awkwardly, when I asked for a tonic water with a slice of lime. A tattoo on his left arm said, "baby"; the one on his right "hey!" That cracked me up.

Edith Pilaf played over the jukebox and men swayed with the music, filling the dance floor with French kisses. A gray haze floated about the ceiling's high wood beams and beer steins on the bar's top shelf. I handed the bartender a ten spot. "Keep it." I lowered my voice. "I got some questions." I flashed my lopsided grin. "Hayden Fuller."

"I know who you are." His wide-set eyes looked right through me. "Won the Cup with Montreal. 1966. And then retired. Before that you played for the Leafs. Seven years. Left winger. Tough guy." He smiled. Some of his teeth were gold. "What I don't get, for a tough guy what the fuck were you doing wearing a number like 28 with Montreal. Isn't that a fucking goalie's number?"

I smiled wanly. "Yeah. Believe me. I've heard that one before."

"Canada looked good last night, huh?"

"Maybe. Kharlamov was in the box for a ten-minute misconduct."

"Yeah. He ran an official. Serves the bastard right."

"You think he's going to do that again in the next six games? We scored three times with him in the box." I held up a fistful of fingers. "Three."

"Yeah, I get your thought." Like most Canadians, he enjoyed talking hockey, but he mentioned nothing about Stana's articles and my revelations of sexual abuse.

"I ain't here to bust heads or bring vice down." Sal was my friend, but I knew all about police profiling of minorities and homosexuals. "I'm trying to solve a murder." I slid newspaper clippings across the granite-topped bar.

"The shoeshine kill—"

"Yeah. I understand the kid was doing *research* here."

Again his eyes looked through me. "Well, you understand wrong."

I held up both hands. "Just telling you what I know—C. Thomas Everly."

"Yeah, yeah. C.T. helped set it up." He rubbed the counter vigorously. "But we didn't do the interviews in the bar. Orlando had a place in the back. Everyone went through the alley, behind the joint, knocked at the door, and went in. His office. The kid never walked through the bar. His office was like a separate apartment." Now *he* was holding up his hands. "We all called him Orlando or The Professor. We all liked the kid. Nobody would hurt him."

I nodded and sipped tonic water.

"The kid was a scientist. Tables and charts, you know? I even talked to him about my fantasies, sexual preferences." He shrugged, the tattoo on his right arm flexing a little, the "hey" becoming "he," the "y" lost behind a cuffed mask of a shirt sleeve. "Geno Seven. That's my name. Actually Severinski, but my parents changed it to fit in." That cracked him up. "Fit in." He was still laughing.

It was a pretty good joke.

Fit in. I knew all about that too. Fuller wasn't the surname my Zeyda brought with him from the old country.

"Like I said, people loved that kid—"

"You said something about charts—so you saw the notebook?"

"Notebooks. There was more than one."

"They here?"

"No. The kid always took them home with him, in a briefcase."

"Anybody want him dead? The cigarette burns. Naked body. Sounds like a sex crime."

"Or hate crime," Geno said.

"Yeah."

"A hate crime made to look like a sex crime, made to bring heat down on us."

"And no one here held a grudge against the kid?"

"All I know is he understood, got us, you know? No judgment. That kid was special. We called him The Professor." He rubbed at the tip of his nose. "But I already told you that. If anything we all hoped he'd find himself and join our tribe."

Special. The kid was special. There it was again. Special. Sexual predator talk?

"Orly? Grudges? No," Geno said.

"Did he have any boyfriends? This Everly?"

"Everly? Yeah, back in the day. He and that Gomery fella, the one that got all knifed up on Front Street? They were lovers. Hung out here, 1950s. Always cried when that Judy Garland song, 'Somewhere Over the Rainbow,' played on the jukebox."

1955-1959. That was the pairing. Gomery and Everly—

"So, Everly, still has male lovers?"

"I don't think Everly was ever bisexual. I think he just loved J. Douglas. If Douglas was a woman he would have loved her." He laughed. "It was the person he loved, not the plumbing. She/he who cares? But now, he's come back to the mean. He's, let me put this in quotes, *cured*." He rolled his eyes. "The guy is fucking boring now. Straight, button-down kind of guy. Voted for Stanfield in '68."

"Somebody gave the kid a bunch of jewelry, "I said.

"We all loved him. I gave him a ring for chrissakes. Nothing romantic. Just—we liked him. He got us." He shrugged.

"He was sodomized—"

"From what I heard, that wasn't love. *That* was rape."

"Cops or anyone else search the stuff in the back?" I gestured with my head.

"No." His lips pressed tightly. "Cops don't even know about it. But there ain't no notebooks there." He finished rubbing the counter, tossed the rag in a dry bucket. "The kid took them home every night, in a locked suitcase."

"I thought you said briefcase—"

"Suitcase. Sorry."

I hated when folks get facts mixed up. It questions the validity of their stories.

I finished my tonic water and asked for the back door key.

"You have a cop's eyes, but they're full of pain." He smiled dimly. "I trust you." He slid me the key. The fob was a half-dollar sized "Golden Dreams" Marilyn Monroe. She was naked against a red curtain.

"Besides," I said. "How tough can a fella be who wore number 28, a goddamn goalie's number?"

That cracked him up.

THE ROOM WAS LIKE THE INSIDE of a photo lab, red and more red: the walls, the shelves, the carpeting, from candy apple to crimson to a touch of fuchsia. Even the lights were red, an old New Orleans *Streetcar Named Desire* feel, Stanley and Stella style.

The only outlier, by a red, wood-stained desk: a white Hepplewhite chair.

The kid was neat, that's for sure. Clothes, dress pants, hung by their seams, in a makeshift closet. There was even a suit still in its One Hour Martinizing plastic wrap with a tight three-corner handkerchief peeking from the breast pocket.

On his work desk was a microscope, slides, and yet another copy of *Grey's Anatomy*. A string of Parker pens were circling around in a small Ball jar. There was, however, as Geno warned me, no notebooks. Who had them? Maceo? Orly lived with him? Everly? He attended some of the interview sessions. Or Abby? She was his girlfriend and confidant and maybe every night the locked suitcase was at her pad. Maybe she kept the notebooks from the police?

I exhaled sharply. On the shelves were a lot of books, including Hemingway's *The Sun Also Rises*, the collected Poe (a Park District School copy that Orly had apparently lifted), and Ray Bradbury. On the anchoring shelf were the heavier books, offset by two bowling pins.

I had never held a bowling pin before, but right away I knew the balance was off. The pin wobbled unevenly across my flat palm. I shook it. Slight shifts of sand or powder slid inside.

Drugs?

I figured I'd have Sal and Toronto PD X-ray this thing pronto and then I noticed the seam.

A deep breath and I turned the pin left and right simultaneously and the outer casing opened like a Matryoshka doll. Inside, several sealed plastic bags. Cocaine.

No need for X-rays.

Babe Migano was right. Maceo didn't hire me to get back $20,000. This is what Maceo wanted. And this is how he was distributing the drugs, inside of faux bowling pins.

Fitzpatrick had a bowling pin in his classroom, near his row of books. Fitzpatrick bowled at Danforth. Fitzpatrick was seen at the back door loading dock, placing boxes in his car. Bowling pins loaded with snow?

The surveillance security tapes that captured Orly stealing cash from a safe were a phony, a setup. Orly was probably asked by Maceo to grab something from the safe. Christ. He was framed.

MRS. WHITELAW CALLED ME LATER that afternoon. She and Susan Gomery walked together in Wilket Creek Park two times a week. Often they started at Edward's Garden and then strolled the paths, pausing to take in their favorite trees: sugar maple and red oak. "Susan didn't show up. Just wasn't there," Mrs. Whitelaw said. "Been trying to reach her for over five hours now. I'm worried—really worried—" The day before as she headed to Becker's for a jug of milk Susan had the strong sense of being followed, a man in a blue cashmere sweater.

"What did this man look like?"

"A red mop of hair like the Beatles sported in the mid-1960s. Susan thought it looked fake."

Dana Carr thought the same thing about the mustache on the fella who visited North York General. "Probably was—a fake." That early mod look was gone. Now it was long, shaggy hair, thick sideburns, and it seemed every hipster chewed gum with rigor. "Age?"

"Anywhere from thirty to fifty—she didn't get a great look."

"Right."

"Goddamn, I'm scared."

"Was the person white or from the islands?"

"Not sure," she said. "He also wore a Walrus-size mustache and sunglasses."

The True Suns were fond of Ray-Bans.

I didn't tell her that this was the second woman in the workshop who had been followed by someone in blue cashmere. And then there was the gym bag in the back of Chunky's white Galaxie. Was someone in the True Suns terrorizing these women? Why?

"I'm going to keep my head down," she said. "Maybe go to Guelph for a while. I got family in Guelph." There was a catch to her voice, the emotion climbing into a scratchy nervousness.

"Go to Guelph," I said.

"Susan is so reliable. She always calls. I think something terrible has happened."

"Go to Guelph."

SEEMS ABBY'S DAD BOWLS in the Danforth league on Thursdays too.

Abby and I were alone in her room and she held herself tightly, catching the undertow of my mood.

I clutched a heavy paper bag in my left hand. "Why did you hire me?" Battery acid dripped from my words. "I mean really."

She backed into a dresser drawer. A dainty vanity was to her left, a wall mirror hung crookedly on a closet door. The room was lacking any frills: plain white, no accents, no photos, nothing but glare. She played with the necklace, rubbing an edge along the left side of her jawline. "To find Orly's killers and to prove—to prove his innocence." She gestured with a small hand, a sparrow's wing.

"By innocence, you mean prove that he's straight. Funny thing about that. Fitzpatrick rolled his eyes at the concept of you being his girlfriend."

"I *was* his girlfriend."

"Okay. If you say so." I pushed back the brim of my porkpie and plunked a bowling pin on her beige vanity. "Innocence? You know what I found in this, in his Kinsey lab in back of TomBoys and Dicks? Cocaine. An avalanche of snow—"

She gasped and moved closer to the mirror, a faint tremor pulsing through her jawline, the double-helix of her necklace dusky.

"Orly wanted to get you away from all this—" My arms were stretched wide. "All of this. A white father who beats you because you're colored." I bit my lower lip, dropping both hands by my hips. "Here's the story, the way I figure it. The kid didn't steal cold cash from his surrogate father, he stole a different kind of money, money deferred, drugs, hidden in bowling pins. How many, I don't know. He stole them for you, to help you get away, but before he could cash in, someone cashed him in."

Her shoulders rounded, warding off a blow.

"That's what I want to know. Who killed him, and why. Maceo? Chunky and the True Suns on Maceo's orders? Everly? He loved the kid. Maybe more than just admiration. Trinkets, jewelry, *special. Had to kill the kid to keep their love a secret?*"

"He didn't love Orly, not that way—"

"Uh-huh."

The light in the room was a burning red sun. "Twenty pins are missing," she said. "Orly told me."

"He stole them for you."

"Yes." Tears crowded the edges of her eyes. "To help me."

"Where did he hide them?"

Algonquin Park, she said. The day before he died he borrowed Maceo's car and took the pins with him to that place we stayed, that retreat, where we sang and camped. "That's all I know." She couldn't look at me. Her hands pushed against the top of her arms, leaving strong imprints, dry gully marks.

"Maceo said Orly took the car on a round trip of 120 miles. Algonquin is twice as far, round trip."

"Maybe he met someone somewhere and took a second car."

"So someone else knows the secret of the pins?"

"Yes."

"Who?"

"I don't know."

I didn't believe her. I told her so.

"I don't care what you believe."

She was too defensive.

"And what about the notebooks? They're not in Orly's lab? They weren't at Maceo's. That leaves you—"

"He did hide them here, but—"

"Yes?"

She bit her lower lip. "My father has one of them. He was always going through my things. Ever since he found a compact full of birth control pills in my underwear drawer." She looked away. "My name was in it. The notebook. My fantasies. Orly didn't want anyone else to find that—Dad hit me with his belt after that."

"A belt?"

"Leather."

"How many other notebooks are there?"

"Three."

"You must have an idea where Orly hid the pins out in Algonquin—*Think, damn it, think.*"

"I can't drive a car or else I had gone out there myself—and searched."

"You been biding your time?"

"I guess."

"Or hoping I'd find out where they were?"

"Maybe."

"You didn't go with Orly when he hid the stash?"

"No way. My dad was home. I could never have got out of the apartment—After Dad saw that notebook, he hated Orly. Wouldn't let me see him."

"Orly must have dropped hints as to ideal hiding places."

"My guess would be the boiler room." She laughed absently. "We had fun in that room, sneaking in, hiding out from the cold. And that's when he first talked about the drugs, inside of bowling pins, and stealing them, for me. He did love me—"

"But you weren't his girlfriend."

"No."

We didn't know it at the time, she said, but that boiler room is now condemned. The whole building, the mess hall, shut down. Abandoned. No more field trips. She laughed. "God I hated that place, the first time I saw it. White, colonial-like. The whole thing is shut down, and it could have toppled on us last fall, capturing us forever in our criminal exploits." She followed the fissured lines of the drop ceiling. "Sometimes I wish it had."

THE CAMPGROUND MESS HALL, white limestone, resembled a human femur, no covering, no skin of life. The windows were just as desolate, bare, no curtains, and the parking lot was a gray stretch of patches of grass peeking through cracked concrete. The cabins in the distance were wet, empty boxes.

Condemned signs were posted on the twin doors.

Loons on a nearby lake quietly wailed.

I went in.

The main space in the hall had racks of chairs lined along a near wall in a series of carts. Long Masonite tables were collapsed and leaning against an opposite wall. A clock in a wire cage wasn't working. The fluorescent lights flickered and slowly breathed to life.

Squirrels scurried over bits of brush scattered across a scuffed floor that hadn't been waxed in a while. I checked the cabinets, cupboards, and closets. Nothing. In the kitchen were old abandoned aluminum pots and pans. The refrigerator: a box of baking soda, various sauces, and orange juice with something green like a mini-city floating at the top, just under the cap.

I shut off the lights, stepped back outside, and clicked on my flashlight. I moved in the direction of the cabins. Abby told me she stayed in #4 and Orly in #7. If he backtracked here, maybe he placed the pins in one of those rooms.

Cabin four was colder inside than out. It had no insulation, just a dirt floor and three bunk beds and four windows. No wonder the vocal kids froze their asses off in late October, just ten months ago.

Nothing.

Cabin seven. I didn't find any pins. But I did find the suitcase.

It was hidden deep under a bunk bed. I broke the lock off with the butt-end of my .38.

Three notebooks, his research. I flipped pages, the flashlight creating a circle that looked like the bottom of a shimmering glass of water. Initials. GS. And then a series of notes; direct quotes; reflections on, from what I could make out, various fantasies, desires, sexual confessions from three-ways to bathroom encounters to hookups in parks late at night. The forbidden was laid bare but in such a way that wasn't puerile but honest, emotional, and forthcoming. JF. AT. Initials for names, I guess.

There were also nine or ten books in the suitcase, including Will and Ariel Durant's *The Age of Voltaire*. No wonder the suitcase was so heavy.

The rest of the cabins were empty.

The sky was dark black, as if it were a painted canvas by Rothko.

I headed back to the mess hall.

Time for the boiler room.

The ground beneath me was uneven. The floor, like that in the cabins, was dirt, not a tile anywhere, and the air was cool, brisk. The boiler hadn't been on for months. A perforated curtain of dust and dirt fell gently from the tin drop ceiling.

I peeled back one of the tiles. It looked like a metal plate riveted to a battleship. The arc of my flashlight revealed dust and dirt up there but no pins.

I slowed my breathing.

Orly did come out here. The suitcase proved it. But maybe he left the pins where he switched cars, sixty miles out of Toronto. But why would he come all this way to hide a suitcase and not the pins? I shook my head. Who can figure out the thinking of a sixteen-year-old.

I wanted to find a soft spot, fresh markings, a darker grade of dirt that might suggest digging and lead to the pins buried somewhere.

I scratched at surfaces with my feet, clawed with my hands, searching for fresh, damp, dank ground.

Suddenly under a whisk of dirt that appeared brushed with a broom I found a trap door.

There was a padlock on it the size of a Stetson hat.

"An old storm cellar," I muttered to myself. "Or maybe a fall-out shelter."

I shot that lock off, metal fireflies lighting up the darkness.

It hurt to pull back the door.

I shoved myself through the hole, walked down thirteen steps, bits of dust and dirt contrails arcing around me, and immediately the air assailed me with its dank excrement, and piss, and blood. I coughed, the odor clinging to me like a shadowy web. My flashlight limned the dents and gouges in the wall.

I moved to the limestone wall and saw it: blood, skin, fingernails.

Orly's fingernails were broken off, limestone powder under his fingers. Silica. Limestone. Orly was buried alive here. Died here and then was moved to Charles Street. No doubt about it.

I bumped into a bunk bed. There were several down there and all around the edges of the heavy limestone foundation was wet moisture, gray discolored lakes.

And then—

Three garment bags dripped down, stalactites on meat

hooks. Shadows crowded the bags' insides. They weren't full of suits and dresses.

Instead, that smell: bagged, decomposing corpses, skin dripping off skulls; angles of hair dry and brittle; bones sticking through forearms and legs. Two of the missing girls.

I would bet money on it.

The girls that had gone missing from Park District School.

I coughed, trying to keep from throwing up.

And the third bag: the vinyl fresher, eyes open, hair watery like floating jellyfish tendrils. She was naked. Pregnant. Scarred. A large X, very noticeable, was cut deeply between her breasts.

Susan Gomery.

Game Three

Friday, September 8, 1972

In the morning I found Stana slouched in the comfy chair of the living room, feet up on an Ottoman, a plaid blanket covering her hips and legs.

"How long have you been up?"

"I didn't sleep." Her face was weighted with worry. On the coffee table to her left were the six books in the Chance Serchuk series and the alleged J. Douglas Gomery manuscript. "Oh, Sal called. He and Miriam are coming over for the game tonight. And Kittle has an alibi for last night and the previous night, the nights of the Susan Gomery heist and death."

"What death, Mommy?" Connie was on a shag rug in the living room playing a concentration game with a deck of cards. Mom had helped set it up, twenty or so cards, face down and Connie had to find various pairs. She was doing pretty damn good.

"Four matches already, honey, that's great," I said.

"What death, Mommy? Who died?"

"A person was murdered, Sweetie—you don't know them." Instead of tiptoeing around topics, Stana often stated things directly to Connie. It was a very successful strategy in avoiding heavy discussions. Meet her at the pass, head-on.

Connie jammed her tongue out the side of her mouth. And returned to flipping cards.

"I don't think he wrote it," Stana said. "Professor Hampton."

She gently tossed off a ream's worth of yellowed paper on the adjacent wooden chair to her right. "The style *is* different—but not different enough."

"Coffee?" I scratched behind an ear, my eyes and mouth dry. It was a warm September and yet my feet were cold.

"Please."

In the kitchen I turned on the kettle and dropped a mound of grounds into the French press. Outside the sky was a bright blue, faded denim jeans. Little chevrons of light graced the window. I rubbed my tired eyes.

It had been a long night. After discovering Susan Gomery's corpse I called the nearest branch of the OPP. And Sal. I was interviewed for over two hours and this morning every Toronto daily ran a story on the possibility of a serial killer in our midst. One reporter even wondered or hinted at a connection with Professor Hampton's "Freedom Writers Society," the fact that Susan's husband was linked to the workshop and she had attended briefly and was now dead. Professor Hampton was unavailable for comment. Kittle put out a statement that in effect said all of us at Greenway Publishing and in Professor Hampton's workshop are both saddened and shocked by the news, and hope that the blue cashmere killer will soon be found.

"I just—it hurts me to say it," Stana's voice stuttered. "But Chip stole that boy's work."

"How can you tell?"

She sat forward in the chair.

"All done, Mommy."

"Good, good. Here, let's see how quickly you can do these puzzles."

"Oh, that's easy," Connie said.

I hated puzzles. Then and now. Bore the fuck out of me. But Connie loves them. I beamed briefly at my daughter and then smiled over at Stana. "You were saying?"

"Three ways, all of them global revisions," she said. "Mere

fine tuning. One, flashbacks. Gomery's are clumsy, round-about: 'Sitting in the living room made him think back to a time when—' versus, 'Two years ago, Chance figured—' You feel the difference, hon? Professor Gomery's flashbacks are more direct, less filtered."

I nodded.

"They're clearly the revised versions because the others are so clunky." She rifled through more yellow pages. "Two—" She held up two fingers of her right hand. "Dialogue."

The kettle whistled. I poured hot water into the press and set the timer for five minutes. "You were, saying, two—" I held up two fingers of my right hand.

Her lips punched together. "Sorry." Tears brimmed at the edges of her eyes. She breathed heavily, waited, and then spoke. "In The Professor's dialogue he doesn't use tags much. He has dialogue, and then a short description of some action as a kind of dramatic beat, and then more dialogue." She licked a finger and skittered through a bunch of pages from the published book. "Here we go: 'I don't care what you think.' David leaned forward, his eyes narrowed. 'You'll do as we say.' You got that?"

"Yeah." I nodded.

She held up a hand as if stopping a row of traffic. "Okay, okay. Here's the same passage in Gomery's manuscript, page 37: 'I don't care what you think,' David said, leaning forward, eyes narrowing, 'You'll do as we say.'" Chip likes removing said constructions. Gomery has them all over the place."

"Hmm."

"It's a subtle difference, but it's a difference. The Professor's prose moves more quickly, but it's just doctored-up Gomery prose." She sighed heavily. "God, I feel sick."

The timer beeped and I poured a cup of coffee and brought it to her. "I'm sorry, honey, I know how much you admired him."

"We all did."

I nodded. "Uh-huh."

"Gomery also uses adverbs like crazy," she said. "I counted twenty-one in one chapter. The Professor rarely uses them. He cut most of them from the manuscript."

She sipped slowly. "Two more things." She held up two fingers from her other hand. "I don't think he wrote the fifth and sixth books. Or, at least, I think they were largely co-written. The voice is much more interior, narrative telling as opposed to showing and scene work, and Kitsey has a much more dramatic role in both plots."

"You don't think The Professor evolved as a writer?" I sat next to her, reaching for her hand.

She pulled away, and got up and crossed slowly toward the TV and the runner's lip that led to the hallway. "I so wanted to find him innocent, to find that The Professor is noble; J. Douglas Gomery is an imposter. But—damn, damn, damn—"

"Why don't you get some sleep—we'll—"

"No goddamn it. No." She turned, her fists tight at her sides. "Sorry, Connie."

Connie looked up, laughed, and then fit a wheel into a car. One puzzle to go.

"No. I'm going to confront him. I'm—I want answers."

"Okay, but why don't you cool off first?"

"I don't want to cool off—I'm mad damn it—sorry, Connie." She stabbed at the floor with her foot, like she were slowly hammering a nail. "Real mad."

"Maybe coffee isn't such a good idea."

"That's not funny."

"I'm sorry."

We didn't say anything for several seconds. Her breathing slowed down. She sipped more coffee. "You know what really chaps my ass? For a man of integrity, how could he steal this person's work?"

"I thought you always said that he said characters don't have to be moral, they just have to be interesting."

"But how could *he*?"

"Tenure," I said. "And the promise, with promotion, of an office with windows."

"Tenure." She shook her head.

"You said you were going to say two more things—what was your last point?"

"There's a gambling subplot The Professor didn't borrow, involving threats on Chance's life, a nasty fella wearing a blue cashmere sweater."

"What?" I rubbed at the edges of my mouth. "Talk about life imitating art."

"The gamblers want Serchuk to throw a hockey game—and they slash the tires of his father's car, which the kid has borrowed, to make their point." She sipped more coffee. "One of the gamblers is a medium-built guy, wears a blue cashmere sweater, and wields a stiletto."

"And Susan told us someone slashed her husband's tires recently—"

"It was Professor Hampton who told you that," Stana corrected.

"Right."

"Someone aping the MO of the blue cashmere villain in the book: serial killer or copycat artist?"

"So who killed Susan?" A bunch of Hampton admirers, the Freedom Writers Society, made a point of running J. Douglas down, saying he was drug-addled, a liar, and *peevish*. Did one of them go so far as to kill Susan because she was leveling charges against The Professor and Greenway Press? What about Kittle? He was motivated to kill Susan. But, the serial kills, the three bodies found in the mess hall in Algonquin Park, pushed the answer away from the group. How could the two be connected unless one of the writers was also a serial killer.

"I have no idea." Stana's lips pushed together. "I looked into Fitzpatrick—"

"Uh-huh."

"Get this, yesterday I did some digging. Old yearbooks, phone calls, the reporter pipeline. J. Douglas was a student at Park District School. He was one of Fitzy's students, 1942. Fitzy was only twenty-two at the time." She lit a cigarette, sharply exhaled.

"That's interesting. What about Susan?"

"No. She comes from money. She went to Leaside."

I nodded. "Hmm."

"But I also looked into his finances," she said.

"You and your reporter friends."

"And my cop friends—Fitzpatrick bought a house in Toronto, 1957 for $16,900. Affordable for a teacher. But did you know he also owns a house in Peterborough, Ontario, and we're not talking about a small cottage either, we're talking about a big house, valued at $49,000. Where does an English teacher get that kind of money? Huh?"

"Drugs?"

"Maybe. He bought the Peterborough home sixty days ago."

"Babe said he saw him collecting boxes in back of Danforth Bowl—"

"Look, remember the Edna St. Vincent Millay story Stewart Kittle told us?"

"Sure," I said.

"How the poet's rewrite wound up being better than the original that was lost in a fire?" She placed her coffee cup on the TV stand, took a puff off her cigarette, the buttons on her pink pajama top mis-alinged. She was tired.

"Yeah?"

Stana punched a fist into a palm. "The argument that Kittle gave you, that Gomery was a peevish lover who sought revenge, stealing The Professor's prized manuscript, just doesn't wash." The cigarette daubed at her lower lip. "The Professor's *new* version wouldn't be that close to the original. Couldn't be, unless he were looking at the original while writing *his* version. The words are *too* close. No. Hampton photocopied Gomery's original during that trip to Santa Monica, and then rewrote, polishing up Gomery's prose and passing it off as his own. He's a fucking thief."

"Sorry, Connie," I said.

The three of us laughed and then played a quick round of *Candy Land.*

I ARRIVED AT THE PROFESSOR'S HOME on Walmer Road to be greeted, surprise, surprise, by Stewart Kittle.

"What do you want, shamus?" Lines furrowed across his forehead. The shape of his neatly sprayed white hair strangely resembled a nipple from a standing baby bottle.

"I want to talk to The Professor."

"I told you and your wife over the phone, The Professor is not giving any interviews at this time." His face darkened. "He's in mourning."

He had a foot in front and behind the door. There was no way he was letting me in.

A buttered crumpet was in his left hand. He took a bite, wiped away the schmutz at the edges of his mouth. "As I said then, he's not seeing anyone. He's, as they say, incommunicado, sequestered. He's under the counsel of his lawyers and his publicist. I'm his publisher, and publicist, dig?"

I smiled, my lopsided grin. 'He better talk to me, soon," I said. "Evidence is mounting."

"What evidence?"

"The manuscript's not his—it's Gomery's."

"That hack. Everything he wrote is overwrought. He couldn't write a clean paragraph, let alone *A Boy on the Leaf's Blue Line.*"

"Gomery caught lightning in a bottle once, and The Professor stole that lightning from him."

"Says who? Gomery? I don't hear him talking." He gestured

as if he were catching rain. "He's dead. Oh, wait, it's Susan Gomery talking. Nope. She's dead too." He finished his crumpet and scrubbed away the remains from fingertips with a short series of slaps, a drummer hitting a run of flams.

"Convenient for you, and The Professor."

"Yes, it is—but that doesn't mean we killed them." He smiled, hand on the hip of his Haggar slacks, as if he were preparing to tell a dirty joke. "And if we did: *prove it*. I have an alibi, The Professor has an alibi at the time of Susan's death." He rubbed the underside of his chin. "Have you?"

"Fuck you. That's not funny."

"I'm not a writer, just a humble editor." A quick short bow.

"There's no way, in terms of syntax and structure, the two manuscripts could be that similar. No way," I said. "Your Edna St. Vincent Millay story doesn't wash."

"What story is that?"

"The one about the stolen manuscript and The Professor having to write the whole thing again from scratch."

"Did I say that? I must have misspoke."

I shook my head. "You said it."

"I don't recall. Funny how that is. And there's no one alive to validate the other position." Now both hands were on his hips. He leaned back. "Your star witness is dead. And so are her claims. The Professor will speak to this tragedy as we move closer to publication."

"Vetted by you."

"Of course." He shrugged. "After all, I am his publicist."

"You're a real piece of work, you know that."

"Thank you." He slipped into his dirty joke smile again. "You doing anything tonight, Superstar?" The students from the workshop were getting together at his place to watch game three, Canada-Russia. "Love to have you." Mrs. Whitelaw was going to be there. Coming all the way from Guelph.

How did he know she was in Guelph? People with power seem

wired into information systems that the rest of us have no access to.

"No thanks, I'm getting together with friends."

He got my meaning, and smiled. "That was good, very good. Maybe you are a writer, after all."

The door closed.

THE BOWLING PIN FELT RIGHT in my left hand. Balanced. There were no seams.

"What the hell are you doing?"

Fitzpatrick entered his classroom, huffing, hands in pockets of his brown wool suit. "Did I say you could touch that?"

Cigarette smoke clung around him like a thin gray curtain.

"I have some follow-up questions."

"I'm busy."

"That's a nice place you got in Peterborough—a mansion on a hill."

"It's not on a hill." He sat behind his desk, hands on the table. He was also wearing a tweed jacket with creased black patches on the elbows. His fingers now slapped atop the desk blotter like typewriter keys across a platen.

"It's still a mansion."

"I earned that money, years and years of hard work," he said. "Years—it's called saving for tomorrow, and sometimes tomorrow comes."

"Sure. And you drive a Mercedes."

"Since when are my finances your concern?" He pointed with a stubby, yellowed finger, his splash of red hair bristling with sweat.

I rubbed at the edges of my mouth. "Since there's been two murders. Since I just discovered J. Douglas Gomery was a student of yours."

"It was just Douglas back then. Dougie actually."

"What kind of a writer was he?"

"Writer?" He shook his head with disbelief. "Writer? Sentence fragments everywhere," Fitzpatrick said. "Incomprehensible prose. Run-ons. He was a worse writer than you." For some reason that really cracked him up.

"What about blue cashmere? Did he ever write about it?"

"Where did you dig up that idea?" The tapping of his fingers grew heavier, staccato downbeats. "You really should write for the movies."

"Yeah. I get that a lot. I wonder what Warners, Mr. F, would think of a schoolteacher, hanging out in back of Danforth Bowl and wandering off with boxes, boxes possibly containing coke inside of bowling pins—snow, as they say on the street."

"That's why you were messing with that pin—" He stood up, sighed, and looked at his watch. Homeroom would commence in fifteen minutes.

"That's why."

"But it's just a pin, isn't it?" Smugness tightened across his face.

"It's just a pin."

He took a big gulp of coffee from a large orange, ceramic mug. "And the boxes I picked up, they were just boxes?"

"Uh-huh."

"How did you get that information?"

"I got my sources."

He sat. "They're American cigarettes," he said. "Cigarettes that fell off the back of a truck, if you get my meaning. Our government charges so damn much in taxes for a pack of smokes. I don't feel guilty about it." He reached inside for a shirt pocket and showcased a pack from his breast pocket. They were Kools, all right. He lit one. "I don't feel guilty at all." He puffed savagely.

"Good for you."

"Any more questions, Mr. Detective?"

"Not now, Mr. Teacher. But there will be." I pulled on the brim of my porkpie. "Count on it."

THE SKY WAS LIGHTER than it was this morning, a soft fade of blue. And before I could fully lean into my communion with nature two fellas in jean jackets and True Suns colors jumped me. Right on the school's front steps. One fella stamped sharply on my instep, sending shivers up my back and neck, causing me to wobble. Suddenly the other fella worked me over with five or six body punches, and I bent and twisted and turned awkwardly, and then my kidneys hurt like hell. Rabbit punches. I fell to my knees, pain everywhere, stars and black spots bouncing before me, and a third fella, much older than the other two, kicked me in the face. I flew back.

The sky turned sideways.

"Enough talking to my daughter. Enough, wiseguy. You hear me?"

His breath in my face was coffee and bad eggs. A lot of bad eggs.

"You talk to her again, and I'll kill ya."

He had black beady eyes and teeth that were too big for his mouth.

"Who the fuck are you?" The words came out of my mouth in blood bubbles. I mean, he told me who he was with the stay-away-from-my-daughter demand, but I wasn't exactly thinking straight.

"Tom Munro."

"Tom Munro, huh? I know you?"

Now, I was thinking straight and being a smart-ass.

One more kick and the black spots spread—

THERE WAS A LINE.

Then another line.

Wood beams.

White plaster. Bumpy texture. Popcorn finish.

"Aw, here he is."

I recognized that purr anywhere. Babe Migano, his voice a fine European sports car. His arms were folded across his broad chest. He was in slacks and suspenders and a white shirt, the cuffs rolled back, French style. Must be a casual day. Well, it *was* Saturday.

Standing at both of his shoulders were Tan Mylow and a sidekick straight out of Toho Studios, shaped like Godzilla, big and brutal, with a white man's overbite and a flattened nose that had been broken more than once. The Red Dragons. Fatigues, black boots, and a crest of a shield on their arm that said "Always Vigilant."

Mylow wore a scarf that flowed to his knees. "You're not looking so good today, Superstar."

The other Dragon was bald with elaborate spider-webbing tattooed atop his dome.

"We saw what happened, and messed up those two punk asses good," Mylow said, a bemused smile on his face.

"That's nice. You couldn't have jumped in a little sooner?" My jaw hurt and my head was a thousand tympani going off at once and none of them in rhythm.

"We had to see how it played out," the Toho extra said. "When a guy makes a play, you let him play it."

"Play it? I was getting played like I was a set of bongos while looking at the goddamn sky."

"You went to the school, uninvited," Mylow reminded me.

"Great." I tried sitting up and almost threw up in my mouth. I lay back down on the small couch. The room was no longer a teeter-totter ride. "Just great. What about Munro—Tom Munro?"

"We were told not to mess him up—" Spider-Man said.

"Much." Mylow finished the first Dragon's thoughts.

"We're in negotiations." Babe motioned with his eyes for the two Dragons to exit. They did.

"Negotiations?"

"Here—" He handed me two diamond-shaped pills. "Take these."

I didn't know what the hell they were, but I dry-swallowed them.

"You'll feel better in a few minutes. At least you'll be able to sit up." He pulled up a metal chair and sat across from me, a leg atop his knee.

"You didn't answer my question."

"I don't intend to," he said.

"What time is it?"

"Four, four-thirty."

"God, I've been out that long?"

"You've been out that long."

"Okay, sensei, what have you got for me?"

He smiled. "I understand you went out to Algonquin Park. Found the notebooks—"

"How do you know that?" *I hadn't even told the police.*

"My boys," he said, "are keeping an eye out for you, and on you."

"Hmm."

"Have you read them?"

"Yeah."

"Carefully?"

"Well—"

"You're not following me, read them carefully, closely."

"Okay."

"You went to Algonquin, via Highway 400?"

"Yeah?"

"You go through Barrie?"

"Yeah?"

"Who has a hamburger stand in Barrie called Shambles?"

"Shit." I snapped my fingers. "Shitshitshitshit. Everly. C. Thomas Everly. He's the one who went with Orly to Algonquin. He's the one—the car swap."

"Yes."

"Are the bowling pins?"

"No." He walked over to his cabriolet, poured a scotch, neat. Sipped. "We already checked. No pins at Shambles. My Dragons tore the place down."

I nodded. "Did Everly kill Susan Gomery?"

"And/or J. Douglas?" Migano shrugged. "Probably not—But he stole the pins from Maceo. With Orly's help. Why?"

"I don't know—why?"

"You can probably sit up. Christ, with you lying there I feel like I'm your goddamn therapist."

I sat up. It wasn't too bad. My head was full of spun cotton candy but the drumming was now more of a set of quiet wind chimes. In rhythm. I planted my feet. The left instep still hurt like fuck. "Everly stole the pins. Why? He was blackmailed?"

Migano nodded, lit a cigar, puffing several times gently until the end was a glowing blister of red. "Check the notebooks."

"I have been, I will."

"He's in there"

"He is—?"

"Certain fantasies—let's just say, the kind of stuff that would not sit well with the Board of Education."

"But they're just fantasies—"

"Not when you're a schoolteacher, working with kids—" Another red glow followed by a puff, followed by a heavy wash of smoke curling around him like a hangman's noose.

I leaned forward. *Abby said her dad had one of the notebooks. He'd read the fantasies. Shared them with Babe.* "Tom Munro. He's blackmailing Everly?"

"Maybe."

"He has the pins—negotiations, my ass."

"I offered him a third of what they're worth." Babe finished his scotch. "But he's playing it a little too cute—way too cute for my taste."

I just shook my head. "He doesn't know you the way I do."

"Meaning?"

"You're not a guy to be played—cute or otherwise."

He lifted his chin and gave an approving, tight smile.

"Am I free to go now?"

Babe nodded.

Seconds later Lou arrived, his pompadour higher than ever.

"Nobody light a match," I said.

"Get some new material, wiseguy," Lou muttered.

I don't know how the hell Babe signaled him to come and get me, but somehow he did.

EVERYTHING IN THE ROOM WAS BLUE: cerulean shelves, periwinkle drapes, powder blue lampshades; midnight-blue carpet. It resembled the strange loud austerity of Orly's red lab room and I had no doubt who the interior decorator of the two settings was: C. Thomas Everly. What tied the two rooms together? A matching white Hepplewhite chair pushed against a gunmetal-blue desk.

Everly's wife, fortyish and plump with a gentle curve to her smile, was in the next room, watching CBC's evening news.

My wife was at home probably watching the news too. She said she had some fried chicken waiting on a warming plate, and hurry home, the game starts at eight, and Miriam and Sal would be arriving any time, closer to 7:30, knowing them. I didn't tell her about the beating I took.

Everly wore a red rayon bowling shirt with twill embroidery, yoke collar, and smiley pockets. It had a 1950s vibe, aided and abetted by an ample brunette in fishnets and splashing pins scrambled across his back.

It was brand new, custom-made, and he'd just been modeling it for his wife. "It will debut next week, league play."

"Who would want to kill Susan Gomery?"

"I had heard about that, but I don't know her. Our paths never crossed."

"That's not true—"

"Huh?"

"According to Geno Seven, you and J. Douglas had an affair from 1955–59, and spilled tears over a Judy Garland song."

"That was a long time ago."

"Yes. And while you two were carrying on J. Douglas was married. Married to Susan."

The walls around him were accented with iconic photographs: Lewis Hine's construction workers erecting the Empire State Building, balancing sturdily on girders, arc lines painting the sky; Dorothea Lange's tenant farmers, strong and dignified, faces touched by shadows of earth; and Ansel Adams's almost bleach-bone landscapes under a white-hot moon. The outlier: vague nude pinups, including a twenty-something, head tilted right, pulled down by a fierce Indian headdress. She had a ballerina's body, and no hair down there.

"Edmund Leja. A great photographer of the female form," he said, noticing that I had noticed. "A real artist."

Art. It was soft porn. "Hmm. She looks like a girl," I said.

"Lois Bishop, 1948." He smiled faraway. "I assure you, she's all woman." His translucent eyebrows arched like the backs of two cats. "All woman. And what happened with J. Douglas, our encounters, are no more. That was just a one-time thing."

"Was there also a one-time thing with Orly?"

"What. No. He's just a kid. And no—no way."

"Does Abby know you're married?"

He staggered into the tight Hepplewhite chair. "Nobody knows I'm married. And that includes my wife." He shrugged off his joke. His marriage was an open marriage. As his hands pressed together, I noticed he wore no ring. His wife puffed up when they were dating like she was pregnant, "and then we got married and she puffed up no more." A desultory shrug. "Twenty years. A Boston marriage, you understand? She's got different needs."

"How old are you anyway?"

"Of a certain age—"

"What has Tom Munro got on you?"

"Huh?"

"The notebooks. He has one of them. And you must be in it."

"Now, wait a minute—"

"Wait nothing—Do you desire, Orly, is that it? A sixteen-year-old boy."

He swallowed hard, lips drained of color. "I'm a Charles Street regular, okay? But I'm not bisexual." His shoulders shook with nervous vigor. "I'm just, well, curious. I had a one-time thing with a man. If that man was a woman, I would have had that one-time thing with her."

The exact thing Geno thinks—

Everly admitted he had bought Orly gifts, trinkets, encouraging him, in his research. "Keep digging—I told the kid. Keep digging—But it was always platonic, above board—I'm a schoolteacher for chrissakes."

"Uh-huh." I figured C. Thomas wanted Orly to delve into a lifestyle that Everly himself was too afraid to embrace. "But, c'mon, C.T, the trinkets, the gifts found among Orly's things, could easily indicate gifts from a lover."

And then there was the necklace Orly had given to Abby. Had Everly given the necklace to Orly first and then he handed it down to Abby?

"How dare you? You're no Sigmund Freud, and I'm not your patient."

"What's Munro got on you?"

He shrugged, the dip below his lip quivering.

"Were you and Orly lovers—did you want to be his lover?"

"We were just friends."

"Uh-huh. I assure you, pal, the Toronto Board of Education is not going to be too crazy about all this."

"I've done nothing wrong."

"Then why did you allow Munro to blackmail you?"

"What?"

"There's something in those notebooks—"

He looked down at his fingers.

"I also found a bowling pin among Orly's effects. They're kind of like those Russian dolls, dolls within dolls. Well, inside the pin wasn't another pin, or a doll, for that matter, but coke," I said. "A lot of coke."

He was now chewing his fingers.

"You and Orly stole pins from Maceo to buy off Munro. Now for the third time, I ask, what does Munro have on you? Danforth Bowl is a distribution center. Soon, the fuzz is going to hit Maceo and his lanes, knocking them down, and where will you be? Talk."

Sal told me when I told him what I knew courtesy of Babe Migano that they were setting up surveillance, tracking Maceo's every move, and they might even put a sting operation in play. So much of this case appeared to be people following other people, knowing things well in advance of the persons pursued. The cops wanted to catch the bastard passing the stuff. "I can't help you, unless you tell me what you know." I slammed my hands in my pockets. "What does Fitzpatrick know? He's your bowling buddy, your friend."

He said nothing.

"Not very talkative, huh? I thought you were a teacher."

The heating fan in the room clicked and chugged, a slow-moving freight train. Like a lot of older people, Everly and his wife liked the temperature ten-to-fifteen degrees above comfortable.

I glanced over at Lois Bishop, the lack of pubic hair. "Abby—"

"Abby. No. Fitzpatrick doesn't know. He doesn't know—I never touched her."

"She's only fifteen."

"I know, I know."

"But Munro knows about your desires—read about them in the notebook."

"Yes."

"And blackmailed you."

"Yes."

"And Fitzpatrick doesn't know? You sure?"

"I don't know—you think he knows?"

"What do you think?"

He nodded. "Yeah. He knows."

"What did you say in these notebooks?"

"Nothing—just having a crush on the girl—that's all—a crush—like I'm sixteen again." He hadn't had sex with a woman until he was thirty, he said. "I often fantasize about being sixteen again and having sex, with a girl, going back in time and having a second chance at what hadn't passed before."

"*You're not sixteen*. Who else knows?" My shoulders hurt and my cheeks burned.

"Tom Munro wanted cash, a lot of cash. I told Orly about it, not Fitzy, and Orly said we could steal some pins, or he could steal them. From Maceo. He knew what his uncle was doing, dealing, distributing coke all around the north end to other distribution centers, bowling alleys. Who expects bowling alleys to be a drop? Anyway, Orly cared, the boy cared for me. And he stole twenty pins. For me. He wanted three for himself and Abby—to get away. That was his cut. Three pins. He hid them out at Algonquin. But the other seventeen, he did it for me. Munro got all seventeen of them, the payout, and then Orly was killed."

"By Munro?"

"Maybe—my money's on the True Suns."

The chugging fan grew heavier. "I'm going to nail Orly's killer."

"Saba took Orly away, tortured him first. Probably killed him later," Everly said. "Saba and Chunky did it, under Maceo's orders."

"Orly never gave me up, or else I'd be dead."

"Munro still has the pins." It wasn't a question, but he took it that way. I knew the answer from conversations with Babe.

"I don't think he could fence them," Everly said. "He tried, but no one wanted to piss off Maceo." He chewed his lower lip. "Yeah, I think he's still got them. The bastard's stuck with them."

"You owe that kid." I pointed a stubby finger. "They tortured, sodomized, and killed him, and he never gave you up. He loved you."

"Yeah."

"You owe him."

"Yeah."

"Call the police. Go into protective custody. Tell your story, help us—Your story would help Abby rest easier. Call the police."

"I will," he promised. "I will." His voice was a dim echo, lost in the catacombs of thoughts and fears.

"SURE YOUR TV'S BIG ENOUGH, Superstar?" A mischievous gleam passed over Sal's face like the shadow cast by a low-flying jet. I was adjusting the vertical hold on the TV. It was a 14–inch Zenith, black-and-white. "We all can't be rich like you, pal."

Our living room was off-white with a coffee table, two floor lamps, a shag rug, a couch and two chairs. Next to the TV, Orly's bowling pin. In one of the corners a plastic potted palm tree. On the dining room table was our Singer sewing machine. Stana had been doing some last-minute work hemming a dress for work tomorrow. Tonight she was wearing bell-bottom jeans and a pink halter top.

She looked terrific.

"When you going to come into the 20th Century?"

"With my husband's buzzcut, a part of him is forever in the 1950s." Stana laughed, hauling in a large fondue pot with their metal forks already resting inside along the lip.

I shrugged. I wasn't into the whole long hair and chewing gum thing like the fellas on Team Canada had going on.

Miriam followed behind Stana with a china plate piled with brownie-size squares of croutons.

We sat around the TV waiting for the game to start. Sal and Miriam on the couch; Stana in the La-Z-Boy; me and Connie on the floor.

A moment of silence before puck drop: in observance of the murdered Israeli athletes at the Summer Olympic Games. Chills pinched at the back of my neck and along the tops of my arms.

Cheese dripped from Connie's chin. "Who was murdered?"

I told her.

"Why?"

That I had a harder time telling her.

The game started and the Soviets were pressuring us from the drop. They were forechecking and sharply passing and nearly scored, if not for a big pad save by Tony O. Canada countered and a Bill White shot from the point had Tretiak flailing, struggling to handle it cleanly. It bounced off the fat cuff of his glove, rattled around his feet, and was knocked home by J.P. Parisé. Miriam jumped from the couch. Sal and I missed connecting on our high-fives. "How many beers have you had, pal?"

"Four," Sal said. "Maybe seven, eight—who's counting?"

In the next five minutes we had a powerplay and were looking forward to going up by a couple of goals. But a bad cross pass in our zone led to Petrov breaking in untouched on Espo and the Soviet sniper fired one through Tony's legs as he dropped to the butterfly.

"Your guy Mahovlich coughed up the puck," Sal said.

Frank did.

"A lazy pass."

"Okay, okay."

"Tony should have had it," Stana said. "Went right through

him."

"No, that one's on Frank," Sal corrected. "It's too bad you never got to see your pop play, Connie. He never would have made that pass. Your father was one of the best defensive forwards to ever play."

I shook my head. Another shortie given up by Team Canada. "Damn," I muttered.

Connie's head tilted left. "Defensive forward?"

"That means I stopped the other team from scoring," I said. "I saw my job as protecting our goalie." *And creating space for our playmakers.*

Connie smiled and wondered if she could have something else. She wasn't too crazy about the fondue. It was too gooey and made her mouth feel all mumbly-crumbly. I made her a PBJ.

The first period ended with Canada leading 2-1, Jean Ratelle top corner on a pretty feed from Brad Park.

This was my night to put Connie to bed so I told her that it had better be quick, kiddo, the intermission is only eighteen-minutes long.

Her room was pink and blue with unicorns and dinosaur cutouts on the walls. I sang her our *Rio Bravo* song, and then she told me that sometimes there were monsters on the ceiling.

"Monsters?"

"I see them on the ceiling and I can't sleep."

"Do you see them now?"

She looked up. "They're kind of all dissolve-y like when you put Alka-Seltzer in a glass of water."

"That's a cool image, honey."

"Why do some people murder other people?"

"I don't know, Sweetie. Humans have been trying to figure that out for years."

"You know chimpanzees have bad monkeys too, who go all scary—" She mentioned something about a book Mommy had read to her on Jane Goodall.

"Yeah—"

"This boy that was killed, the shoeshine boy, were you trying to protect him too, like you protected goalies?"

"I didn't know him until he was killed," I said.

"But you're trying to find out who murdered him?"

"Yes, I am." *And J. Douglas Gomery. And Susan Gomery.*

"Do you like doing that kind of work?" Her face drooped with sleepiness.

I swept hair from her eyes. "Someone has to do it, and it gives me purpose." I looked at my fingers. "I want the world to be a safer place for everyone."

"Like a superhero."

"I'm no superhero."

"Frank made a bad play, didn't he?"

"Yeah, he did. We all make mistakes."

"Is he still your favorite player?"

I laughed. "Of course. You make mistakes, and you're still my favorite girl." I leaned over and kissed the top of her forehead.

She nodded, and smiled. "I love you, Daddy."

"I love you too."

She concentrated at the ceiling. "They're all still dissolve-y."

"I'll make them go away." I broadly gestured at the ceiling with Bob Fosse–like hands, stood up, danced a few steps, not at all like Bob Fosse really. More like Baloo the bear, and Connie laughed at my antics. "They gone?"

I scratched my back along the edge of the door's frame like Baloo rubbing up against a tree.

She laughed some more. "Yes—Can you stay with me, until I fall asleep?"

"Yes."

WHEN I RETURNED TO GAME ACTION it was the second period and we were up 3-1 and on another powerplay. We had the puck deep around Tretiak, but four of our guys were down low, including D-man Brad Park. Boris Mikhailov checked the puck from one of our guys in the corner and fired a long pass up to a breaking Kharlamov. He took it in stride, outskated an out-of-position Park and broke in on Tony, forehand, backhand, and scored. 3-2.

Both goals were shorties.

"Maybe Park should have stayed back at the point," Sal said.

I sat dejectedly on the couch. "Park was down low and nobody rotated back."

Nobody said anything for a while. The game was slipping away. The Soviets just kept coming.

"Speaking of shorties, do you guys mind if I light up a cigar?" Sal played with his picket fence of his Hemingway beard.

"Please don't." Miriam made a face.

"Last time I smoked a Short Story cigar, Stana told you she was pregnant, remember? It's been awhile—since we all just kicked back."

The Gray Hearse case.

I remembered.

"Go ahead." Stana reached for a Parliament.

"Oh, okay, but blow the smoke that way—" Miriam pointed to the sliding doors that led to the backyard.

Stana lit up. So did Sal. "How'd it go, with Connie?"

I gave Stana a brief smile. "Monsters on the ceiling—they're gone now."

"I remember those days," Miriam said. Her boys were now twelve and fourteen.

Sal reached for his wife's hand. "Next weekend we're going to take a trip to Niagara Falls. Just the two of us."

Miriam raised her chin and the light of the room glinted off the dimples at the corners of her mouth. "I bought a new outfit."

"I hope it's one of those see-through nighties."

"Sal!"

He winked at me.

"Niagara Falls. That sounds lovely," Stana said.

Sal wondered if we were up to talking shop, about the case. Put our heads together, now that Connie was asleep. "I know I've had a few beers, but I think I'm relatively lucid—"

"Bullshit," I said.

"Okay, okay." He reached for his Molson's Export, and another puff.

Miriam moved to the front edge of the couch. "Let's compare notes." The tips of her fingers shook with excitement and some anger. "What if the three murders were unrelated?"

"That might be," I said. "I'm pretty sure Maceo and the True Suns killed Orly. I just need to find the proof."

Sal rubbed at his scrubby beard. "Three variables: the True Suns, the Red Dragons, and those damn workshoppers—Two kills belonged to one grouping and one to another."

"It made sense but who do you put in what group?"

It was a mess to figure, one big mishegoss. Susan and Orly, sex crimes, and a serial killer. Doug, workshoppers. But Stana said that the blue cashmere angle made it possible to place Doug's murder also in the sex-crime category. And yet, who benefits from all this? Greenway Publishing? At least in terms of the two Gomery deaths. That leaves the shoeshine killing a sex crime or maybe a crime of vengeance, the True Suns getting even for stealing all those drug-laced bowling pins.

Paul Henderson on a pass from Bobby Clarke that bounced off a Soviet defender's skate suddenly made it 4-2 Canada. "How's the surveillance going at Danforth Bowl?" I asked.

"Nothing so far," Sal said. "It's set up and rolling."

"Did Everly talk to you?"

"The biology teacher?"

"Yeah. I gave him your card—he knows some shit."

"No. No call."

I hadn't shared with Sal the three notebooks. Maybe I should—I also hadn't shared about Everly's crush on Abby.

"You ready for a real bombshell, Superstar?"

"Always—"

"I've been looking into the various personalities in this case shall we say," Sal said. "Kittle, Fitzpatrick, Everly, Whitelaw. Bank records. We know Fitzpatrick came into a lot of money recently. Bought a nice home in Peterborough. That's got us digging—Into bank deposits, credit-card records, receipts from Eaton's. And—" he held up four fingers. "Guess who bought four cashmere sweaters, blue, from Eaton's four months ago?"

Nobody said anything. A gentle wind tapped at the sliding glass door that led to the backyard.

"Stewart Kittle," Sal said.

"But he has an alibi for both of the Gomery murders," I said.

The Soviets scored to make it 4-3. "Two goal-leads just don't hold up against them." Stana frowned.

Sal wondered aloud if Kittle knew the killer or gave the sweaters to the killer?

"Kittle—" Miriam tapped her chin and shifted on the couch. "He's a huge fan of that 120-adjectives exercise where we're to pick three and make them a part of who and what our lead character is. Remember 'peevish'?"

We all nodded.

"Obviously, the workshop made Doug into a character, a narrative. Three adjectives. A second one for Doug might be a hounded man. A past enemy, a sexual predator from 1947, hunted him down and killed him in 1972. What if the blue cashmere angle is all a construction, a story made to distract us from the real story? There is no blue cashmere killer. Yes, there's a killer out there who targets women but blue cashmere has nothing to do with it."

"I like your thinking, Miriam," I said.

Suddenly the Soviets made the game 4–4.

"Fuck," Stana yelled. "That blows—"

Miriam continued, her eyes widening, "That person was Kittle. In a wig. Pursuing Susan at the Park and Mrs. Whitelaw and me. Building the narrative. He has to destroy Doug's reputation in order to protect The Professor's. If you take away the walrus mustache and the moptop wig, the build and walk is Kittle's."

"Walk?" I asked.

"I remember now," she said. "The fella had a side-to-side, arrogant male walk."

"Of course, so Kittle's building a false narrative, but someone still killed Doug? Who?

Professional or personal motivations," I said. "Kittle fits the former. Mrs. Hampton, fits the latter."

"We need to look into Mrs. Hampton," Sal said.

"For Susan it was personal, too." Miriam said. "Her husband's reputation."

"What about Mrs. Whitelaw?" Stana said. "I can't figure her out."

"She's in the middle. She was best friends with Susan but Kittle had also promised her a chance to ghostwrite one of the new, upcoming novels. Divided loyalties."

"Yeah—and Fitzpatrick knew Doug Gomery," Stana said. "A student of his. What else does Fitzy know?"

THE THIRD PERIOD WAS SCORELESS. Stana whipped up a quick batch of Jiffy Pop popcorn, and we munched away, and when the CTV cameras showed Bobby Hull in attendance, cheering Canada, my wife let out a violent sigh. Hull had signed with the Winnipeg Jets of the rival WHA and the NHL owners wouldn't let him play for Team Canada. Most of Canada was outraged. And Bobby Orr had a bad knee. Two of our best players weren't dressed. No one was that worried, until the Soviets blew us out in game one, and now the commentators on TV were woefully wishing Hull could suit up. But not Stana. A few years back she had written an article on domestic violence, interviewing several current and ex-hockey wives, and her editors at *The Toronto*

Telegram, the paper she worked for at the time that closed its shop in 1971, killed the story.

"Well that was fun," Sal zipped up his leather jacket. "Next time I'll bring a telescope to keep a better eye on the TV."

I punched him in the shoulder. "You fucking guy."

"How can a tie feel like such a loss, but it does," he said.

"We blew two, two-goal leads," I said. "That's how. Both teams almost scored in the last minute of play. Tony made a tremendous in-close save with 13 seconds to go."

Miriam grabbed the car keys from Sal. "I'm driving."

"Okay, warden."

Miriam and Stana hugged and then the Lambertinos left.

"We should do something romantic sometime—like Sal and Miriam heading to Niagara Falls—a getaway." She reached for my hand.

"Maybe a date night—we could ask your mom to sit for us—"

"I'd like that." She nuzzled my neck and the side of my face.

I winced.

"What?"

"Nothing."

"Nothing, my ass." She traced a line along my lower jaw. "It's all swollen along here."

I shrugged. "A little fracas, outside of Park District School, it's nothing."

"Jesus, honey."

"No worse than a hockey fight," I lied— "You should see the other guy."

"I've heard that before."

"A run-in with the True Suns—it's all good." I smiled my lopsided grin. "Your friends the Red Dragons."

"My friends?"

"Well, you were waving at them from the window the other night"

"Oh, stop."

"The Dragons came to my rescue."

She shook her head disapprovingly. I squeezed her hand and we sat on the couch, her legs, sideways, over my lap.

"You never said anything about my outfit."

"What? I like it."

She kissed the side of my face. "Do you?"

"Yeah—I've been staring at your nipples all night."

"That was the idea."

"Huh?"

"Some detective you are."

"Oh—"

She stood on her knees, undid the back of the halter and it slipped away. "When do I ever not wear a bra? At least with company around? When do I *ever* wear a halter top?"

"Not now apparently—"

She laughed, leaned into me and my ribs hurt and my lower back pounded from the beating I took, but I didn't say a damn thing about that there because, well because—

"Let's go to bed," I suggested.

"No, I want to do it here." She had my belt off, my pants down passed my hips and then around my thighs. "We need to spice things up a little."

"But Connie—"

"We'll put popcorn on the floor, out in the hallway, like those detectives do in the old movies. We'll hear her if she *breaks* in"

"Can people see us through the sliding glass doors?"

"Oh, shit," she said, covering up with a throw pillow.

There was a part in the curtains. I grabbed the second pillow, covered myself, kicked my pants free from my ankles, and closed up the seam. When I returned to the couch, Stana was naked. "Let's do it missionary, old-fashion style—we seem to like that, a couple of old married folks."

"We're not that old."

"You look beautiful like that."

"I could lose twenty pounds."

"I like the whole look."

I felt heat in my face. I think I was blushing.

I joined her, nibbled at her neck, nipples, kissed her forehead. "You put in your cap?"

"Remember what Sal said, when he was smoking that cigar?"

"No."

"About the last time? The Gray Hearse case?"

"Oh, wait, no—"

Her face brightened.

"Yes. Come April, we're going to have another one."

"That's awesome."

"You sure?"

"Yes."

She guided me in and I sighed deeply.

"I think entering for you is the favorite part of all this—the best—"

It was, I said. It was when I felt the most connected with her and the most comfortable during the sex act. She pulled me in deeper, and after a couple of minutes, we came together.

Believe me, that didn't happen that often.

Saturday

I FOUND IT IN THE MIDDLE of the second notebook.

The nuance. The real truth behind "the crush."

I woke up some time around 2 a.m, the Sominex of sex with Stana had knocked me out for a few hours, but now, three hours later I was wired, the jigsaw pieces to this case's puzzle belonging to two different landscapes that I just couldn't navigate my way across. The pieces wouldn't fit. Not neatly.

C.T. It was a single entry, written in blue ink, dated a year ago. C.T. felt guilty over his conflicted lifestyle and loving a girl. A girl. Fourteen. He had a thing for twelve- to fifteen-year-olds and never acted on those desires, but now there was this one girl, to be fifteen soon, who he couldn't stop thinking about. And she's dark-skinned. Was that part of the appeal? Was he one of those white men, he wondered, full of atavistic desires, a need to return to the jungle, the "primordial ooze of our ancestors," a need for a girl from the islands? The girl was petite, could pass for twelve, but he dreamed about her, not clean dreams either. Sexy dreams. Sex in a hammock, sex on a raft, sex in his kitchen with the refrigerator door open. Dreams. Distractions. Desires. He talked to the girl, praised her work, but never told her how beautiful she was, but he was watching her, the supple lines of her breasts, his breath catching on those days when she arrived to his classroom early. She looked like a gymnast, moved like a ballerina. A girl. A pretty, pretty girl. "I want her. Maybe I should take up a new hobby. To forget her. Photography? How cliché is that?"

C.T. C.T. Everly. The girl: Abby Munro. And that photograph by Edmund Leja hanging on one of Everly's walls, the photograph of Lois Bishop, wearing an Indian headdress, the photograph in which she has no hair down there. Lois Bishop. Young looking. Petite. Like an athlete, a ballerina. C.T. Everly, pedophilic desires. And racist thinking, gussied up as so-called admiration of a people and their culture.

Tom Munro probably had even more lurid entries in the notebook in his possession. Lurid enough to force Everly's hand to steal in return for Munro's silence.

I pushed back from the kitchen table.

Christ.

The box at my feet had one more notebook to lean into. But I had enough for a followup visit with Abby and Everly. Something told me things had turned physical between them. This entry was written a few weeks before that trip in October to Algonquin Park and those cold cabins. What went on in that boiler room? Did they sneak off together at any time?

The books were SF paperbacks. A cloth copy of *Leaves of Grass* had a looseleaf drawing of a motorcycle squeezed inside. It was a guy on a big chopper with a big, bold sun and yellow diagonal lines bleeding everywhere like a Japanese flag. It was such a kid drawing: the macho biker mixed in with the silly junior-high sentimentality, the sun beaming radiant lines that no one can ever really see. The lines kicked the illustration's realism to the curb. Maybe that was the idea: the conflict between life is and what life ought to be. And Orly *did* draw this. He signed his name, bottom left, to the work. This work wanted it both ways: dark truth and bright hope. Maybe. Anyway, I liked Orly more for the idealism under the hurt.

And then—

Another find.

I reached for Will and Ariel Durant's *The Age of Voltaire*.

A 5 x 7 photograph was crushed between the pages like a pressed rose.

It fell from the volume and brushed up against my cup of instant coffee.

C. Thomas Everly stared at me with a bemused smile, hands on hips, a gleam in his eyes that promised to reveal pleasures yet fulfilled.

He wasn't wearing any clothes.

The only thing he had on: the necklace with the jade crescent moon and gold inlay, the one I saw around Abby's neck, the first day in my office, the one she said Orly gave her, but now I knew, it was from Everly, he must have given it to *her* as a testament to their love.

THE THIRD VERSION of the story was the correct version.

Abby didn't hire me to restore Orly's reputation, to prove his innocence or his sexual normativity. She also didn't hire me to recover twenty bowling pins full of coke so that she could get away from Regent Park, and all of this. No, she hired me to protect C. Thomas Everly, who was in over his head.

They were lovers.

She and the teacher. Not, Orly and the teacher. Not she and Orly. Abby and C. T. Everly.

She was wearing gym shorts and an orange T-shirt that went all the way to the top of her knees like a dress. It had a white crew neck collar. We were sitting in the back of Zellers, drinking coffees and eating grilled cheese sandwiches and French fries with gravy. I wanted to meet her without her father overhearing a damn thing.

The booth was candy-apple red with gold trim. The floor in our little corner diner within the low-fi department store was like a chessboard, full of black-and-white squares.

"You got that necklace from him, not from Orly."

She absently stretched the chain in my direction, and agreed with a brief nod. "How did you find out?"

C. Thomas is wearing it, in a very suggestive photograph, I said. I slid the 5 X 7 photograph her way.

She winced.

"Orly must have somehow found the photo, and taken it, to hide it away from your father."

"Yes." She shifted uncomfortably, a hand at the side of her neck, her eyes faraway. "After Dad found one of the notebooks I knew this would be the final tipping point."

"Dad got the notebook and he had leverage over C. Thomas and he was blackmailing him, right?"

She nodded. The brown gravy on the Fries was congealing into a wet mud.

"If he'd seen this photo he might have killed him."

"Yes—He doesn't like me seeing boys," she said.

Across from us in a spinning rack full of cheap Pocket paperbacks was one by Norman Mailer on boxing.

"C. Thomas isn't a boy."

"I know, I know."

"Did you know he was married?"

Her eyes widened. She played with the necklace, jade with gold inlay. "No, I, he is?"

"He is."

Her eyes were wet marbles.

"How many more photos like this did he send you? I'm sure this isn't the only one."

"Several." She pushed aside her sandwich. And in some of them, she said, he has—a—

"Wonderful," I muttered. "I don't need to dust for fingerprints."

"It got kind of creepy," she said. "I turn sixteen in a few weeks, well, November 9th, and he started sending me poems, love poems, that he'd written, and photographs, and little notes at the ends of his love letters that said, forty-five days to go. Thirty-seven days to go—"

"Hmm."

"Until I'm sixteen."

"I figured that."

"We haven't done anything yet. Well, we have, but we haven't done *it*, you know? We've done everything *but it*." It all happened last fall. Out at the cabins. The vocalists retreat. "When everyone else went on that hayride I told you about me and Mr. Everly retreated to the boiler room and made out. It smelled of dust, mold, and wet wool. He was a great kisser. Orly's kisses were sort of naked, something missing. But, C.T.'s—" She shook her head without embarrassment. "I loved him. He's married, huh?"

"He's married."

"The photo? He called the photo a prelude." She laughed nervously. "I'm not even sure I want to do it with him anymore, all those poems and notes were just—"

"Over the top?" I sipped coffee. It was as bitter as a Conservative candidate giving a concession speech.

"He's just twenty-eight. I'll be sixteen soon, but those weird notes—"

"A countdown to sex—"

"You don't need to spell it out."

"Twenty-eight? Is that what he told you? More like thirty-eight going on forty-eight. The guy's been married twenty years."

"Twenty?"

And she was soon-to-be-sixteen, but she could pass for twelve, thirteen.

She followed the lines in the ceiling. "I think Mr. Fitzpatrick figured something was going on between the two of us."

They were best pals, bowling partners.

"Mr. Fitzpatrick used to talk to me all the time," she said, "but after that school trip, he was a little cold. He used to say I was a good writer, but then he never spoke to me. Maybe it had nothing to do with that. The boiler room. You know, after his son died, he died. Inside."

"A car accident," I nodded solemnly.

She couldn't quite look at me, stirring her coffee with a wooden stick. "Rumor had it that the cheerleader his son was with was giving him a blowjob while he was driving and he lost control of the car. That was the buzz all over Park District."

"You really did hire me to help C.T, didn't you?"

She nodded, small breaths, small breaths. She couldn't fully breathe. "After Dad got that notebook, he hit me, cut me—"

"Cut you?"

She pulled down at the crewneck collar. Between her breasts and above the cups of her bra was a scar, an X.

"My God, did you get that treated?"

"I treated it myself. If I reported it, I'd be in a foster home."

"Maybe that's a good thing?"

"No." Even with the brutality of her father, it was a known brutality, and within those boundaries, the days he worked, and was gone, she had a degree of freedom that made it okay. "I was able to find spaces of power within his dictatorship." She laughed bitterly.

"Did your dad know Susan Gomery?"

Abby's eyes narrowed. "Who's she?"

"Her husband years ago was a student of Mr. Fitzpatrick's."

"Never heard of her."

"Well—" The words wouldn't come out and I drank the rest of my coffee. "You've heard of the blue cashmere killer and the bodies found in Algonquin?"

"Yes, of course. The two girls were friends of mine."

"Well, Mrs. Gomery's corpse, the third that was found, had an X carved between her breasts—"

"My God." She covered her mouth. "My dad, a killer?" She shook her head vehemently. "No way, no way."

"Maybe." I shrugged. "There's evidence there. Circumstantial, but—"

"No."

"Orly hid two pins out there. For you and him. Your future, his. Where are they?"

"I don't know."

"He didn't tell you?"

"He told me, but—"

"You don't want to tell me—"

She nodded.

"Fair enough." *I was going to have to report all this to Sal. This wasn't something to keep under wraps.* "Where's your dad hiding the dope?" Rocks were dissolving in my stomach, and I needed an antacid tablet. This was my fourth cup of coffee and that was two cups too many. "I know he has it. He's in conversations with Babe Migano to unload it."

"The gangster?"

"He'd prefer the title, night club owner, or man-about-town, but yes, gangster."

She smiled as an afterthought. "I don't know. I thought maybe Shambles, but Shambles was a shambles." She apologized for the play on words.

"Babe's guys—the Red Dragons gave it a going over—and I searched Algonquin figuring maybe Orly hid all the pins there—that's before I knew your dad had the goods—most of the goods."

"I've checked all over the apartment—believe me."

"What can I do for C.T?"

"Protect him from my Dad, from Fitzpatrick, whoever might try to destroy him."

"The Board of Education is who I'd be worried about. When this story breaks, he'll be broken—" *Not that he doesn't have it coming to him.*

"It doesn't need to break—I'm not going to say anything."

"It isn't just about you."

Her lower lip curled under her teeth. "Then help him get away. Someplace. Anyplace—"

"I've already tried talking sense to him. To make a deal with the police—Nothing."

"I wish he'd listen to you—" You know with C.T, at first, she said, I felt like I was part of something, that love energy that all the poets write about, you know? "I felt alive with him and rescued from all this, from the anger of my father, from—you know how many fights I've had at school with the colored girls because I got a white father? You have any idea?"

She liked Orly a lot, but in the boiler room with C.T, she loved a man. And it was marvelous.

For a time.

AFTER MEETING WITH ABBY and warning her to keep her head down, and take no chances, and if you need to get away, call me, you can stay at my place, I headed to my office to make several phone calls. First I told Sal about the X on Abby's chest, courtesy of her father, perhaps matching the one on Susan Gomery's corpse. And Sal said he was going to bring Munro in—suspicion of murder. I also told Sal all about Everly and the pins and the blackmail threats and how I suspected he had gone missing. Then I called Everly. On the pretense of reaching him, but I really wanted to talk to his wife, fishing for a clue. His wife in a rather thin medicated voice said she hadn't seen him since I last dropped by their home. And then I called Professor Hampton. Kittle answered.

"Don't you ever go home?"

"Not when there's jokers like you in the world." His voice sounded heavy with liquor.

"A little too much celebrating last night—the death of Susan Gomery?"

"No, I was a little down, last night—the Soviets—we should have won that game."

"Oh, yeah, book sales."

"Yeah, book sales. I'm worried—they outskated, and outchanced us. Canadians like them. Did you hear the mixed emotions expressed toward our boys? Especially Bergman."

"Well, Bergie did swing a stick rather violently at a Soviet winger."

"That was just for emphasis. Intimidation. No intent to injure."

We played better than the final score indicated, I said. We can beat these guys.

"They play such an elegant style. They're winning over the public." And all those damn liberal writers, he said. From the workshop. "Freedom Writers Society. Freedom my ass—more like the Brainwashed Writers Society. Celebrating. Celebrating the Russians. Saying this is the death of Canadian hockey, as if that's a good thing. Scratch any liberal and you'll find someone who hates blue-collar hockey."

"I'm a liberal, I *played* hockey."

"And you were tough. You took nothing from nobody—carried a lunch bucket on the ice."

"Yeah—Look, did Hampton know Tom Munro?"

"Never heard of him."

"I'm not asking you, I'm asking The Professor—ask him for me, will ya?"

"I'll give it consideration."

"Do. Susan Gomery was found hanging in the mess hall catacombs of Algonquin Park, an X carved into her chest. Tom Munro, Abby's father, a student of Fitzpatrick's, carved a similar X on his daughter's chest. Fitzpatrick knew Susan Gomery's husband and Abby's father. I'm trying to put some pieces together here."

"We'll have a statement in a few days."

"Great. But I'm going to keep coming. You might all have to talk sooner than that."

"I'll take that under advisement."

I HUNG AROUND MY OFFICE for a couple of hours, and called Everly twice in that time. Nothing. I mindlessly scribbled drawings of hockey sticks, pucks, goalies on my desk blotter. Drank a Coke from the vending machine down the hall. There was no Pepsi available, and I hadn't touched Fresca since the cyclamates scare. Back in the office, I paid some overdue bills: rent; Ontario hydro; and a subscription to *MacLean's*—important to have decent reading material lying around for my clients.

And then there was a gentle knock, very gentle, as if she were embarrassed to be calling on me.

Mrs. Whitelaw.

The sun caught her face as she walked in, lighting the corners of her eyes.

She lowered her head from the light, and snapped her purse closed. Had she just applied some face powder or lipstick? She apologized for bothering me and wondered if I had a minute.

"Of course I do." I directed her to one of the three chairs in my office.

"Busy?"

"Not if you call the art I dashed off on my blotter, scribblings. Can I get you a Coke—there's a vending machine, end of the hall—tea, you brought tea?"

Of course she did. Rue Britannia.

I turned on my hot plate and boiled water in a soup pan I kept around. I'm a Campbell's tomato soup guy.

She placed a tea bag in front of her and wiped at the edges of her mouth. Last time I saw her she wore pince-nez glasses. Today it was harlequins. It was a much better look.

"Thanks."

I guess I said that out loud. Bad habit. "Too many concussions."

"No, I appreciate the compliment." She smiled demurely.

I wanted to tell her she was a good-looking lady, even if what she wore resembled something pulled off the rack from Alice Kramden's closet on *The Honeymooners*.

"You heard I was at the party last night, at Kittle's—"

"Yeah. What brought you out of hiding?"

"Vanity, dare I say, vanity." She smiled deftly and laughed at herself. "I'm fifty-two years old and I still seek validation."

I nodded. I'm like a kid that way too. I love it when my daughter calls me a superhero.

"Mr. Kittle was going to announce to the group that I was set to write the new books, books seven and eight, in the Serchuk series—He called me in Guelph," she said, as an afterthought. "Insisted I show up at his little shindig, as he called it."

He's a goddamn publicist too, I said. "So he's good with the showboat words. Shindig." I shook my head. "How did he know you were in Guelph?"

"Tell me about it." A bemused crinkle spread through her lips. "But, he knows."

"Uh-huh."

She reached into her purse and pulled out a thin tea biscuit and nibbled. "Do you mind?"

"No, no."

"You want one?"

"Just had some French fries with gravy and a grilled-cheese sandwich. It's now sitting in my gut like the wreck of the *Titanic*. When I played hockey, I could eat whatever. Now look at me—" I patted my gut. "I mean who wants to go through life counting calories?"

"Not me," she agreed. "We're a diet-obsessed culture."

"We sure are."

"I don't mind a man with a belly if it makes him gentler, kinder."

I wasn't sure how to take that.

The water boiled and I poured some into a clean Dixie Cup that I doubled to protect her hands from the heat. "Sorry, the only mug I have I'm drinking from."

She dropped in the tea bag. "The party was upsetting," she said. "Very—"

"Yeah, I heard. A bunch of liberals cheering on the Soviets."

"I'm a liberal." She seemed a little offended by my remark.

"So am I. Don't let my buzzcut fool ya."

She stirred her drink with a little baby spoon. I wondered what else she had in her purse. It looked like it could carry a small typewriter. "They just like the Soviet style of playing—no, that's not completely true," she corrected herself. "There's a streak in them that really dislikes hockey players in general because they're so privileged and entitled in our culture."

"Yeah, I get that." When I played I never had to stand in line at the bank. I got free Pepsi at bars, and when I bought furniture or appliances the sales rep often skipped the sales tax.

"It was when the announcement happened—"

"About you ghosting the new books?"

"Yes—I expected people to be happy for me. Maybe that's silly, naive."

"You got a story in *Redbook, Chatelaine,* you know your shit."

"Thank you." She looked down at her lap, her purse, the tea slightly trembling from the noises rising up from Yonge Street. She had just sent off the revisions to a different short story to The New Yorker. "Yes. But if the looks in that room could kill—"

"Who all was in the room?"

"A couple of new people you haven't met yet. Todd Owens and Geno Seven."

"Geno Seven—he runs the bar on Charles Street. Tomboys and Dicks."

"I guess he's a writer too." She slowly sipped tea, and then dunked her biscuit, the gray turning to a dark mud. She nibbled.

"I got sugar cubes if you want—"

"No, I like it like this. Do you have lemon?"

"No."

Something about the timing of my response cracked her up. "You're a very charming young man."

"I'm not that young."

"I'm fifty-two, remember."

"Any more problems with people following you? The guy in the red wig and walrus-sized mustache?"

"And blue cashmere? No."

I told her about Sal looking into sales receipts at Eatons and discovering that Stewart Kittle had bought four such sweaters, medium-size. "Did the fella look like Kittle?"

"He looked like a guy in a Beatles wig and mustache a cowboy at a rodeo would wear."

"How would you describe the fella's walk?"

"Walk?" She tapped at her lower lip. "Side-to-side. Kind of full of himself."

"Could it be Kittle in disguise?"

"He—he—does walk like that."

"Uh-huh."

She said nothing, lips pinched.

"Do you know Tom Munro?"

"No."

"I think he may have killed Susan Gomery. The police are looking to bring him in for questioning."

"Susan never mentioned him either."

"Never?"

"Never."

"What about Fitzpatrick? What did she think about him?"

She didn't like him, Mrs. Whitelaw said. Susan went to him for help, before all this started, this whole who-wrote-the-first-novel thing. "Susan reminded Fitzpatrick that her husband, well ex-husband, wrote a composition in the early 1940s that was pretty much the entire plot of the first Serchuk novel, distilled into five pages for a theme on teamwork."

"Where is this theme?"

"It was thirty or more years ago." She shrugged.

"Fitzpatrick graded this early draft?"

"Yes. But, he claimed to not remember a thing about it—the character's name was Serchuk, there were gamblers and the teenager was a defenseman, a boy on the Leafs blueline."

Everything in the room brightened. "Bullshit, not remember—sorry, Mrs. Whitelaw—Fitzy remembered and he went running to Greenway Publishing, threatened to tell what he remembered, and the press bought him off to the tune of enough money to buy a small mansion in Peterborough and a Mercedes to drive to and from it from Toronto."

"You think?"

"I think."

"And Kittle—you think he's masquerading as the blue cashmere killer?"

"Yes. To create a narrative—"

"He's no killer," she said.

"I'm not so sure. I'm still figuring him as a possibility for the first Gomery kill."

Noises from Yonge Street—people chatting, cars idling—rose louder from down below. The sun burned orange.

"There's something else—I don't know if I'm just being an overly sensitive writer—"

"Is there such a thing?"

She laughed and finished her biscuit. Here's the thing, she said, when Mr. Kittle made that announcement about me being the ghost-writer-to-be, the dirtiest look I got was from Mrs. Hampton—

I rubbed away a fleck of fries that was still stuck to my chin from lunch.

"That's troubling."

"I know."

"What did Professor Hampton think?"

He was glad for me, she said. "He toasted me in front of the whole group. Raised his glass of wine and said I was a fine, fine writer, a real up-and-comer. If you can imagine at fifty-two, being an up-and-comer, he said the series was in good hands."

"But Mrs. Hampton?"

"Daggers—"

I finished my coffee.

"And that's not all. There's a rumor going around and I don't like to gossip but, the rumor is the child that Susan was carrying wasn't Stewart Kittle's."

"Oh, yeah. Whose was it, Fitzpatrick's?"

"No, Hilary 'Chip' Hampton."

AFTER MRS. WHITELAW LEFT. I called Everly again, wanting to help in some way, any way, but he wasn't in, his wife said he'd been gone for over twenty-four hours. Annoyance hummed under her words like telephone lines buzzing during a snowstorm. His last words to me were, she said, "I'm off in search of my youth."

She had no idea what that meant. "He could be a real cryptic son of a bitch, you know that," she muttered.

Stana called twenty minutes later. "Get your ass, home." Her voice was full of breathy grace notes. "Something came in the mail today that's a major game-changer. Major. If Kittle and Hampton don't talk to us now, they're fucked."

"What is it?"

"Evidence that J. Douglas wrote *Blueline*."

"I'm on my way."

WE SAT AT THE DINING ROOM TABLE, the Singer sewing machine pushed to a far edge.

Connie was with Stana's mother for the evening. "I had a crazy idea about date night, but when I returned from Scarborough I found *this* in our mailbox."

I reached for her wrist, squeezed. "*This* is amazing."

It was a five-page theme, written Wednesday, October 14, 1942, on wide-ruled paper. The ink had faded a little, bleeding and blotting here and there, but it appeared authentic. The name in the right hand corner, Dougie Gomery.

I read it four times.

It was like a folk song, like taking the idea for a novel, and distilling it into a three-minute recording.

"It's a fairly accurate plot outline of what *A Boy on the Leafs Blueline* became," Stana said.

I hadn't read the first book in the Serchuk series, but from what Stana had told me about it, this was it in miniature. A young kid of Ukrainian descent playing Junior A, gets a callup from the Leafs, and becomes a regular member of their blueline. Throw in some gamblers, a fella in a blue cashmere sweater, an injured goalie, and the kid scoring a big goal in the final game of the season to lift the Leafs into the playoffs, and you have the novel. Oh, and the girlfriend's name: Kitsey. And like classic representations of Lois Lane in the old comic books Kitsey's always in constant trouble and in need of rescue.

"And the themes," Stana added. "Perseverance, sacrifice, dedication. It's all there."

"We'll have to have the boys in Sal's lab check the fibers in the paper—but I think this was written, no doubt about it, in 1942. Did Susan Gomery ship this to us before she was murdered?"

Stana's lips pressed against one another. "No way—no stamps." She turned the envelope over, pointed. "See. This was hand-delivered to our mailbox."

I worried my upper lip. Susan Gomery was dead. She accused Fitzpatrick of knowing about this composition—possibly even taking a buyout from Greenway Publishing to keep quiet. There's no way he would have handed it over to us. If he had the manuscript it would be ashes in the bottom of a trash can.

I paced. Someone else in the workshop? Mrs. Whitelaw, Susan's good friend?

I rushed to the telephone to call her apartment. The light of our Phone Mate 400 was blinking. It was a new device, reel-to-reel tape, that a reporter like Stana needed for her job. "Did you see this?" I pointed to the "messages" light.

She had been mesmerized by the five-page theme and hadn't bothered to check.

I switched to "rewind" and then "playback calls." I cranked the volume.

"Fuller, this is Everly. Did you get the MacGuffin? Dougie gave me a key six months ago, when he was fearing for his life. The key was to a safe deposit box at the Royal Bank on Bloor. Anyway, it doesn't matter where the bank is. Christ. I hate talking to machines. Dougie told me when he gave me that key that in the event of his death I was to go to this box and get this thing, and that I would know what to do with it. Kittle and Hampton refuse to budge, but you know how to handle this. I would try myself, but I'm running out of time and options—I—you were right. Fitzpatrick knows and he has put me in a rough spot. I'm finished as a teacher. Well, I'm now turning the tables on him—he knew all along of this manuscript and he's been bought off."

C. Thomas Everly, I mumbled in the direction of Stana. "He and Gomery were lovers back in the 1950s."

"I know. I heard about it from Miriam. Poor C.T. Normal before shock therapy cured and made him straight—talk about sick medical practices." Stana had just written an exposé on compulsory sterilization of the "feeble-minded" in Toronto during the 1950s and 60s. She was also currently looking into the preponderance of targeting indigenous individuals.

"What now?"

"Hampton and Kittle. I'm sure they're still camped out together. Let's wreck their party," she said.

"What about date night?" I smiled, my lopsided grin.

"Are you kidding me? This *is* date night." She kissed my cheek. "Let me change into jeans and grab a sweater. This is so exciting." She ran up the short set of stairs of our split-level bungalow to our bedroom.

I holstered my snub-nosed.

Five minutes later on our way out the door, the phone rang. It was Sal. He had gone to Munro's apartment to interrogate him about the X's and Susan's murder. But now Tom Munro was dead, and Abby was missing.

She probably ran out, I said, given what was going on with C. Thomas.

"She might have been kidnapped. You haven't seen the carnage yet."

I kissed Stana on the nose and promised I'd bring back Chinese from Sai Woo's.

She promised to have John Coltane's *A Love Supreme*, with its scale-based harmonies, playing for me upon my return.

—

YOU CAN FEEL MURDER. The air sometimes just doesn't move.

Even with all that police activity: lab boys photographing the body, detectives searching around for clues, bagging evidence, there was a stillness to it all. The air was heavy.

A small clock, ticking atop the back edge of the stove read 10:47. Easy Listening music, CFRB, 1010 A.M, floated unevenly through the apartment. It must have been the last sounds Tom heard before checking out. What a way to go. Christ.

And the apartment was a wreck. The refrigerator door was open; cabinets tossed; dishes shattered across the floor, and living-room lamps crushed and crumpled on their sides. Several squares from the dropped ceiling were missing, broken up on the floor, like so many bits of paper-like ash. That must have been where the pins were stashed, and found.

Someone now had them, all seventeen, I imagine.

Did Abby take the pins? Or was she taken? Did she kill her father or witness his murder?

"Talking to yourself, Superstar?"

"Sorry."

Sal pushed back his gray fedora and rubbed at the picket fencing to his Hemingway beard. "Dead about an hour. We got a tip."

I nodded. "Male or female?"

"A fella—" Sal half-circled the corpse. "Can someone kill the radio?"

Someone did.

I didn't figure Abby for the femme-fatale type, and once I saw the body I knew it wasn't a female kill. Munro was slumped in a hardback chair, his head bent forward like a marionette that had lost its strings.

The first time I met Tom Munro he was kicking my face in. I barely got a glimpse. Beady eyes. That's all I had time to process.

His white skin was parchment thin, almost see-through. And he looked a bit like his daughter, the parenthetical lines around his mouth, the scythe-shaped birthmark on the left side of his face, a green eye.

Eye. The other one was missing as was half the fella's face, a pulp of fresh grapefruit, ground down to bits of blood, bone, and brains marking a Jackson Pollock flourish across the wall.

This poor bastard was tortured before they killed him, Sal said. He lifted up a stump of the corpse's left hand. "Three of his fingers were cut off. Garden shears. He was still alive when they did it—At least that's what the lab boys say."

"Tortured for coke," I said, and then I pointed at the ceiling and the fallout of tile ash on the floor. "And he gave it up."

"You think the daughter was kidnapped?"

"Maybe."

"You think this was Everly's handiwork? I got an APB out on him."

"No."

"Maceo?"

"He wants the pins, but no—"

The violence matches the violence of the shoeshine kill, Sal said. "Could be the True Suns or Maceo."

If he wanted to think that, that was okay with me, but I knew the real answer and I wasn't going to say a word. Not out loud.

Call it professional courtesy, call it some kind of, for lack of a better word, *pledge of friendship*.

FROM A DRUGSTORE across the street I called Babe Migano at his Etobicoke home.

He was awake.

I wasn't surprised. "You washed Munro's blood from your hands yet?"

"Don't push your luck, shamus. I like you, but not that much."

"You got the pins, didn't you?"

"Did I?"

"The drop ceiling was crushed to ash. There were missing fingers on Munro's left hand. Evidence of torture, a Red Dragons calling card—"

"The man had a chance to negotiate. I gave him every opportunity to negotiate—I'm an easy-going fella."

"You're a regular negotiator, all right. No one ever said you weren't fair."

"Fuller, don't get cute. I hate cute." Migano's voice purred. "Don't push me. In the end I got bored with Munro's negotiations, and his repeated choices of playing it cute." I could sense him shaking his head, as the cubes in his glass of scotch knocked about. "I offered the man a fair price."

"And now that man's dead."

"Now he's dead. Thus runs the world of finance—the guy abused his daughter. Cut her. She's lucky to have him out of her life."

"That's one way to look at it—"

"Look, Gary Cooper, cut the laconic witticisms. What is it you want?" He paused, ice cubes clacking more heavily. "Do I have the pins? I wouldn't know—Is Maceo soon to be out of business? That I do know. Yes."

"I can put him out of business for good."

"You can?" The glass was placed aside. "How?"

"Do me a favor, through your grapevine to gangland, your underworld connections—"

"Now you're being nasty."

"Okay, okay, your pipeline to businessmen who ply their certain *trades*, make it known that I have the pins. I do have one, but let's pretend that I have ten or eleven of them."

"That'll make you a target."

"That's the idea."

"I'll have the Red Dragons surveilling your place on Houston Crescent. Backup. Be careful."

"I will."

"I'll start placing the calls."

I NEVER THOUGHT THE WORD would get out *that* quick.

After stopping for Chinese, it was thirty minutes by the time I got home. Near midnight. I was about to switch on the hall light when I noticed the edges of our white shag rug and a trickle of lamp light bleeding across the floor.

Then I noticed the two fellas in our living room.

Maceo and Saba.

One sat in the big chair across from the TV; the other on the compact couch.

There was a crescent-shaped cut in the sliding glass door, near the handle and locking mechanism.

Stana stood, wearing nothing but panties and my pajama top. Date night.

She couldn't move from their sight lines.

Both fellas had .45's atop their thighs.

Both wore Ray-Bans.

"Welcome home, ese," Maceo's voice was like the frosting on a donut, creamy, and fresh, but lacking in any real substance. First he's a Jew, and now he's Hispanic. This cat had no idea who he was.

I placed the Chinese food cartons on the coffee table.

"Can I sit down now?" Stana said.

Maceo nodded at her with his head, and she sat in the chair nearest the TV. She crossed her legs and tugged at the ends of her pajama top.

"I didn't know you were married to such a babe." Saba's sunglasses slid down his nose slightly. "She's a real woman. Unlike no-tits Munro. She's built like a boy. No wonder Orly dug her. Fruit."

"No gutter talk." Maceo raised a hand the size of a pork loin. "And let's not speak ill of the dead. Respect."

Saba shrugged reluctantly and gave me a newscaster smile, empty and waiting on the next camera cue. "After all that stuff in the paper about you and your dad diddling you I never thought such a woman would want *you*." Saba shook his head. "Shows how you can't make assumptions." He laughed.

My lips pinched together and my jaw tightened. *Assumptions*. Maceo and Saba with guns drawn were way way too smug, too self-assured. They had the drop, sure, but they should have had me searched, removed my .38. *Never underestimate your opponent.*

Assholes.

"I bet you're lousy in the sack." Saba smiled over at Stana. "You want a real man, sister, call me."

Stana's eyes told him he was already dead. He just hadn't got the memo yet.

"Speaking of assumptions, I thought you were honest." Maceo's voice was now fabric softener. He reached down by his right foot and plunked two halves of a bowling pin on the low-riding coffee table between us. "Look what I found? Right by your television. Just resting by the floor. Weren't you hired to find my stash?"

"You said $20,000, cash."

"A euphemism. Cash/stash. I was talking in riddles, codes." He shrugged and lifted the gun from his thigh. "Where are the others? I heard through the grapevine, you got nine or ten."

"You heard half-right." I shrugged. "Orly held back three. One I found in his back room at Tomboys and Dicks. There were actually two bowling pins in his room. One was just a bowling pin. The other two *fully loaded pins* are hidden out at Algonquin."

"Hidden where?"

"I don't know. Oh, yeah, you can't ask Orly because you killed him."

"We did," Saba said. "The guy wouldn't talk. We burned him with cigarettes. Chunky fucked him in the ass. Nothing. The fruit was tough."

"And you're a boy playing at being a man," Stana said.

"Oh. Did you hear that, patron?"

Now one of Maceo's fuckers was French. Patron. Give me a break. None of them knew who they were—

"Did you hear that? Big talk coming from the little woman."

She's not little, I said. She can kick your ass. "How are you doing, Sweetie?" I smiled at Stana. Her eyes were full of dancing freckles, directing me to the standing lamp on my left. It leaned right, loosely anchored to its base.

"She's a curvy woman, that's for sure—" Saba gave Stana the once over twice.

"Enough talk. We want the pins, ese," Maceo said.

"What I've got is the notebooks. The ones with all the personal confessions. I've also got the gym bag with the blue cashmere sweater, the one in Chunky's Ford Galaxie, the one that ties you into terrorizing members of the workshop."

"That wasn't us, that's just a sweater." He pushed his sunglasses back against his eyebrows.

"I've also got film, lots of film, showing you two and the rest of the True Suns loading boxes upon boxes into trucks and assorted road vehicles, boxes full of coke."

"Those are just boxes, boxes on film," he said. "Nothing more."

"I also have a partner. Babe Migano. He's got my back. Dig?"

Maceo's smile was suddenly full of knots.

"Not so sure of yourself now, are you? Where's Abby?"

Maceo didn't know. "She was gone when we got there. So were the pins. Tom Munro was greased when we got there, ese. Nothing but a stain on the floor."

"On the wall, actually."

"Yes, yes. A stain on the wall." He sighed with sad resignation. "Orly betrayed me. That's why he had to get got. My nephew. That wasn't easy—"

"I didn't spill any tears," Saba said, the gun clamped to his hand. He leered over at Stana and the puffy part in the top of her pajama top. It was buttoned but some skin showed because of her curves.

Maceo, an ankle atop his knee, flashed his gun with forced menace. "Seems Orly had an accomplice. Our good friend, C. Thomas Everly. How do you figure that cat, bubbeleh? He calls me, tells me he's ratting me out to the police. He wanted to give me a heads up so I could make a getaway. Real gent, that fegele. Class. You know? Some people got it. Anyway, I need those pins before the police close in and the noose tightens." The pretend menace faded. "You got connections with Migano? Like what?"

"I ain't got the pins, ese."

"Huh?"

"Babe Migano does. And you're out of business, thief—"

Maceo shifted in his chair. "What, so your friends with Migano? So what. That's some kind of get-out-of-jail-free card? That's going to save you, now?" He leaned forward and snapped his fingers. He was like an ornery kid readying to blow out some birthday candles. "Friend." He laughed. "I'll negotiate with him directly. Cut out the middle man." The knots in his smile tightened. "Saba. Kill them, kill them both—"

Saba was still smitten with the curves of Stana's chest, the skin showing through the inadvertent part in the pajama top, and his distracted gaze was enough.

I knocked over the floor lamp with my left hand, shattering the bulb. Stana cleared, diving behind a third chair.

I popped into a three-point stance.

These fellas had on Ray-Bans, ese, bubbeleh, patron—

For them, the room was briefly the black of a cold, cold lake, but I knew the room, this was my pad, and my .38 was barking in the direction of the armchair and couch.

An anguished scream from Saba followed by Maceo's muffled grunts as he crumpled to the shag floor and then the smell of shit mixed with death's cooling stillness.

My body was no longer a part of me. I was nothing but cold trembles, drifting, drifting.

Wind gently tapped at the glass of the sliding porch door with the cutaway crescent moon.

Stana huddled by me and we waited, wind tap-tapping.

Her breath warmed my face, bringing me back from dark, cool drifts.

Eventually Stana stumbled up against a small coffee table by the overturned third chair. She reached for a Parliament and Zippo. The flame was low.

We saw enough.

Half of Saba's face was now resting on his chest, the lenses of his Ray-Bans stippled to his eyes, like peppered coffee grounds.

Maceo curled on the floor, fetal hands gripping tips of pointy boots. Two holes bled through his back. One of the heels of his boots had broken free.

Game Four

Sunday, September 8, 1972

Something C. Thomas said had grabbed a hold of me. "In search of my youth." A cornball line from a not so cornball film, *Citizen Kane*.

In a way C. Thomas was like Charles Foster Kane, a man in a loveless marriage, looking for something he had lost. He hadn't had sex with a woman until he was thirty, and maybe that reality had him longing to rewrite, relive an obscured past. In his fantasies he was fifteen, sixteen again, seeking intimacy with 14-16 year old girls. He projected himself into spaces that he had never lived in, a failed past that he wants to rewrite. That's the youth he seeks, a love that was never lost because it was never there.

Fantasy is one thing, but acting on those fantasies, writing treacly love poems and sending inappropriate photographs and countdown-to-sex notes, well, that makes for a sick fucko.

Anyway, I had convinced myself and Stana that the dark wishes in Everly's mind had crossed over into reality and that he was headed to Algonquin, to be forever sixteen.

He was also headed there to find the cocaine, turn it into money and drive north and start over.

He had taken Abby on his trek.

Stana hugged the arm I wasn't driving with and rubbed my shoulder. "Pretty fast thinking back there—with the lamp."

"They were victims of fashion—them and their god damn Ray-Bans." I shook my head. "Maybe having you dive clear was a bad idea. With you preggers and all. I'm really sorry about that."

"You warned me. I was ready, bracing."

"Warned you, how?"

"A signal."

"What signal?"

"With your eyes. You glanced at me, the lamp, me. Very quickly. I got it, read the moment."

"I don't recall doing that." I had been glancing at the open buttons on her pajama top.

"I recall it—a real fast look—We've been married now for six years. We got all kinds of shorthand." She smiled pleasantly.

I laughed and then it turned kind of sludgy. I had just killed a kid, a minor. It doesn't matter what I thought of him or what he'd done. Yeah, he was a punk ass, but he was just a kid. Heavy rocks, breaking apart, drifted about in my stomach.

TWO HOURS OUT FROM THE CITY, we called the police, told them what had happened, left the door open for them, and we'd answer all questions upon our return in a few hours. Return from where? Sorry, can't hear you—

THE MESS HALL, even in the inky black night was still a glowing human femur.

Two cars were parked all akimbo on the cracked concrete out front:. an orange Datsun 240Z (C. Thomas must have taken his wife's wheels) and a Mercedes (Fitzpatrick was here too).

Fitzy's car was warm. That meant he had got here later and got the drop on the biology teacher.

I unholstered my gun and Stana dug the back-up .45 out from the glovebox.

We moved slowly between the shadows of birch trees.

Police tape covered the doors in an X pattern and "This Property Is Condemned" signs were posted on several windows.

We entered quietly.

It didn't take long to hear the clawing cries, half-human, half-animal, rising up through the floor.

We rushed to the kitchen and down the steps that led to the boiler room, the ground beneath us was uneven, causing our footing to slide and slip. Dust and dirt fell from the ceiling like thin fishing lines.

The claw of cries grew more urgent.

I wanted to shout, tell Abby we were here, but we needed to be covert. What was the setup? Where was Fitzy? Everly? We found the open storm cellar door and descended thirteen steps. Stana cocked the hammer on the .45. It clicked gently.

Bits of dust and dirt contrails arced around us. Immediately the air, the same air I smelled a few days ago, assailed us. Nothing had changed. Heavy excrement, piss, and blood filled the air. Abby was naked, hands roped around a meat hook screwed into a wood beam.

Abby's hair was matted, her lower lip cracked, and the scar, X'd between her tiny breasts was reopened, blood glazed around her navel. She sobbed with thankfulness upon seeing us.

Stana untied Abby's hands.

I worried where Fitzy might be, my gun raking the area.

I didn't need to wonder about Everly—

He was naked, hanging from another hook, ten feet away. The poor bastard had been gutted, a flap of skin peeled back like a tent flap, his intestines spilling onto the dusky dirt.

Gunk gathered at the edges of his mouth and nostrils.

Stana and Abby hugged. The girl's fingers were dried with caked blood, nails broken off. She pointed a few feet behind her, at a spot we couldn't quite see, but she could, because she had been walled up down here for several hours. "I think Orly's fingernails are in the limestone over there. The foundation. He tried to dig his way out."

I coughed, yeah, I said. "This is where they tortured and

killed him. Saba, Chunky, the True Suns. They admitted to the killing. Under Maceo's orders. They killed him." She deserved to know the truth.

"I thought so." She cried on Stana's shoulder.

And then I told her what had happened at our home, Saba's and Maceo's long goodbyes.

"Look, we gotta get out of here. Fitzy might be hovering above, ready to drop the storm cellar door on us, and lock us in."

Stana shuddered. "Meat hooks. And fingernails in the wall. Something right out of—"

"Poe?"

"Auschwitz and Zyklon B, gas chambers. People trying desperately to get out before suffocating," Stana said.

After marrying me, my wife has converted to Judaism and at times, I swear, is more of a Jew than I'll ever be.

I zipped Abby up in my red windbreaker. It didn't cover everything. So I removed my shirt. She tied it around her hips like a beach towel. Thankfully for all present, given my 215 pounds, I happened to also be wearing a T-shirt.

We slowly climbed back to the boiler room.

Abby's eyes narrowed and she hissed, loud and feral.

And then we all saw what she saw.

I wanted to hiss too.

Frank Fitzpatrick was in front of the boiler, his jacket puffed out at the shoulders. By his feet, spiked into the dirt, a burning Tiki torch. He wore gray jodhpurs and his hands cradled a 12-gauge, the tip waving us down like a large road flare. "One of my favorite writers. Poe. Glad to hear he still has currency, still being read today. Real sense of the macabre. Like a young man with a bright future dying because he was fellated while driving."

He backed against the boiler. "Drop the heaters," he said. It was like he was playing at being tough, his lines borrowed from B-movies, and his grimace: low-rent Lawrence Tierney.

We did as he said. "Such a waste," I acknowledged.

His son. The lacrosse star.

"Perverse is what it was. Perverse. The car rolled and rolled. Caught fire. Trapped, my son died in a wall of flames. And now all three of you will be buried, walled up, here." He laughed, and then said something about the wickedness of women, his son's death, and the wickedness of women again. Suddenly he was babbling in tongues, the words a choogle of noise, no breaths, no beats, just venom about women. Evil, evil women. Women had to be punished. Like those two girls he killed—and Abby for sleeping with a teacher—and—

"Susan Gomery?"

"Yes."

"What she ever do to you?"

He cut a tight half-circle to my left. Dirt fell in heavier, blurred lines. "I killed the girls, I killed Gomery. And now you all. Those five pages—yeah, yeah, Everly confessed that he gave you the Gomery original, 1942, but it will never be seen by the public." He stretched out his arms, waving the shotgun. "Consider all this my love letter to urban renewal." He laughed again, leveling the shotgun at me. The city needed some cleaning, and this was his rain of judgment. "I knew of the drugs," he said, "because I knew of the ring-a-ding-ding between Everly and Abby and Tom Munro's blackmailing of the teacher. So I wanted in on that action too. Money does what money does."

Beaded dust continued falling, more quickly now. "Everly and his fantasies. They destroyed him. Pedophilic desires. A real sick bastard."

"And what does that make you?" Stana's eyes narrowed.

"Everly told his story to the police, confessed to it all over the telephone, including my involvement in blackmail. He spilled his guts to them, and I made the figurative literal." His macabre sense of humor was just too much for him. With smug satisfaction, he raised his trowel-shaped face and defiantly howled into the beams above.

I dove for the ground, swept up a handful of dirt and tossed heavy, brown hailstones of dust into his eyes. "Get down!"

Stana and Abby dropped and Fitzy staggered, the shotgun exploding a round into the ceiling, dotting the dirt above with pock marks of powder, and then he clawed at his eyes.

I found my .38 and parked one in Fitzy's head and he dropped to his knees, blood spurting, words burbling from his mouth. My bullet was messing with his synapses. He didn't have long. I grabbed the 12-gauge, Stana the .45, and we ran for the opening, Fitzy mewling behind us.

The shotgun blast forced bricks of dirt and bits of beams to fall in chunks. The whole room wobbled and thudded.

Fitzy was still gurgling and burbling, choking on blood, scratching the ground, struggling to stand.

He never made it.

The basement collapsed behind us, as we ran and ran and ran. Limestone walls cracked at their joists. His final burbles were lost in dust, dirt, and blubbering earth.

Outside, rain fell.

Inside, walls were still rumbling, as half of the human femur of a mess hall caved.

STANA BROUGHT ASHKENAZI–STYLE stuffed cabbage rolls to her mother's. She also made a chicken liver spread for matzo crackers. Like I said, she had become more of a Jew than me.

Connie was glad to see us, jumping up and down, asking Stana to read her a story, and leading her to the living room. Ma asked me if I wanted a snack, something to nosh on before dinner.

Nosh. I smiled at her. Everyone was getting into the Yiddish-dictionary act.

She squeezed my wrist. Her gray hair parachuted her face, setting off her blue eyes, eyes that took you all in. "I'm so pleased you're going to be a father—again. You're a good man. My daughter, she glows. I never thought I'd see that again."

I nodded my appreciation and sat at the circular black table in the kitchen. I nibbled on celery that was crammed in a small Mason jar, half-filled with water. "You got any peanut butter?"

She handed me some and I spread it along the celery stick's trench.

"And you're a great dad. You listen to Connie, really listen. I wish my husband was still alive to experience this—you two as parents—" Kindness spread to the corners of her eyes.

He got to be with Connie for the first two, two-and-a-half years of her life.

"You want a boy this time?"

"I'm fine, either way."

"Doesn't every dad want a boy?" Her smile wobbled a little. "I know my husband did."

"I'm good with girls."

She kissed the top of my head. "I knew I loved you."

The bread was ready in the oven. She took it out with pillows for gloves and asked me to cut it into thick slices to soak up the stew's tomato-based sauce. It was on the stovetop, filling the house with the pleasant smells of potatoes, beef, okra, and barley.

Ma placed Stana's cabbage rolls in the oven to stay warm and checked on the stew, stirring it, making sure none of it was sticking to the bottom of the pot. She turned the heat to simmer. "I'm so glad you're okay—and the girl, Abby—it was all over the news—"

The police, in Algonquin and later back in Toronto, gave us a hard time for going rogue, handling things ourselves. But television stations and press reporters called us heroes for saving a young woman from the sad fates of two of her classmates. One television anchor went a little off the rails, ranting on and on about whether or not we can really trust teachers. Look at the facts: "One of the teachers at Park District School had a yen for underage students and may have been involved inappropriately with a fifteen year old; and another was a blackmailer, a killer, and a huge follower of the writings of Edgar Allan Poe. Maybe we need to look into the process of those folks that matriculate to be teachers and ask ourselves, Education or Indoctrination? Maybe we ought not to be teaching Poe in our schools."

"All that press, good for business, I guess—the PI business."

She nodded and sprinkled pepper into the stew. "Is Abby going to be okay?"

Trauma sticks. It never goes away. "I hope, someday. She's a ward of the Children's Aid right now. They're going to take her out of that school district. A new start—"

"Does she want a new start?" Ma gently stirred the stew and then shut off the stovetop.

"I don't know."

"It's funny how adults always think they know what's best for kids."

"Always—" My body ached from all I'd been through in the past few days. "Yeah." I shrugged. "Anyway, Professor Hampton's going down, too." We got a manuscript, I said, an early early draft, five-pages long, that shows he stole the idea and overall plot of his first novel from Douglas Gomery.

"Stana really liked him."

I shrugged again. "The guy's a thief."

She patted my shoulder. "Don't be too harsh. We're all lost souls, in some way."

AFTER DINNER WE WATCHED the game in the living room on Ma's 24-inch color, solid-state television. It was one of the big perks about visiting her in Scarborough.

"Guess what, Connie?"

"What, Daddy?" She was sitting crosslegged on the floor, rocking a little, excited for the game to start. She was playing with the ends of her toes in her Pippi Longstocking socks.

"You get to see the whole game tonight." I laughed.

Excited, she scooched across the hardwood floor towards me.

"It won't be over until 10:30, 10:45," Stana said. "And she has school tomorrow—"

"It'll be okay, just for tonight—one night—it's Team Canada—"

Stana said all right and the game started.

I WASN'T TOO HAPPY. Guy Lapointe and Serge Savard weren't in the lineup. Next to Brad Park and Bergy they were our best defense pair. I had been busy working two cases, and hadn't the time to read all the hockey scuttlebutt. Were they injured, needing rest, or was this a coaching decision?

Moreover, the crowd was in a sulky mood. Later during the broadcast McClelland Stuart, voice of the Leafs and hockey Canada, praised the Soviet's team play, and how they passed the puck and waited for good, meaningful shots on goal. Unlike the Canadians, who he criticized for lacking team play and dumping and chasing the puck to very limited success. "That just isn't working in this series—The difference between the two teams' style of play is very apparent." The subtext: their style of play was better, more productive, and more exciting and enchanting than our style. What McClelland put to words was the overall feeling the crowd had at puck drop: "I like this new thing I'm seeing. It's exciting. *I want that.*"

It also didn't help with the crowd's sulkiness that in the first six or so minutes Bill Goldsworthy, over-eager to impress his coaches with his tenacity and everyman, working-class ethos, took two very stupid penalties, one for elbowing that could have easily been a boarding call. The Soviets scored on both power-plays, tip-ins by Boris Mikhailov on shots from the point. 2-0 Soviets.

Our aggressive style of heavy hockey, Canadian grit, was

pissing people off.

Usually when you're the home team and take a penalty the fans boo the call, mad at the refs for giving the opponents the opportunity to go on the man advantage. But in Vancouver, they booed Canada for taking the penalties in the manner that they did. Okay, maybe Goldsworthy shouldn't have punched Maltsev in the head after the Canadian forward was whistled for roughing, but the crowd rained down a torrent of boos on him and later even bagged on Rod Gilbert. Rod was one of the true gentlemen of the game. But the fans gave it to him for a non-call, following an after-the-whistle scrum in which he punched another Soviet player in the back of the head behind their own net.

We were the *villains*.

I could no longer sit on the couch. I was pacing. "Vancouver sucks. Listen to them, listen—"

"We're playing like a bunch of hooligans," Ma said. "I'm embarrassed for us, for Canada."

I said nothing and headed to the kitchen and opened a bag of Cheesies. I brought back the bag and a separate bowl for Connie.

I munched Cheesies, angrily.

CANADA SHOWED FLASHES of brilliance in the second period.

The Soviets were up 3-1 when we suddenly came to life, playing a feverish, free-wheeling game. Twice Yvan Counoyer, once on a brilliantly threaded pass by Rod Seiling, broke in all alone on Tretiak only to be stoned by their young netminder. Between these two breakaway chances, Phil Esposito, rushing down the left wing, nearly scored on another great one-on-one moment. Tretiak, however, didn't flinch, holding his ground. The crowd applauded Canada's hustle but also Tretiak's stellar play.

Moments later: "What's Mahovlich doing out there?" Stana yelled at the screen. "Sitting on Tretiak like that."

Mahovlich was draped over the back of a crouched Tretiak,

boxing him in, not letting him up.

"He came out to play the puck, that makes the goalie fair game," I said, feebly.

"He was holding him down—not letting him return to the crease—that's not hockey, that's Whipper Billy Watson shit."

"Frank's not a wrestler," Ma said. "He's trying."

"The whole team's trying," I said. "Frank's just frustrated. The whole team is. There's a lot of pressure on the boys."

"It is a little embarrassing," Ma said.

"I'm with Ma, this is embarrassing," Stana said.

Connie glanced up at me, waiting for me to say something, something to defend our favorite player—

AND THEN CAME THE MOMENT that put the game out of reach: with the faceoff deep in their end, Paul Henderson lost control of the puck, it bounced off a Soviet player's stick, off Whitey Stapleton's stick, and suddenly they had a two on one. They skated fast and loose, and with a pretty pass, put one in the back of our net. Dryden had no chance.

But Tretiak had stopped three breakaways. *Three.*

The crowd noticed the difference and wouldn't forgive our guy, Kenny, for being human.

Seconds later, a long lob of a shot from outside our blue line arced and dipped like a pop-up in baseball. Dryden caught the puck in his trapper and as he dropped it to his skates the crowd cheered with mockery. It was as if their jeers shouted, "Why can't you make the big saves, like their goalie? You're ruining our party. *You*—" Within the next couple of minutes Dryden made two more routine saves that were met with cheerful derision.

Christ.

Assholes.

Fucking fans.

I wanted to punch them all out. I really did.

Connie sensed my fury and decided to curl up against her

mother instead of me.

I went back to the kitchen and spread chicken liver all over a matzo cracker. I sat at the table, away from the television.

I ate a second cracker. Alone.

But I returned in time to see Don Awrey, who struggled in game one in Montreal, make a great defensive play. When a shot trickled through Dryden, Awrey reached behind and knocked the puck off our goal line, keeping the score close. It went relatively unnoticed because of the fog of despair filling the Pacific Coliseum.

MCCLELLAND STUART PILED-ON during the third.

He was obviously dismayed and disappointed over what was happening. We all had swallowed the myth of Canadian hockey, the greatest brand and style in the world. And yet here were these Russians beating us at our game and charming the fans in the process. Midway through the third, Petrov bear-hugged Phil Esposito to the ice and took a penalty. He raised his arms, apologetically shrugged, and appeared to be saying, what else could I do? This *is* a big man. The crowd loved it. And cheered. Cheered *him*.

And for the fans at home, McClelland's words reflected and encouraged their shifting allegiances, here's a list of his comments: "The Soviets have an edge in the definite margin of play—in every department"; "Cournoyer showing lots of speed but not too accurate on the net"; "the Soviet passing is making the Canada team a bit dizzy at times"; "the Soviets have a commanding lead but it's not just the score, it's the way they're doing it"; "Tretiak is giving the goal-keeping that you have to have to win a championship—"; "right from the drop of the hat there hasn't been any doubt as who is the better team—they seem to have complete control of the game."

Stuart's words belied his irritability and feeling of betrayal at Team Canada's apparent lack of effort.

Dennis Hull potted one in the last seconds "to make the score look more respectable than it really is—"

Thanks, McClelland.

On the final whistle the crowd jeered, applauding the end.

5–3 Soviets.

I hoped we never play another international game in Vancouver—fuck them.

Stana, her mother, and Connie said nothing.

I shook my head and went back to the kitchen, grabbed a Pepsi. Nobody else wanted anything.

When I returned, Phil Esposito dejectedly lumbered in a sort of half-glide toward broadcaster Johnny Esaw who was standing on the ice, microphone in hand. Head tilted left, black hair spritzed with sweat that also dripped down his face, Phil spoke from the heart, and what he had to say went something like this: "To the people of Canada, I say we tried. We did our best— We're really disheartened, disappointed, and disillusioned! We can't believe we're getting booed in our building— I am really, really disappointed—I can't believe it. Some of our guys are really down in the dumps—Let's face facts. They have a good team—We came because we love Canada. And I don't think it's fair that we should be booed!"

Wow. The rant, the apology, the imploring of all of us to get behind the team, resonated. I had chills.

Connie and Stana and Ma were quite still.

"I'm the one who should be ashamed," Ma said.

Monday

ESPO'S POST-GAME COMMENTS were a real punch in the mouth, a patriotic rallying cry.

The next day, the dailies were buzzing with comments over Esposito's speech and how we had, some of us, given up too quickly on the team. The North York Board of Education announced that when the series resumed in Moscow on September 22 for a slate of four games, three during the school week, classes will be marshaled to the gym or the library to watch the mid-afternoon contests. This was about nation building, Canadian identity.

Moreover, the Canadian government announced 3,000 tickets for sale, a travel package, sending Canadians overseas to cheer on our boys in all four games.

Milt Dunnell of *The Star* called just after the neighborhood girls had come by to walk Connie to school, and the daily was wanting to send Stana to Moscow to get her spin on the series, the woman's angle. She was known for her hard-hitting exposés and maybe she could do something that explores the fragility of our collective identity and investigates the mythos of hockey as "our game."

"What do you think?" She was wearing a powder-blue set of pajamas and showing just a little.

I was sitting at the breakfast table finishing some eggs and orange juice. "Yeah—do it."

"You want to come?"

"What about Connie?"

"Ma can take care of her for a week or so—they'd both love it." She pulled herself to my side. "It could be a second honeymoon."

"In Moscow?"

She laughed. "Well, we'd get to see some great hockey. And be part of history—I'll call Ma."

"You think it's okay to travel?"

"I'm only two-and-a-half-months along—yes, it's okay to travel." A squirrely smile crossed her lips. "You get so protective when I'm pregnant."

"Well, yeah."

She called Ma, and ten minutes later we were all set.

STANA'S PLAN FOR THE DAY was to write a column, a personal essay on her journey through the game last night, how she found herself frustrated and angry at the team, feeling they were letting us all down, and then somehow Phil's speech, spun everything, turned the arrows of judgment back on ourselves, made her ashamed for getting down on the boys, and made her realize Canada *is* hockey, and the players need our love. It was an empathy switch that had been shut off by the dazzling play of the Soviets and Phil had turned it back on. She too loved Canada and she loved the men who represent us. "The article is almost already written."

"Sounds like it."

"You wish you were a little younger and could be a part of this?"

"They never would have selected me, but yeah, to play against really good players like that, and to represent your country, I'd love it." To wear *that* flag on your chest—

She kissed me, and said she needed to shower.

I had some loose ends I wanted to tie together with Professor Hampton. The five-page theme, for one.

"Can't that wait until tomorrow?" She wanted to confront Hampton too, but she had to get this article out. Noon deadline.

"Sure—I guess."

"I hear Kittle has gone back to his office to work. No longer needing to run Greenway from Walmer Avenue."

"All the strings are tied, as far as he's concerned, but not as far as I am concerned."

"Tomorrow? Let me get this article done."

"Okay."

"Love you." She kissed my nose and headed upstairs.

Water hushed through the pipes.

I ambled over to the Hi-Fi, my back and neck stiff from our tousle with Frank Fitzpatrick just hours ago, and the pounding I took from Tom Munro hours before that, and put on some

Sonny Clark, Cool Struttin. It is one of my favorite hard-bop records.

I was restless.

I popped two Anacin.

We had solved the question of who killed Orly, and Susan Gomery. But what about J. Douglas? That was still a cold-case file, and Kittle, heading back to his office, was a gesture that oozed too much confidence, a sense of privilege: what was done was done and things have settled back to the norm—time to move on, pal—time to move on.

Not hardly—

There was a knock on the wall, coming from upstairs.

I headed to the bathroom.

The water pounded and Stana stuck her head out from behind the curtain that she had folded in front of her like an accordion. One eye was closed because of shampoo trickling down—freckles dotted her shoulder. "You want to join me?"

"Yeah—of course."

"Give me five minutes—I'll be done with my hair."

"Can you make it three?"

She laughed. "Put on Coltrane and turn it up—"

THE PHONE WAS RINGING insistently when we climbed out of the shower. I turned down the stereo, a towel covering my modesty, and picked up the receiver.

There were gasps on the other side of the line. "I've—been—poisoned—"

I recognized Mrs. Whitelaw's voice.

And then she gurgled and vomited, I think, and then, there was a thud and something shattering.

She lived in Don Mills. Just a mile or so away.

I called for an ambulance.

We arrived first.

WITH STANA'S SHELL OIL CARD I cracked open the door. The click was a fallen icicle.

All the lights were out except for a swatch of yellowy gold from an open refrigerator door. Hulking lines of lumpy shadows spread across the gray linoleum floor. Next to the lumpiness were the remains of a cup with a broken-off handle, and two halves of a cracked tea saucer. The lumpy shadows resembled a pile of uneven blankets.

Stana turned on the hall light.

Tea and death and vomit filled the air.

The lumpy blankets were Donna Whitelaw, fish eyes open and blood at the corners of her lips. A stiletto was stuck between her breasts.

We edged closer.

The "blue cashmere killer," if there ever was such a thing, was allegedly Frank Fitzpatrick. In a hateful diatribe he had admitted to killing two young women from Park District School and Susan Gomery. His motive, apparently, vengeance against female sexuality in all its forms and the "fallen world" they create through their lusty, promiscuous temptations.

So how could this be?

Two cashmere killers?

On the table: a teapot, a cast-aside cozy, three lonely sugar cubes, and sparkles of sugar dust that glinted like specks of glass. A spoon sat in the ceramic mug. And a small pond of vomit.

Why was the refrigerator door open? I leaned and looked in. Next to Tupperware containers and a jar of kosher pickles, a blue cashmere sweater.

This whole thing was too orchestrated, overdetermined.

Bad writing.

I closed the refrigerator door.

"You're not going to believe what I found in there—a cashmere sweater."

"Pure workshop gimmickry?"

I think so, I said.

Stana crouched near the body, staring into faraway eyes. "Someone wanted to keep the myth of the blue cashmere killer alive—" She pointed at the stiletto.

"Absolutely." Writers can be a stubborn bunch, I said. "Some hate to revise their damn plot lines."

That cracked her up. "You're terrible," she said.

"Well, someone really wants us to believe in the story they spun."

"Mrs. Whitelaw was a part of that spin—and now—" Stana reached into her handbag, the size of a milk crate, and shook a cigarette from the pack. She lit it. What did Donna know that killed her? "She must have been involved in the first killing." The cigarette dangled from her lower lip.

"I don't know about that." I liked her. In the two times I met with Mrs. Whitelaw one-on-one there was just something so real about her. Honest and vulnerable. A killer. No.

"No, not a killer. But she knew things. And remained silent. An unwilling accessory, silenced by the promise to get to write a couple of the new Serchuk books." Stana blew smoke into a far corner of the kitchen. "Or maybe, she was more directly involved. What if Kittle, after taking Miriam home, planned to return to the writers' retreat and pick up Donna at Tony's? What if he brought Donna to the apartment?"

"No. I don't buy it—not Mrs. Whitelaw, and Kittle had an alibi, the police said."

"We never checked on it and anyone can buy an alibi, if the price is right. Alibi, my ass." Stana took another quick pull off her Parliament.

"Your mother says you should cut back on the smoking now that you're pregnant."

"You and my mother have been trying to get me to quit smoking for five years."

"Ever since you were pregnant with Connie."

"Okay, okay." She butted the cigarette, and turned back to the corpse. "I don't want to be hassled about smoking. You knew when you married me I like a cigarette, now and then."

"I know, I know."

"I'll cut back."

"That's all I'm asking."

She smiled warmly and returned to Mrs. Whitelaw. "I bet she was given secobarbital. Like our first victim, and then stabbed," Stana said.

"No," I said. "This was something stronger."

We heard the medical guys running down the hall, steps thudding closer—

"On the phone she said she was poisoned." I rubbed at the edges of my mouth. "I think she was given something like cyanide—and she didn't expect the person to kill her. She let them in. This is no B and E."

I glanced at the two halves of a plate on the floor, the C-shape handle broken away from its cup. The clean Formica table. She was reaching for something, I said, and that something had been removed from the crime scene. Look at the positioning of the body. I kneeled next to Mrs. Whitelaw, and spoke to her. "What were you reaching for?"

The medical guys entered.

I crouched near Stana and opened Donna's hands. Inside the left palm was a muddy smudge, like traces of wet beach sand.

"What's that?"

"What she was reaching for—" Beige. I recognized it. The damp remains of a tea biscuit.

MRS. HAMPTON OFFERED US COOKIES as soon as we came through her door, but I wasn't hungry and Stana was too mad to eat. Negative energy radiated from my wife's whole body, the freckles on her face vibrating. I took off my porkpie hat and loosened my tie. The warmth in their home was uncomfortable.

It wasn't even winter for chrissakes. I undid the top two buttons of my flannel shirt.

The place smelled of porridge and moth balls.

"Donna Whitelaw is dead," I said. "Murdered. Don Mills. The police are there now." The back of my shoulders hurt. Tension ran through my arms. "They'll be coming here—next."

"Huh?" Professor Hampton turned from the window, his eyes looking through my shoulder, his face full of abstract lines, obscured meanings. "Here?"

"And I don't think it's going to be to have you autograph a few books."

"I—I—" His hands fell to their sides.

"The writing isn't yours, Professor." Stana reached into her purse and pulled out the five-page theme. "C. Thomas Everly gave this to us before he was disemboweled by Frank Fitzpatrick. Frank was J. Douglas's tenth-grade teacher back in 1942, and Dougie wrote this for him—it's Blueline—in miniature." She held it up. It looked like a standard raised in battle.

"Kittle doesn't know about this yet," I said. "But when he does his lawyers will be coming up with some kind of control spin—but this whole Serchuk enterprise is in for a crash landing—from Blueline to bread line."

He shook his head vehemently in the direction of the theme.

"That's just an outline, a scenario," his wife jumped in. "What in Hollywood they call a pitch—that's hardly proof of plagiarism."

"It's actually a treatment, a pitch is something you say aloud," Stana corrected Mrs. Hampton.

The Professor's wife took it with bad grace and huffed in her seat, arms crossed dramatically.

Stana wanted to piss her off. And she did let Mrs. Hampton know we're running the damn show. "I've also read the original copy," Stana said. "The early draft. The prose of the original is too near, too precise, when placed next to your revised prose.

Sure, your revisions are much better, cleaner, more efficient, direct, lyrical. But line-for-line, the words are too alike. You couldn't have lost the original manuscript and then recreated it so perfectly."

"Simply put, we don't believe the *peevish* lover angle." I moved toward the glass case, the bookshelf full of classic books, the porkpie tapping my thighs.

"They *were never* lovers," Mrs. Hampton's eyes narrowed. "That was Kittle's idea." J. Douglas had gone gay for several years, until the "wonders" of shock therapy "cured" him, she said. "Kittle suggested that we tap into that back story, and use it."

"*Peevish*? Really? That word popped up too many times on this caper and it was all of your undoing. Peevish," I said. "Don't you teach in your workshops how to make characters three-dimensional and rounded? Complexities? When all the arrows point in one direction, I get suspicious, Professor. Peevish? It was on your list of 120 adjectives. Susan mentioned it. So did Mrs. Whitelaw. And Kittle, I believe. And the blue-cashmere angle? Another overdetermined detail. Bad plotting. Bad writing."

"Peevish was *never* my idea," Mrs. Hampton said. She sat in the chair across from us and tucked her legs closer, a green plastic plate balancing on her thighs. It was piled with four or five sugar cookies under cellophane with a red bow precariously tipped on top like a fedora's edge. "And it got overplayed—You're right—You're very smart, Mr. Fuller." And the sweater? "An unwanted gift," she said. "Buried in our cedar chest for years."

I wasn't sure which sweater she was talking about: the one in the Valiant or in Mrs. Whitelaw's refrigerator?

"What about all those sweaters Kittle bought?"

"That was to create the fear, the presence, of a serial killer."

"Too much," I said. "No nuance—"

"The police are coming to arrest me—for Doug's death and Donna's?" A thick strand of Chip's slick-backed hair had broken free and fallen down his face.

"Why did you do it, Professor?" Stana leaned in with her shoulders. She wore a black beret, a pleated skirt, and an orange-and-black cardigan sweater, the pattern of which resembled a bunch of flying swallows.

"I didn't kill anyone—I—Tenure. I needed to get tenure." Back then he had a cramped office, but soon he'd have no office and no job. "In the summer of '47 Doug shared his book with me. The writing was very rough. But what a plot. The kid could write a gripping narrative." He invited us to sit down. "It's ironic isn't it? The first story *was* his, but the next three were mine, all mine. It's like I needed that first plot to jumpstart my imagination." His hands fluttered. "I justified it to myself, you know, saying I was Shakespeare, taking someone else's plot and making it more beautiful, which I did. You can't deny that. The irony? He saved *me*. Writing that book gave me the courage to write the next three on my own. It was like a catalyst. *Overtime* and *Five Minutes for Fighting* are all mine. So's *Shot on Goal*. It was like drinking a magic elixir. Right out of a fairytale: the student was the teacher and the teacher was the writer-student. That's called situational irony," he said.

I was thinking of Poe's "The Oval Portrait," and how in order for the artist to live, his muse must die.

"The fifth and sixth books, I wrote," his wife said, finishing a cookie. "More or less."

"That accounts for Kitsey having more of a role and the greater interiority overall," Stana muttered.

"Thanks for noticing." She started a second cookie. "Chip, of course, worked with my work. He revised it, smoothed it out—he's so wonderfully lyrical."

"Yeah, a regular William Wordsworth," I said.

"You sure you don't want a cookie?" She gently set the Saran Wrap and bow aside. "I made them yesterday. They're still fresh."

"No thanks," Stana said. "You're a thief, Professor."

He winced at the words. "Don't say that."

"He's an artist," his wife corrected.

"Your husband's a Hallmark hack, putting greeting card words to other people's narrative pictures," I said.

"That's not fair." The Professor's voice cracked.

"And you're also a murderer. That's why"—I glanced at my Timex—"the police should be here any minute."

"I didn't—" He bit heavily on his pipe. "I told you, I didn't, I didn't."

"The Freedom Writers Society?" Stana asked.

The floor of the room felt as if it were bending toward the sun. It was damn hot in there.

"Greenway was going to use my husband's work, our work, to celebrate Canada," Mrs. Hampton said. Cultural identity. "Susan Gomery threatened to ruin that and she had to—" Suddenly, Mrs. H's accent slipped from its refined origins of privilege into the clipped argot of Cabbagetown and Regent Park, where I grew up. "She was a real bitch." Mrs. Hampton held the green plastic plate tightly, one of the cookies teetering near the edge. "I didn't kill her as you know. Thank god for Mr. Fitzpatrick and his demons. He did what I wanted to do, what I *should have* done."

She took another bite of the cookie. "Yes, my husband stole that boy's blueprint, but he transformed it into something beautiful. That should count for something."

Her husband couldn't look at her; the pipe trembled in his hands. "The child—why did this Mr. Fitzpatrick—"

He hated women, I said.

"Do you know how many men she slept with, and how many different fathers that prospective child had?" Professor Hampton said. "I'm not sure that I was the one—that I was the father—but to murder a child—and if it were mine—"

"You slept with her then?"

"So did Kittle—and Fitzpatrick."

Susan wanted to assure her cut of the profits from the reprinted Serchuk books, Mrs. Hampton said with a dismissive left-handed wave, steering the conversation away from Susan's womb. The North York Board of Education was going to put money in all our pockets. Kittle wanted Doug dead to keep the book project alive and vital. "I wanted him dead too. So, you're right, we, the workshop, concocted a narrative, invented the fella in the blue cashmere sweater, taking a character from Doug's earlier draft, and making him real. Kittle came up with the peevish-lover and me the queer angle." She dusted chips of cookies from her fingers. "Hilary had no idea what we were up to. He went along with the queer-lover angle to protect himself from being suspected of stealing that boy's work."

"Blaming the real victim—" Stana's lips pushed into a thin line.

"Yes." She took another bite of a cookie.

"But why Mrs. Whitelaw, why kill her?" I stared in Mrs. Hampton's direction.

"Kill her, me?"

"Yes, you have a penchant for making cookies, cookies for all kinds of occasions. They're great cookies. I've had some here. Here's how it figures." I planted my feet and took a step in her direction. "You doctored some cookies with secobarbital. Knocked Dougie boy unconscious and then Kittle stabbed him, mortally wounding the fella. Later, like this morning—you went out—" I turned to The Professor. "She went out this morning, didn't she?"

"Marketing," The Professor said. "We needed some milk, and bread."

"Right. Marketing? She went to Don Mills. But instead of secobarbital you gave Mrs. Whitelaw, what, cyanide?"

Mrs. Hampton sat back in her chair. "Yes."

"And tried to make the whole thing look like the blue cashmere killer."

"Sticking a stiletto through someone's chest is a lot harder than writers make it out to be," she bragged. "Took some work—"

The stabbing was postmortem.

The room fell silent.

"I enjoyed killing her." Mrs. Hampton stared at the empty plate. "Donna was getting far too entitled. She was going to write the seventh and eighth book. All because she had a story in *RedBook*. Can you believe that? The seventh and eighth books? Kittle had initially promised those books to me."

"She also has a story coming out in The New Yorker," I said.

"A revise and resubmit. It's not a done deal," she corrected.

"But the child—" Professor Hampton's lower lip quavered. "Why did Fitzpatrick kill an unborn child?"

"You never wanted one with me," Mrs. Hampton said.

"But—"

"So, Professor, you had no idea about these killings?" Stana's words were full of hard rain.

"He didn't. The great writer, oblivious to all around him. Cookies—*my calling card.*"

Her trademark and that's why Mrs. Whitelaw reached for a wet tea biscuit, a kind of cookie, a final clue—

"Finished? Are you finished with your recitation? I admit it all," she said. "And I'm finished here too, done talking."

"I *am* complicit." The Professor was lost in the carpet's wavy weave.

"Now that's what we call understatement." Mrs. Hampton wagged a finger in his direction.

"The police are on their way?" Professor Hampton asked.

"Yeah."

Suddenly, Mrs. Hampton squeezed into a tight knot, her hands tensing, the plastic plate dropping blithely to the floor. Her mouth moved and there was no sound, her lips pinched, and her body was a wringing towel. Slowly her face glazed into a ceramic mask and she curled to the floor.

"She's having a heart attack." Hilary Chip Hampton reached

for the phone and dialed the operator. He talked quickly, a voice spackled with helium.

"It's not a heart attack—" Those cookies, like the ones she gave Mrs. Whitelaw, were laced with cyanide.

And just a few minutes earlier she had tried serving some to Stana and me. Red bow and all.

Mrs. Hampton, now from the floor, focused sharply on us, her heart and lungs failing, a series of theater lights dim-dim-ming.

Cyanide is a long goodbye.

It took her two to five minutes, and she was well aware of the pain.

When she did die, she died before the medics, before the police arrived.

And with her death went her story, the accusations leveled at Kittle, the last standing workshop killer.

But I knew the story. Stana knew the story. And Kittle was about to know it.

HE CONGRATULATED US on figuring it all out, as he licked bits of apple tart shortbread frangipani off his fingers. "As you can see they're still bringing birthday treats to the office. Hate celebrating my birthday." He laughed at his joke, patted his belly. "Come on you two, lighten up." He grinned, a political candidate seeking re-election. "Get a little fun out of life."

Fun? Doug, Susan, Mrs. Whitelaw, Mrs. H. Four on the floor. And now, maybe, Kittle.

He was sitting on a leather couch with pillows the size of a Buick's bumper. On his left was a cabriolet, Babe–Migano style, with a bottle of J & B Scotch. In front of him, a blunt coffee table decked out with fudge, lemon tarts, and a green plate piled with sugar cookies. "Sit down. Sit down. Suicide, huh? Pills?"

"Yeah, you could say that."

"That's too bad—too bad. Nice lady—"

"She's a murderer," Stana said.

"Dropped by this morning. Brought me some cookies." He pointed at the plastic plate. "A little late getting me my birthday treats, but better late than sorry, huh? Love that old broad. Sad to see her check out."

"She named names." I flashed my lopsided grin. "Said you and her knocked off Gomery—secobarbital. You stabbed him with a stiletto."

"Funny what comes from a delusional mind. What comes from a woman planning her September farewell."

"We have her confession," Stana said.

"What have you got, really?" He sat forward. "Her word. My word. Who's the public going to believe?"

"We've also got—"

"You've also got nothing. That's tough. Real tough. But, hey, you figured it all out. You should be proud of that. But there's nothing you can do. You win—I win." He placed a hand to his heart. "Winners everywhere, baby."

We didn't sit.

"My lawyers are with Chip right now. He's distraught, and he'll answer all the questions tomorrow. In the meantime, the doctors have given him a sedative. He'll collect himself, and in the morning he'll realize that all of this can just go away." He waved a hand, fluttered some fingers. "Magic dust. It all can be pinned on a jealous wife. *She* killed Doug. With the help of, get this, Mrs. Whitelaw. Whitelaw needed Doug gone so that she could write books seven and eight, right? If the project goes under, her chance at fame is poof, gone. So the two of them do in Doug. And then, because I agreed to let Mrs. Whitelaw write two of the new forthcoming Serchuk books, *Mrs. H* killed her too," he said. "Just showed up at her apartment. A friend—and stabbed her, huh?"

"Mrs. Whitelaw is no killer," I said.

"It'll play that way." He smiled mischievously. "My lawyers

are a creative bunch."

"What about the guy in the red wig and Walrus mustache and blue cashmere killer?"

"Off the record?" He winked.

We said nothing.

"Either of you wearing a wire?" He held up a hand as if preparing to take an oath. "You have to tell me, otherwise it's entrapment."

"Neither of us is wearing a wire," I said.

"Yeah, I followed her, Miriam, and Susan. Trying to build up a narrative of some crazy fucker out there hunting workshop members. This guy, a fellow queer, killed J. Douglas. A full-blown queen."

"Please don't—it's offensive," Stana said.

"What? I don't care if a guy's a fruit. I got two fruits on my staff—great copy editors."

"And I bet they sing and dance and smile real good too," Stana said.

He pointed at her. "Touché." You got a smart wife here, he said. "Bright, very bright—but don't confuse smart with smart-ass, sweetheart. My lawyers might sue—slander." He chuckled. The fact that Susan Gomery was pregnant with possibly this Frank Fitzpatrick's child didn't help Susan, vis-à-vis Mr. Fitzpatrick, with her long-term life expectancy." He shrugged and smiled sheepishly.

"It's unclear as to whose child she was carrying," Stana said.

"Right, right. But we can keep all that part out of the papers, can't we?" He winked again.

"You got something in your eye? I think Stana has some Visine in her purse."

That cracked him up. "You got great comic timing. Roll over Lenny Bruce and tell Mort Sahl the news."

"*You* killed Douglas. *You* were there when Lady Macbeth killed him. She told us," Stana said.

"Right, right. Hypothetically possible. But where's your witness, witnesses?" He smiled. It wasn't pretty. "This frangipani is delicious. You should try it. Delicious." He scraped shortbread crumbs from his fingers with a quick brush of his hands. "I have people who will vouch for where I was at the time of both deaths." He shrugged. "I can assure you I wasn't there when Whitelaw was killed. I was here, preparing Hampton's communiqué to the media tomorrow. I was on the phone, dictating to my secretary the whole time."

"We have the manuscript," Stana said. "It proves—"

"What does it prove?" He cut her off. "What? Let's just say Hampton wrote all the drafts. J. Douglas stole the first draft from Hampton, and Hampton had an affair with Susan, and she surrendered it back to him. You like that story? I do. It's a good one. Box-office boffo."

"But he didn't write the five-page theme. Dougie Gomery did. 1942."

"Huh?"

"I have it," Stana said. "Dougie handed it C.T. Everly and he handed it to us. The novel's ideas, trajectory, distilled in a five-page theme—" From the depths of her purse, Stana held up Gomery's theme written in 1942—"Titled: 'Boy on the Leaf's Blueline.'"

"Let me see that—" He reached.

Stana pulled it away. "You can see it from a distance—we haven't made a photostat yet."

"What is it, really?"

"I told you," Stana said.

"You told me—give it a rest—it's an outline. What Hollywood calls a treatment. That's all—a summary."

"Look," I said. "Professor Hampton admitted to us that the first draft wasn't his, that the talents of Gomery jump-started Hampton's creativity. If not for Hampton there would be no books, two through six. Gomery was a catalyst."

"Gomery was a jackass who had delusions of grandeur."

"But The Professor admitted—"

"He won't after tonight," Kittle said. "My lawyers will have a prepared statement. Like I said, a good night's sleep will get his mind right." He laughed. "Your victory is a private one. Everything you surmised is highly probable, but that's all I'm willing to say—And the death of Mrs. Hampton will create sympathy around The Professor and boost the sales of his books. Win, win, baby."

"Mrs. Whitelaw was no killer—she was a victim."

"And the victors tell the stories, and in our workshop story Mrs. Whitelaw is the antagonist—You want to take some of this with you? I can't, or I should say, I shouldn't eat all this—"

"The police will be here soon," Stana said.

"I'm always willing to welcome the boys in blue. Always." He gestured with an inviting hand. "You have no witnesses. Bupkis, baby. The coveted manuscript you have? That's a first draft. Written by The Professor—and the five-page theme? Coincidentals. That's all. Coincidentals. Something Fitzpatrick mentioned to The Professor in passing and it triggered The Professor's idea for the novel—"

"Fitzpatrick didn't know The Professor." I rubbed the edges of my mouth.

"We'll find a way to make that possibility inevitable."

"You fucker," I said.

"Like I said before. Lighten up. Canada, overall, is better off," he said. "A hockey series to celebrate the Summit Series."

"Yeah, and how's that working for you, so far?" I asked. The Soviets were up 1–2–1.

"We'll win it. Phil Esposito won't let us lose. Hockey is Canada's game," he said. "Just you wait and see. We'll gel as a team in Moscow." He sipped J&B Scotch. "The time is right for a return to traditional values. The Serchuk stories are morality plays." He laughed at the situational irony.

"You killed Douglas Gomery," Stana said.

"Right. Where's your facts? Mrs. Hampton is dead. Susan is dead. Doug is dead. Mrs. Whitelaw, dead. The Professor will have a new story tomorrow for the press. The jealous-wife angle works for me, jealous that her husband endorsed Mrs. Whitelaw to write books seven and eight, instead of lobbying for her. I was at the party where he toasted Donna. It was right here. The press will eat that up." He winked again. "Jealous wife kills woman who took her place—Christ, I'm glad I live alone—Jealousy's a bitch."

I reached across the table and grabbed some fudge, a butter tart, pushed aside a red bow and nabbed three cookies off a green plate.

"Hey, easy on the cookies—I haven't had any yet."

"You're a real fucking prick."

"Happy birthday to me," he said.

We headed out. He didn't show us the way.

It was cold for September, the wind kicking up, and dust from the street sprayed around us. Across the way ran the back of a scraggly strip of stores in dirty white brick: a donut shop, a One Hour Martinizing, a Chinese food joint. An open dumpster sat crookedly by brown, dead grass.

"God," Stana sighed. "What a douche—" She kicked at the ground, bits of chocolate-bar wrappers and half-pint milk cartons splashed at the edge of the street. "Maybe we can work on The Professor—"

"If we can get close to him—"

We headed toward our car.

"What was with the cookies?"

I stared down at the three of them in my hand. "He's a covetous son of a bitch." I flexed numb fingers and wished I had worn my leather jacket instead of my light windbreaker. I sidearmed the cookies toward the empty dumpster across the way. I watched them arc like wobbly clay pigeons and double thud into the metal box. "You saw the green plate?" I said.

"Yeah," she said. "Red bow."

"You didn't say a thing about it—"

"No—"

I nodded. "Can I buy you a late lunch?'

"Yeah," she said and glanced at her Longines watch. "Missed my deadline—fuck it—"

IN THE EARLY EVENING, before 6:30 p.m, when the police arrived for questioning, Stewart Kittle would disappoint them, because he was dead.

A cyanide goodbye.

He should have let Mrs. Hampton write the seventh and eighth books.

A Hayden Fuller Timeline

July 17, 1935, Hayden Fuller born in Cabbagetown, Toronto, Ontario, Canada.

March 17, 1955, Rocket Richard Riot in Montreal.

1957–58, Hayden's first season with the Toronto Maple Leafs.

April, 1962, wins Stanley Cup with the Leafs over Chicago.

Spring, 1962, begins a relationship with *Toronto Telegram* beat reporter Stana Younger and pursues a hobby in photography.

April, 1962, wins Stanley Cup with the Leafs; scoring the winning overtime goal of game two of the finals.

Spring, 1964, sent to the minors, the Rochester Americans of the AHL, for "moral turpitude."

Spring, 1964, retires from hockey following the end of the AHL season. NHL totals: 458 consecutive games played; 107 goals; 318 points.

Summer, 1964, earns his PI license after taking courses at York University, Toronto.

January, 1965, Sarah Kerr murdered (this was Fuller's first case).

April, 1965, events of *Cheap Amusements* take place. The novel introduces a recurring set of characters: gangster Babe Migano, reporter Stana Younger, and Toronto's Top Cop and personal friend, Sal Lambertino.

July, 1965, events of *A Fourth Face* take place. The novel introduces more supporting characters to Hayden's universe: his therapist, Dr. Jeannette Cohen, and the RCMP's head of counter-terrorism, Anne Chevalier.

Summer, 1965, Hayden, reinstated in the NHL, with the help of Anne Chevalier, following the events of *A Fourth Face.*

November 7–8, 1965, Hayden's father Ira is murdered.

November 11–15, 1965, the events of *Neon Kiss* take place.

November 11, 1965, Remembrance Day, Hayden returns to Maple Leaf Gardens, wearing Montreal Canadiens colors and is named the game's third star.

February, 1966, the events of *Day of the Dragons* take place in Bannerville, Ontario, Pop 1201, a small town some 85 miles northeast of Toronto.

February, 1966, Hayden contemplates retiring from hockey for the second time.

May, 1966, the events of "Shot, Reverse Shot" take place. Hayden lives on St Urbain-Street, Montreal.

May 5, 1966, Hayden wins the Stanley Cup with Montreal, figuring prominently in the last three games of the series.

May 6, 1966, Hayden retires from the NHL for the second and final time, and returns to his Bloor-Yonge PI office in Toronto.

June 6, 1966, Hayden and Stana get married at a small ceremony in Toronto. Sal Lambertino is the best man. Jean Béliveau and Frank Mahovlich are in attendance.

Late September, 1966, the events of "The Gray Hearse" (published in *Mag Pie* magazine #19) take place. Sal Lambertino figures prominently. Stana announces she's pregnant.

December, 1966, with celebration for Expo '67 in the works, the events of "Four on the Floor" (published in *Groovy Gumshoes*, 2022 edition) take place.

April 15, 1967, Connie Fuller, daughter of Stana Younger and Hayden Fuller, is born.

September, 1970, the events of "The Final Portrait" (published in *Twelve Winters Journal*) take place. Kim Stabulus and Athol Leighton return in an art gallery / murder mystery story. Hayden kills Leighton.

September 2–9, 1972, the events of *A Shoeshine Kill* take place. Sal Lambertino and his wife Miriam figure in the plot. Action is set around the first four games of the 1972 Canada–Russia Summit Series.

The novella *Day of the Dragons* and the story "Shot, Reverse Shot" are available in the Hayden Fuller collection *Five Hard Bites*, from Twelve Winters.

Four Eddie Sands Stories

This Place Called Winsome
A Cap for Tom
A Stretch of Ground
Artifacts

This Town Called Winsome

–1–

usan Norget was quiet, lost in shadows.

I was worried about her.

She arrived by train from Niagara Falls wearing a wool coat with an imitation fur collar, ankle-high boots, and a modest gray dress with a sash stretched across her body that read, "We're *United* Postal Workers." She had been at a convention there to strengthen their union or something. She worked the desk at the Winsome PO.

"See the Falls?"

Seen them before, many times, no need, she said, her lips pinching with the dips of winged lines of street lights. Her glasses were small-framed and her blonde hair swept like a scarf to the right. "I just went to meetings and in my free time stayed in the hotel—ordered room service." My cab filled with the tincture of whiskey.

I smiled my smudge of a grin. "You okay?"

"I will be—" Her voice was parchment thin. "Do I know you?"

There was a touch of push back to her tone so I shrugged with a hand. "Eddie Sands—you probably heard about me, I'm the guy who had his picture in the paper for rescuing Irene Sizemore from an ice house—" Vic, her abusive husband, had kidnapped and planned to kill her and frame me for the murder. With flares and a .45, I killed him, and two accomplices.

"Yeah, I read about that—who didn't in a small city like this?"

Winsome's pop is 58,000.

"Did you love her?"

"Irene? Yeah—"

"I remember where I saw you." She snapped her fingers and the sash trembled. "You bought Girl Scout cookies from my daughters, twelve and ten, a few weeks ago, when you drove them to the Bijou to see a Tommy Kirk double feature." A smile was in her words. "Saturday is their movie afternoon." She looked down at her hands. "Live action Disney is awful."

"Yeah, a four year old with Crayolas could write a better script."

"*Writers*—" Her husband Harlan was publisher of *The Advocate*, a small twelve-page paper that came out on Tuesdays and Fridays, she said. It started off as a bi-monthly advertising supplement and then Harlan got the bright idea to get into the business, creating a radical alternative to the mainstream press. With his best friend, Lonergan Bauer, Editor-in-Chief, they tackled the tough questions: Reparations for the American Indian; the Negro Question and Real, *Economic* Integration; and What's Wrong with Falling in Line with the Domino Theory? "The Advocate Club—that was their little group of intellectuals." She made a face, her words drifting away, eyes clouded with amber, focused on some horizon that only she could see. "I was also seeing a man at the convention, not my husband, and we're not on the same page—newspaper people." Them and their spouses, she shook her head—artists, professionals, housewives—pushing boundaries, experimenting with drugs and questioning monogamy and—"The ice house rescue—You're a good man."

Moments later we pulled up at the Daws Motel. Susan didn't have a suitcase or an overnight bag. She tossed a twenty on my front seat.

"I can't break that." My first four calls had cleaned out my cash reserves. Everyone was tossing me twenties tonight.

"Keep it," she said. The drift of an inward gaze darkened her eyes. "I don't need it."

–2–

After changing a couple of twenties at a corner gas station and filling up my thermos with coffee, two quick calls followed: a liquored-up fella wanted KFC and a carton of cigarettes before returning to his trailer-court home; a young woman in fishnet stockings, a plaid skirt, and buzzed platinum hair, was headed to a Labor Day party, "Labor Day Observed." She laughed. College kid.

My clientele, the six-to-six graveyard shift, consisted largely of alcoholics (so-so tippers); strippers (decent tippers so long as you flirted with them); and college kids (the absolute worst tippers in Winsome).

I couldn't stop thinking about Susan Norget. *Keep it. I don't need it.*

SHE WAS AN X ON THE BED, breaths broken and barely there.

I had knocked and knocked and knocked and then kicked in the door like a TV cop. My foot hurt like fuck.

On the floor, an empty bottle of Jack and sleeping pills.

I called the front desk, "get an ambulance, pronto," and then poured coffee from the thermos's plastic cup into her. She coughed and gagged and coughed. "Wake up, wake the fuck up." She slumped against me.

I slapped her four or five times.

Her eyes fluttered, fallen mascara lines now resembled black icicles.

Somehow I got her into the shower. Cold water thudded and I worked her mouth and throat. My fingers must have tasted like gasoline, coffee, and potato chips to her.

Quickly there followed the thick smell of stomach acid. "Eddie?"

"What you do a silly thing like this for—?"

"I am a silly thing," she said.

-3-

The next day I visited Susan at the hospital. Her story wasn't in *The Advocate* but it was second-page news in the *Winsome Mercury*. She had a private room and smiled gently in my direction, veils of hope crowding at the corners of her eyes. She wasn't wearing glasses and I wondered how well she could see me.

She motioned me to sit next to her in a white wooden chair with blue padding.

We talked, for I don't know, forty or fifty-five minutes: movies, books, and how funny *Get Smart* was. It was her daughters' favorite show too.

They and their father had dropped by several times leaving pastel drawings and bright yellow flowers in a vase on the table. Susan's friend Donna, a painter and the wife of *The Advocate's* Editor-in-Chief, brought in an oil painting to cheer her up. It filled the space above a sink.

Donna's painting featured a peasant woman nursing a baby in the middle of a recently plowed field. The sun wobbled in the sky like a communion wafer. The ochre-hued dirt was so real that I could almost smell the turning of the earth.

"My husband's a good man, too—Lots of men are good to me. Some better than others—" Susan stared at the painting. "My origins were anything but idyllic—" She grew up in Winsome's east end, a tough, tough neighborhood, with bald lawns, short gravel driveways, and discarded auto parts in front yards.

I didn't plan to have an affair, she said, but I did, and I loved him, like you loved Irene. "I really loved him." It started at an Advocate Club get-together, a goofy game of naked Twister. Donna was there. So, too, Donna's husband, Lonergan. Harlan wasn't. He was working late on the paper. After Twister the conversation turned to Victorian morality, Alfred E. Kinsey, and the women put their house keys in a hat and whatever key the fella picked—well—"Why do they call it wife swapping. It's so patriarchal."

I tented my fingers together. "Your husband doesn't know, does he?"

"No—Why not husband swapping? Anyway. I really don't like the painting," she said. "Too much wholeness and holiness and self-sacrifice. The sun, the sky, should be flames on fire."

"Take it down, if you don't like it."

"I can't. Donna painted it."

"Take it down."

"Cordell Skinner, that bastard, is blackmailing me." Skinner owned a chain of coffee shops throughout upstate New York. "He hired a detective to follow me and take pictures of me and my lover, together in restaurants, parks, in bed—several photos." She gave Skinner hush jewelry, all her savings to keep quiet, but now he was threatening to tell her husband and take the evidence to the *Mercury* unless Harlan delivers a lot of cash.

"What does the Mercury care? Affairs—" I rubbed at the edges of my mouth.

Her husband is a radical publisher of a rival paper, she said. "His politics are left of left, and it's all about advertising dollars. Shrinking the pie. He rounds up a lot of advertising for *The Advocate*. They'll want to destroy him, to get those dollars back, and close his newspaper down." She positioned a pillow behind her back and sat more upright. "The photographs—" Skinner got in good with Harlan because he bought up chunks of advertising in the paper for his coffee shops. From there, he got himself invited to our club's activities. "It was all a clever sabotage plot."

"Don't worry. I'll deal with Cordell."

I offered her a cigarette.

"This is a no smoking area," she said.

I lit it for her.

She inhaled and exhaled slowly.

"My dad was a cop, a crooked cop in Philly. I never really knew him," I said. "After his death in 1934, my mom moved us to Iowa where a series of 'uncles' beat me regularly, one even broke my left arm—" I reached for her cigarette, took a drag, handed it back—"No one's going to hurt you."

–4–

It wasn't until Saturday that I met up with Cordell Skinner. He lived up in Parkhill, a rich exurb with brick streets and turn of the century hexagonal lamp light. His home resembled a castle, loudly distanced from the Victorian homes that filled the block. Instead of square lines and stacked boxes, his home had a giant turret, a wide curve of a front porch, and an equally wide archway.

He was slunk back in a chair, a bruised plum rising under his left eye.

I have an unconventional way of knocking.

"You sonofabitch." He readjusted his red kimono, tightening the sash. A dragon, precariously perched and ready to spring, filled his chest.

"Lay off Susan Norget. You talk to her husband, I'll finish what I started."

"It's not her husband I'm after, it's the paper."

"So I hear."

His eyes glazed over with a lazy days gaze.

His living room was crowded with Eisenhower–era furniture: a low-slung coffee table; black Hi-Fi unit with silver speakers; Eames chairs; and floor-to-ceiling lamps with five different colored cones of light. On the bookshelf: wood sculptures by Jose P. Alcantara.

I get the dope on his wife, a rival paper uses it, destroys the publisher's credibility, he said. "His competitors want all of the advertising dollars." He smiled. It was dirty. "And I hear the Advocate Club is into some kinky shit."

I pulled him and his smug smile up out of his leather upholstered chair and tossed him sideways like he were an army duffle bag landing on a bottom bunk. I saw action in Korea, 1952–53. Pork Chop Hill. Radio operator.

He slammed against a coffee table.

A Howard Miller clock followed him down.

California lilacs, a heady smell, like boiling honey, filled the air. It wasn't spring time. "You got a girl in here?"

"I'm generally working on something."

The door across from us, nearest the kitchen, was locked. "He's not worth it, sweetheart. He'll take everything you own." I turned to Skinner. "You threaten Norget or talk to her husband, you'll be done talking, pal—"

"Is that a threat—?"

"Yes."

He shook his head. "I take what I want."

"That's for sure," said the female voice on the other side of the door.

–5–

Within hours, Cordell Skinner was dead.

The *Mercury* splashed his death in lurid headlines in Sunday's dailies. Skinner was found in his upholstered chair by a business associate, late Saturday. Two in the chest. Two in the groin. .38 shells scattered throughout the room. "This kill was real personal," the Chief of Police said. "Real personal." One article made a passing reference to *The Advocate* and strange goings on in an exclusive club that Skinner was a fringe member of and that his death might be related to an affair he allegedly had with the spouse of a prominent person on the *Advocate*'s editorial staff.

Cordell? I thought he was blackmailing Susan, not sleeping with her. This is who she loved?

There was no mention of yours truly in the stories, but the police had questioned me for two hours that morning. They knew I had rescued Susan from a suicide attempt and that I had visited her several times at the hospital.

They also knew I rescued Irene from her kidnapper husband. Killed the son of a bitch. And they connected the loose dots, as police will.

What they didn't know? I had tossed Skinner about like a duffle bag. Threatened him. And there was a girl behind the door.

But if they found her, what might she say?

HUNGOVER AND MY MOUTH full of dust that just wouldn't go away, I visited Susan after my run-in with the gendarmes at the cop shop. Pain pounded behind my eyes. I dry swallowed two Anacin.

It wasn't me, Susan, I said.

She was glad Cordell was dead. Blackmailers. And she hadn't slept with him, ever. "My husband has an alibi. He was with his kids. A show at the Bijou. Some Disney shit."

I sat in the chair next to her. "What happened to your hair—they do that?"

Gone was the soft swoop of a scarf. In its place: a jagged pixie cut.

"No, no I did." She smiled a lopsided grin. "I cut it myself. I know, I know, don't say it—it shows—" She laughed. "The cops have been asking you questions—?"

"Yeah." I tapped my fingers together and absently shrugged. "They haven't connected me with Skinner *yet*—I like your hair."

"Liar." She squeezed my arm.

I don't know why, but at that moment, I think I fell in love with her. I know it's weird, but I'm an impulsive fella. I wanted to kiss her—

"That's not all I did—" She nodded in the direction of the

wall above the sink.

The painting was gone.

"Good for you," I said.

Suddenly a woman appeared at the threshold of the door. She wore a dress the color of autumn leaves, with purple paisley patterns floating around like so many amoeba. Pushed back on her fine dark hair was a Robin Hood hat.

Donna Bauer.

"So, you're the gall–ant fella who rescued our Susan—from her excesses." Her accent was slightly put on, a nod back to 1940s Mid-Atlantic with clipped words and em-dashes of Shakespeare.

They talked for twenty or so minutes about Harlan, how he still loves Susan, and Donna suggested several splendid ways, darling, to win back his trust. Feign interest in the paper—contribute to an article on postal rights and women workers.

"I don't need ink on my hands to prove I love my husband," she said.

"He knows about the affair, darling,—the cryptic hints in the *Mercury*." In a seam to her Robin Hood hat was a silver brooch that sparkled with chips of diamond: a dragonfly.

Susan shook her head sadly and eventually grew tired and dozed off.

Donna and I headed to a vending machine for coffee.

After you left, Skinner told Harlan, she said, called him—on the phone. Gave him the damn photos. For a price.

"*After I left*—so, it was you behind the door—"

"Relax, handsome. I said nada to the cops."

"You killed Cordell—"

"Oh, bless your heart. Don't be a chump."

"Where are you from, really? That accent is all Bette Davis or William F. Buckley in drag—*bless your heart*." I put some apple pan dowdy into the last three words.

She said nothing. "People with Southern accents aren't seen as credible." She worked years at losing it.

"Uh-huh." I directed her to a round table and four chairs. "The dragonfly. Cordell was into Oriental kitsch. *He* gave that to you."

"He did."

"He blackmailed your friend."

She collapsed into one of the chairs. "I loved him. Don't ask me why, but I did. Have you ever loved someone so much that you forgive them their faults?"

Irene Sizemore. But killing her husband killed us.

"So you and Cordell?"

"Yes."

"And Susan?"

Donna sat up, wiped the edges of her eyes and took a long slow drink of coffee. "I carried on with Cordell. Susan carried on with my husband—"

–6–

"You killed the wrong man."

Harlan Norget flinched and his upper lip curled back slightly. He was middle-aged, wore Lombardi glasses, and what hair he had was a laurel cluster, tight Brillo curls running barely above the collar line of his freshly pressed shirt. The bright light of his home office shone a spit mark atop his head.

Beyond the closed mahogany door, in the living room, his two girls were playing RISK. Every now and then one of their voices rose to protest a move, a decision to conquer a continent.

Skinner was getting dope on your wife to use against you and your paper—advertising dollars—but Susan didn't sleep with him, I said.

"Look, I don't know what you're talking—"

"Let's not play this game. Your alibi doesn't wash, Harlan. When you drive a cab you get to know a lot of stories, you get to know a lot of people. Believe me. Mary Swann works the ticket window at the Bijou on Saturdays. I drive her to Bingo, Tuesday nights." I shook free a cigarette from my pack of Luckies. "She says the girls went to the show—alone—arrived in a taxi—alone. Cops can check that. We hackies log all our calls." I shrugged. Lit my Lucky. "But the cops won't check as long as I keep my yap shut."

He shifted uneasily in his chair, reached for a cigar, left hand tapping a sloppy rhythm on his desk blotter. His bookshelves were full of best sellers and picture frames of commemorative postage stamps. He *did* love her. "What do you want?"

"I'm not putting the squeeze on you, I'm doing this for her."

"You love her too, don't you?"

"Forgiveness—a chance for a new beginning—"

"Huh?"

"Forget what she did, and I'll forget what you did."

"I'm not following, not completely."

"You killed Skinner. He was blackmailing your wife. You thought he was sleeping with her. He wasn't. It was Lonergan. Only, Susan didn't tell you it was Lonergan, because she loves you and values the friendship you two men have."

He nodded, said it was possible, probably true. He couldn't see the man's face in any of the photos.

The room shrank in the silence that followed.

"I never thanked you for saving my wife's life."

I smudged an eyelash of tobacco off my tongue. "Forget about it." Forgiveness for you and Susan, that's what I want. "That's my price—"

Somebody beyond the mahogany door had just conquered another continent.

Harlan quit rolling the cigar between thumb and finger, dropping it on the blotter, unlit.

I couldn't place Donna's role in all this. How could she stand idly by while Cordell blackmailed her best friend? Did she secretly resent Susan for messing around with Lonergan and wanted to see her punished?

Sweat dotted Harlan's upper lip. "What about you? How will you fix things if the police—make you—a person of interest?"

I took a quick drag, sharply exhaled. "I'll get by. I always have. Susan tried to kill herself because she loves you, and hurt you. Go see her."

He said he would.

On the way out I waved at the girls and said they were playing a French game invented by Albert Lamorisse, a film director over there. "'The Red Balloon?'"

The girls looked at each other, and then me, sideways smiles.

The things you pick up driving a hack in a small town like this, this town called Winsome.

A Cap for Tom

Nurses and interns rushed Tom Reynolds down the hall, one of the gurney's wheels sticking, stuttering.

Everything was a blur of white: tiles, walls, track lights.

A knife was in Tom's leg

I brought him here in my cab, shouting, "Apply pressure, dammit, apply pressure—"

Now I lit a Lucky, ambled to the lobby. The Po-lice wanted a word.

OFFICER MOONEY, a young fella with a jarhead cut and a scalp line dusted with copper filings, asked me to repeat the story three times.

Mooney, three hours ago I picked up a different Tom. I knew his name because it was embroidered on his filling station shirt. He'd been drinking, his jittery hands tracing rapid half-circles above my heating vents. From his wallet he read an address off a ribbon of paper. Take me there, he said.

Daws Motel, on the other side of Winsome. He sat forward in the front seat. I usually don't let folks sit there but he was six-five, six-six, and said there wasn't enough leg room in back. Late autumn wind whipped candy wrappers along the roadside. The closer we edged to the motel, the more desolate the area became: no sidewalks, no trees.

Within minutes we were there, and he hopped from my hack while it was rolling to a stop. He hugged the gym bag as if it were a small bomb. I wondered if I should reach for my .45 in the glove box.

A lanky guy in black plaid stood in the arc of the motel room's dim backlighting. His right eyebrow arched higher than his left as the dramatic monologue before him tumbled.

Tom's feet were planted to the front patio as if it were flypaper, his free hand drawing louder and louder half-circles.

A woman's voice, from beyond the door, climbed above Tom's words.

Penciled streaks of frozen rain fell.

Tom returned, shoulders stained with scales of thin ice, and stretched in the front seat. "Wrong guy—" He laughed. It was full of sad resignation. Drive around, he said. "Wrong guy, wrong guy."

I shrugged vaguely, lit a Lucky, and shook one free for him. "Around it is."

We wandered downtown side streets for forty minutes or so, fishing lines of rain glittering. He gave me an address to an all-night laundromat.

And that's the story, Mooney.

"Hmm—"

"The odd part—"

Mooney's eyes narrowed, face tightening with command presence. "Yeah?"

"The guy in plaid, at the motel, the fella who answered the door? He's the second Tom, the one I later drove to the hospital with a knife in his leg—"

SO WHAT DID I not tell Officer Mooney?

Me and the first Tom didn't drive for forty minutes before hitting a laundromat. More like ten. I pulled over near a deserted phone booth that shook in the shimmer of a street light.

The sidestreets were now painted black. I hoped plows were salting the roads.

"You served, didn't you?" He held the gym bag to his chest.

"Yeah. Korea. Pork Chop Hill." Occasionally, I still slept with a gun under my pillow.

"Christ, that was a meat grinder."

"You?"

"Big Red One. WWII. North Africa. Czechoslovakia. Italy. Liberated Jews from Faulkaneau." When he came home he sat on his mother's porch for days clutching his carbine, catching the bend of the evening sun. "You got someone, somebody?"

"No," I said.

"You like being alone?"

"No."

He nodded. He knew the Susan Norget story. The paper loved to cover my "exploits." Two months ago, I rescued her from a suicide attempt, the Daws Motel. She checked in without a bag and gave me too big of a tip to warrant the three-and-a-half-dollar call.

He rubbed at the scraped spaces around his mouth. I figured the fella must shave 3-4 times a day—there were no traces of licorice stubble. "You like her?"

"Susan? Yeah, yeah I do—" But she's married.

"You like me?"

There was so much desperation behind the question that I wasn't quite sure how to take it. "I don't know—you seem like a nice fella."

Tom's wife Emily was the supportive type—a school teacher, third grade. "Anyway, she read all that Jack in *McCall's*. You know, about helping veterans feel at home?" His right hand circling was now drawing a series of small stones. "You feel at home?"

"Sometimes—"

His lips were a broken line, sticking to parts of his teeth. I wondered if he were getting help from the VA.

"Help?"

Shit, that shut him down.

I offered to buy him dinner at Gus's.

"No-no. Thanks. I just got laundry I want to do—that's all."

"Laundry? There can't be much in that bag."

"There's enough," he said.

AN HOUR AFTER LEAVING the other Tom at the hospital, I had a run of calls. The bars had just closed. The last of those calls was Janice Pilgrim, a regular fixture of Winsome's nightlife. Her serrated laughter could be heard a block away, and she painted every side comment with lipstick traces.

She wasn't laughing now.

She had fallen asleep in my hack, the red tip of her cigarette burning a hole.

Her house, along the river, was surrounded by short trees with stubby branches. The house was small, blue, wood-framed, with white trim and a shallow gravel driveway. The front lawn was bald with dust. Through curtains of cold rain, a single streetlight cast silky shadows of marionette strings.

I lugged her sideways from the cab, leaned her standing by the screen door, while I knocked.

A ten-, eleven-year-old skinny kid with wide set eyes and short hair sighed. I couldn't tell if they were a boy or a girl but the sigh revealed a rinse and repeat cycle: this scene with Mom had played out before.

They guided their mother to the couch, covered with magazines, a crumpled-up Aztec blanket, and a bowl of soggy cereal.

We cleared a space, laid Mom down, and covered her to the chin with the blanket.

"You going to be okay?"

The kid grinned and nodded grimly. "How much does she owe you?"

On the coffee table: a row of pop bottles marked by bits of dead leaves that resembled dried specks of black flies.

Breakfast.

Many a night, following a long shift, I returned to the cab stand only to see them, kids in the light of early morning, walking with their empties to get deposit money and maybe a candy bar. "Don't worry about it—I'll square with her later."

They nodded.

I pulled a crumpled one from my jacket. "That's for you." I smiled my smudge of a grin. "Get yourself something."

The kid looked at their bare feet, ashamed.

That wasn't my intent.

I FINISHED FILLING OUT my call sheet, cleared, and listened to everyone on their car radios gabbing over the stabbing. Emily Logan was in police custody. Her husband Tom wasn't the assailant. Tom Logan didn't stab Tom Reynolds. Emily Logan did, trying to break up a fight between her husband and lover.

"Who did the knife belong to?" I wondered, was it in Tom Logan's bag the whole time we talked alongside a phone booth.

Nobody knew who the knife belonged to.

And why would Tom Logan say Tom Reynolds was the wrong guy when Reynolds was sleeping with his wife? Helluva way for Emily to break up a fight, stabbing her lover.

I had planned on doubling back to the hospital, but now that I knew Emily Logan, and not Tom Logan, had stabbed Reynolds I saw no need. I no longer worried about what Tom Logan might do to his wife's lover. I worried what Tom Logan might do to Tom Logan.

I DROVE AIMLESSLY for another hour or so when the call came, Shell Station on Roosevelt behind the Armory. Tom was working late. Spray job. Just walk in and get him, I was told.

It didn't make sense. You don't do a spray job in the morning, following a hard rain when the sky's wet.

It took five minutes. The Shell station still echoed its Art Deco origins with its strong curves and heavy lines of chrome. Inside, the station's white light burned brightly, and the thick smell of paint filled the spaces between me and the car inspection pits.

The tips of my ears and chest burned. I lit a Lucky to calm myself.

A Buick 55 sat in the light's glare, gleaming a metallic blue. Sprawled on a wooden work bench was a spray gun and cans of motor oil and wrenches. On the end of the work bench was a pile of neatly folded clothes: trousers, dress shirt, underwear, socks.

Dangling down one of the grease pits was Tom Logan. His neck twisted up in coiled wires. He had rigged himself to an engine hoist at the edge of the pit and then stepped off.

His hands were cuffed in front of him and he wore a white bathing cap and a woman's one piece black-and-white swimsuit. He was a big man and the fabric struggled to contain him.

Under the empty gym bag, I found a note: "Emily, I'm the wrong guy for you. Nature let us down."

I jumped into the grease pit.

He swayed gently.

Wrong guy. Earlier that night Logan wasn't talking about Reynolds, he was talking about himself: *the wrong guy.* I finished my cigarette.

Briefly I thought of unstrapping Tom from this grisly gizmo and dressing him back in his trousers and dress shirt, returning him to mid-1960s "respectability," but there was something to this art tableau, something he wanted to say. And I guess, he trusted me to find him, and make sure that he had his say.

Eventually, I called the police, but not right away. Instead, I sat with Tom for thirty or forty minutes, sat in the pockets of quiet, and from deep in the hole I saw the morning sky turn from a pastel orange to a cornflower blue, and the city's street lights silently shutting off.

A Stretch of Ground

–1–

He was a thin scarf bending with the lines of snow.

The call came twenty minutes ago, north, twelve miles from Winsome, on one of them numbered county roads, 215. His red windbreaker had a stuck zipper so he held it closed with a gloveless hand. Why he didn't wait in the small house on the hill, I don't know.

He crumpled into my hack, words clouded with liquor. He pointed at his car, a Ford Falcon pressed into a large oak tree. The headlights and grill were now a lopsided grin. Take me to the Daws Motel, he said, words crashing hiccups.

He was on the run from Mike Dietrichson, owner of Winsome Pontiac Buick on Franklin. I bowled against his team now and then, Wednesdays, Mohawk Lanes. Mike hated to lose. He had big hunching shoulders, a hard stomach, and heavy hands. He always talked trash, badgering us to pick up 7-10 splits.

My fare rubbed at the cold spots on his face with shaky fingers. A white beaded wristband puffed against the fleshy part of his hand. The band was full of letters—some I could make out: ANA.

"How much have you been drinking, cowboy?"

"Drinking?" His eyes darkened. "I don't drink—" He introduced himself.

Jimmy Feddersen? A week or so ago, his face was under the yellow glare of WKLL's news cameras. He had found $2300 in a black doctor's bag near a storm drain on Water Street.

Word had it the money was dividends from a high-stakes poker game Dietrichson ran above the Armory. Nelson Griggs of Young and Beggert Realty was there. Winsome's Chief of Police was there too.

The black bag should have carried $12,300, he admitted. That meant ten large was unaccounted for.

Two hours ago Dietrichson grew tired of Jimmy's good Samaritan bit. Two of his boys rousted Feddersen from Regehr's and brought him to the dealership. In a back room, they worked him over with sawed-off baseball bats. "Where's the rest of the money, thief," they asked between full-barreled swats.

"Did you take it?" I asked.

He looked away. Two bandits in Mardi-Gras masks had broken in on the poker game and hijacked the winnings. Jimmy—narrow shoulders, small hands—fit the bill. The other bandit was a woman.

His hiccups returned. "I don't know how I got away—" He coughed. "I needed the money," he mumbled, something about a stretch of ground.

He had a family forty-five minutes east of here that he wanted to give back to. He was working at the Sizemore pulp and paper mill but the returns were slim, slow. He needed a bigger stake. He missed his girls, six and ten. Maybe I could drive him there?

We never made it.

Jimmy's hiccuping slid into wobbly laughter and then burbles of blood.

He crumpled against the dash—dead.

There was no money in his pockets.

–2–

Some fucker was tap-tapping my face like a drummer riding his hi-hat too damn long—

They sat at the couch's edge, guns on their thighs. The room was full of cigarettes and coffee. "Wake up, soldier." The older fella's face barely moved, lower lip loose. He must have had some form of palsy.

Thin sands of light filtered through my trailer's musty windows.

I'd seen these guys before, Mohawk Lanes, Wednesday Night Bowling, Dietrichson's posse. The one with the drooping lip was Kyle Kangas. His eyebrows were a heavy zipper and his pockmarked face looked like a dry lung. Terry Jack Kotter was in his early twenties, with gray eyes the color of rain and the fragile skin of a Hummel. He sported a bolo tie, cowboy hat, with an Aztec band. Several razor nicks dotted his chin. A spot of Kleenex was stuck to one of them. "Where's the money, soldier?"

The tap became a stinging slap. "Ten G's—"

Under my pillow was my Army-issued .45. I had slept with it since the Ice House incident several months back. Keep talking assholes.

"Jimmy didn't leave it with you before he, uh, checked out, did he?"

"He barely said anything—you guys gave him a real working over—"

"So, he did talk?"

"Nothing about money—"

Another short lash—my head exploded with scorpions.

They had searched Jimmy's apartment—nothing. Talked to the girl in the farmhouse—Ellana. Another fat nothing.

One of the poker night robbers was a woman, Kangas reminded me. And Jimmy's car crashed into a tree by Ellana's pad. "Coincidence?" He shrugged with sulky languor.

She said she'd never seen him before, Terry Jack added, the gun raised like a semaphore flag. "But we didn't believe her. Worked her over a little—" There were some shadows in his smile.

The beaded wristband. ANA. Ellana. "You give her the Louisville Slugger treatment too?"

"My technique is varied." Kyle rubbed his chin. "Relax, soldier. She's still alive."

"The soldier bit. You overuse it," I said.

Bronze Star, Korea. Greased a few Red Chinese, huh? He smirked. You were a real bad-ass.

"I was a radio operator—"

Truth be told, I had killed more since coming back. Three in an ice house rescue a few months ago on the Mohawk reservation. That "operation" put me in the hospital for four weeks—flashbacks, nervous breakdown. "What did you do to Ellana?"

"Relax—" Terry Jack straightened the shoestrings on his bolo so that the aiguillettes lined up. He gently tapped them together.

Kangas's lips barely parted. "Maybe it's all like she says. Just a coincidence."

"Right." Terry Jack laughed, air slipping slowly from a slashed tire. The sand in the room grew thicker. "Dietrichson wants the money."

"I'm telling you, I know nothing about the money, Jimmy said dick about the money," I lied.

The gun under my pillow was too far away. *Keep talking—*

"Our boss hates to lose," Kangas said. "You hear anything, you see anything, money-wise, you let us know? Dig?"

"The guy was a real loser," Kotter said. "And the boss hates losing to losers."

"I only met Jimmy yesterday—"

"That's enough time to learn a dying loser's secrets—you don't want to be a loser too, do you?"

My mouth was full of bile. "If I find the money, you'll leave the girl alone—"

They looked at each other. "Maybe—"

"Yeah—maybe," Kangas winked. "Life's full of uncertainties, motherfucker."

They laughed.

Then Terry Jack handed me a wad of Kleenex. "Now, clean up your face—"

-3-

"They cut off two of my fingers," Ellana said.

Her left hand was wrapped in a bandage the size of a cave man's club. Spots of blood showed through the mummified gauze.

We were in back at Regehr's, red-lined booth, yellow Formica table. We were drinking orange egg creams from glasses with more curved rings than the Michelin Man.

She sipped and swallowed two painkillers. "I think I've passed my limit on these but it hurts like a motherfucker." She grimaced. "What the hell do you want? The goddamn money?"

"I want to help you—"

"You work for them?"

"Fuck no."

She smiled, suddenly recognizing me. You're the fella who punched-out that schoolteacher for sleeping with his daughter. And you rescued Irene Sizemore from her sadistic husband and his ice house of horrors. Killed three, she said.

"Yeah." I rubbed at the edges of my mouth. *Funny how it works: after bringing Irene and her son safely back home the alleged charges against me for supertuning fellas who supertuned women suddenly disappeared.* Cabbie turned hero. My war record helped. Two Bronze Stars. And the four-week stay in the hospital generated quite a bit of sympathy. "Tell me about Feddersen—"

She flicked curled ends of blonde hair away from her black eyes. Look, she said, me and Jimmy did the robbery—but you already knew that. I wasn't going to tell those bastards—she looked at her club for a hand. "He needed the money for a stake for his family. A stretch of ground, he called it. A farm or some damn dream. Me, I just wanted money. Nothing noble." She shrugged effortlessly and sipped more egg cream.

Ellana was a waitress at Gus's Diner and was tired of a life clearing tables and plates dotted with cigarettes buried in mashed potatoes. And there she heard talk of a poker game, Thursdays above the Armory. "So we got a couple of Mardi Gras masks—"

"Was Jimmy in love with you?" I told her about the wristband.

"Yes." They had a thing. "Like you and Irene had."

"Yeah—" *Killing her husband who had been plotting to kill her kind of ended our thing.*

Jimmy's wife and kids live above a grocery store, a short hour from here, Bingston, she said. Jimmy came here to make more money to buy his own place— "He wrote letters home every day." She reached into her bag. "I haven't had a chance to get a stamp for this but—it's to his wife—"

It lay on the table between us as her voice sank down a well. I noted the address.

"Why the whole black bag ruse?"

She popped a third painkiller. The bottle now had a very thin rattle. She shrugged at it vaguely. If Jimmy "found" some money it might divert suspicion from us, from me. "That was the thinking—Jimmy was worried for me—"

"But $2300 ain't going to placate Mike. He wants it all—all back."

She nodded and played with the charm of a dolphin on her necklace. "Yes. The cheap S.O.B. I'd wait on him at Gus's. Seven per cent tip he left, like paying a goddamn sales tax. Seven per cent."

I shook out my pack of Luckies, offered her one, lit it for her.

"I'm not giving that bastard back my share of the money." They each pocketed five.

"Jimmy send his share to the wife?"

She puffed quickly. "Yeah—I think so." Another puff. Her words were muddy.

"You should slow down on those pain meds."

"Who asked you?"

I leaned back, took a long slow pull, my eyes narrowing. "I'm offering you the same protection I offered Irene—"

It had been just over a year since the ice-house incident, and three months since the Salinger Files, a caper involving a manuscript written by that *Catcher in the Rye* fella that was stolen from Polis College on the hill. A librarian, a college prof, and a student from the rich exurbs, Colin K. Hoops, were involved in the shenanigans that devolved into sexual assault, kidnapping, and killing. The librarian was dead, the prof dismissed by the Board of Regents and sent to prison, and the student, the rapist? Well, he walked free of all charges because his family could afford the best lawyers. That is, he walked, until he met up with me in a ski mask late one night under the shadows of the campanile and I broke his legs.

"I won't let Dietrichson or his boys hurt you anymore."

She smiled dimly, and then popped the last painkiller in the bottle.

–4–

I don't know why it hadn't occurred to me before, but when it did, I called in sick and drove east to Bingston and the address on the letter Ellana had yet to post.

It was a small town of about 3500 with a motel, a bar, hardware store, and four-corner gas station. The mom and pop grocery was right next to a Rexall. I drove down Main Street and on over to an excluded spot on Taft and Third. Lit a Lucky. The sun was high and bright and the street was empty.

If I had a horse I'd be looking for a goddamn hitching post.

I tugged at the back of my leather jacket, covering up the .45 in the waistband of my khakis.

Jimmy's wife was behind the grocery counter. She had a plain face, chestnut hair, and tortoise-shell glasses with wide frames that showed off her blue eyes.

I grabbed a box of popcorn with an elephant on it and a bottle of Pepsi. "Rebekah?"

She nodded. The smell of bubblegum and detergent filled the spaces between us.

I was the cabbie who was with your husband when he died, I said, and regardless of the bogus police story that it was a mix of alcohol and the crackup that led to the brain trauma that killed him, I told her that was all bullshit. He had been beaten to death by Dietrichson's boys, only he didn't know he was dead yet until he was in my hack. I lied a little and said his last words were about her, and the girls.

She smiled awkwardly. "You don't have to say that for me." Her teeth were narrow and her chin dipped as she spoke. "Jimmy was drifting away from me, from us—"

The tops of several cans along the shelves were flecked with fly matter. Beyond her swayed a frayed curtain. Behind it, cinder block walls, a cot, and a hot plate.

I took a short drag of what was left of my cigarette and offered her one. She didn't smoke. She used to, but Jimmy quit so she did too.

"He was sending you money, right?"

"Yes—"

"To buy a stretch of ground—"

"Yes—"

"Did he ever send a large lump sum, like 5 K? I'm not with Diestrichson or the cops. But, a couple of beefy guys are going to come this way—if I figured it out, they will—and—they cut off some fingers of a friend of mine."

She shuddered and glanced down at the cash register and rang up no sale. From under the drawer she pulled out a short letter. "This arrived last week—"

It was a long goodbye from Jimmy:

"Dearest Becca. I don't know how to begin and this isn't what I want to tell you but I must. I'm in love with someone else. I love you too, and I think maybe a person can love two people, at the same time, but I'm afraid I love Ellana more, and I, I, want you to have this money, $3,000, to have a new start for you and the two girls. I remember so many great things about life with you, and I'll always remember those great things, but—things change, I don't know why. Maybe it's part of God's plan. I don't know. I still love you, but, like I said, I love Ellana more. Money has no conscience. I took it for you. Please put it toward something good. Sorry I lost my way. Sorry I lost you. Hug the girls for me. Love, Jimmy."

The letter shook in my hands. The money was severance pay. *Three K? That meant he held back 2 large ones for himself, his own nest egg.*

With Jimmy dead, Rebekah was re-thinking the dream of a farm, and instead wanted to move west to Winsome or North to Watertown. The suburbs. But she couldn't just up and leave, she said, the kids liked it here. They had friends.

Sure. You got friends, family in the Midwest? Those guys will be coming, they're killers, I muttered. Let me stay in the back room. I'll camp out there. Soup, sandwiches, I'll get by—

She showed me to the room.

I smoked a half a pack of cigarettes, the .45 on my thigh.

The Pepsi had turned warm.

–5–

On the third day, they arrived in Sloan Wilson grays, flipping over the open sign on the door to "Sorry, we're closed." They wore gloves. Terry Jack still sported the black cowboy hat with the Aztec band. It was parked in a jaunty manner on the squared-off shelf of his head.

All the light in the room dimmed, disappearing behind the heavy shadows of their thick shoulders.

"Cold day, huh? Much business?" Kyle smiled faintly, his eyes elsewhere, hands in the pockets of his camel-hair coat.

They spoke barbed-wire fences of menace, commenting on what nice girls Rebekah had, and wasn't that them, playing in the backyard, making a snowman? "It's getting kind of dark." Terry Jack glanced over his shoulder into the thin night.

Kyle picked at a tooth with the corner of a matchbook he'd grabbed off the counter. "Shouldn't they be inside? Safe?"

Rebekah gasped.

Hate to see something happen to them, one of the two said.

"Guess, you can't keep an eye on them girls, because your man's gone, huh?" Kyle closed the matchbook, his face an even dryer lung than it was a few days back. "Give us the money—"

"The money he sent home," Terry Jack said.

"To you."

"Five large."

"It wasn't five, it was three, assholes—" I mumbled loudly.

Terry Jack reached inside his pockets and pulled out a .45, but before he could do anything with it, my gun was barking as I stepped through the part in the curtains. I put two in his chest. His hands folded in front of him and he fell to his knees, vague half-words tumbling from crimped lips.

"Sands—!" Kyle's coat was buttoned too tightly and he never did get his gun free. I took off half his head and he tumbled back, thudding hard on the store's gray-green linoleum, brains and bone, a scraped streak stretching like long fingers.

Terry Jack swayed, and then a big blood bubble burst between his lips and he fell forward.

Rebekah shook against my shoulders, and then asked for a cigarette.

THE STATIES HELD ME for close to three hours. But Rebekah vouched for me, saying I was a friend of the family, had come to visit, had come to give my condolences over Jimmy's tragic death. These two men, whom she had never seen before, came into the grocery store and held her up. "Pulled guns and everything. Threatened my girls." Thank god, Mr. Sands was here, she said. Did you know he was a hero? Two Bronze Stars in Korea? Why these other men would want to rob such a place, she had no idea. "I guess some people think there's a lot of money in groceries. Maybe there used to be, but there ain't no more."

ONCE I GOT HOME I called Mike Dietrichson, told him he'd have to get some new boys, his two had said their long goodbyes. Becca has the money. Consider it payment for the murder of her husband. You do anything to her, or Ellana, I'll kill you.

Sinatra played in the background and Mike didn't say much. "You're a real red-ass, aren't ya?"

"You could say that."

"I understand, you left my name out of it—"

"I did."

"Okay. Okay. Case closed." I could feel him smiling through the phone. "You ever grow tired driving a hack, give me a call—"

THE NEXT NIGHT was bowling night. Dietrichson had a couple of newbies on his team and they couldn't bowl worth a damn. He gave them as hard a time as he gave us, but he was a good sport about it all. Between bawling them out and talking smack to my team, Mike bought us all several rounds of beer. He even tipped the waitress twenty bucks.

Artifacts

I was held by those watchful eyes.

Tall prairie grass, scratchy streaks, heavy brush lines. Mohawk people moving, one of them peering through a sea of yellow gray.

I turned from the painting, wiped at the edges of my mouth, my .45 heavy in my hand. On a black Chippendale chair sat Cheryl Strangeways, lower lip curled under, dented with teeth marks. Her eyes were murky. Cigarette burns dotted her left arm.

"Who did this to you? The fellas from the motel?" A camera on a tripod was to my right. Other paintings, along with Colt Peacemakers, Buffalo pelts, Winchesters, dreamcatchers, and bows and arrows filled the walls.

The eyeliner around Cheryl's lost highway glare was squeezed into bleeding stars and she was reaching for flashing specks that only she could see. "Moth light, moth light," she murmured.

Dangling from her ears, feathered earrings.

She wore nothing else.

Neither did the dead fella sprawled on a white shag rug, bled pink, in front of her: Milton K. Krasner, philanthropist, lawyer, collector of American Indian art. He smelled sour and if I didn't know any better I'd have sworn that fungus was growing beneath him. A tomahawk splintered his face, the right eye wandering from the orbital bone.

Little shadows, pushed by the light behind the fire grate, left a row of small crosses across Krasner's corpse.

Cheryl snatched grimly at the ethereal moths, while I dropped my gun in the pocket of my leather jacket. The camera back was flipped open. The film, gone.

Cheryl had no answers to my questions—her voice, a distant, Morse code bleat.

I stared once again at the brave behind prairie grass, asking him what to do.

He heard every breath I sighed.

IT ALL STARTED about three hours ago on the worst night of the week to be driving hack—Tuesday. A lot of hackies take Tuesdays off—but I needed the money to pay my rent. The landlord had raised the rates out at Cherokee Village where I live in a trailer home.

I had just finished dropping a fare at the Empress Hotel and was filling out my call sheet, watching snow fall in thin fishing lines, when Donna Dodginghorse hopped in, gripped the top, open buttons of her red mackinaw, and shouted, "Follow that car, Eddie—"

Donna recognized me. Winsome's one of those small-town cities, 58,000 people. And if you get your name in the paper and your pan on local television people remember you and your notoriety.

I knew of her too and her rep: a social worker and therapist for the Mohawk people out on the rez, she fought the Winsome City Council to get the necessary funding to build their community center. A recovering alcoholic, Donna ran AA meetings and encouraged youngsters to follow their interests—art, writing, basketball. Say *yes* to something and *no* to alcohol. I liked her.

Anyway, she wanted me to track a '64 or '65 Catalina with a busted taillight and a smear of mud obscuring part of the license plate. Cheryl—nineteen, manic depressive, two years out of reform school, and Donna's sponsoree in the program—was in the car. "She's trying to get the paintings back—"

"Huh?"

Donna's eyes narrowed and she warmed her hands over the heating vents on the dashboard. "She has a gun—she plans to kill him."

"Slow down—kill who? What paintings?"

"Can you pick up the speed of this crate?"

Donna had high cheekbones and dusky pecan skin. Her black hair was pulled back in a ponytail. She was pretty.

"And do what exactly?" *My army-issued .45 was in the glove-box.*

"I don't know, but the paintings belong to us—and you, you're always there—for women." She smiled and recited my rap sheet: how I rescued Rebekah Feddersen and her young daughters from two hit men, shooting them dead in Bingston, upstate New York; and how I saved Irene Sizemore, a past lover of mine, from an ice house where her husband Vic planned to kill her and frame me for it—

Claude Harrison, the artist, had gotten into trouble with the IRS, she said. "He hadn't paid his taxes in years, because, well, he didn't want his money to support the white war machine, muscle for the Fortune 500 club." Claude could get up to seven years in prison and he just couldn't do the time. "Years ago he was driving a delivery truck along back roads slicked over with mud and he slid into the river, almost drowned. Claustrophobia."

I understood that kind of shit. I still slept with a gun under my pillow—the painful fallout from Pork Chop Hill in Korea, and a fucked-up family history, beatings at the hands of a series of men Mother called my uncles. One of them broke my nose; another, my left arm. I always felt trapped. Still do. Maybe that's why I'd taken to helping, hitting back.

Harrison hired the best lawyer in town, Krasner. "Only Claude couldn't pay Krasner or Krasner didn't want Claude's money. Krasner wanted them paintings, the ones Harrison was gifting to the Community Center."

"Of course that's what Krasner wanted." I knew Krasner. A

covetous son of a bitch. He always wanted *more*. He could be found late Saturday nights, in a back booth at Gus's Diner, a hand on some Indian girl's upper thigh, murmuring nasty, intimate things for all to hear.

The Catalina barreled along the brick streets of Parkhill, a rich exurb with hexagonal street lamps and two one-way streets divided by a median you ought to be putting golf balls on. Behind and below the rich neighborhood was a reserve, a hiking trail, full of birch trees, deer, and the occasional black bear.

"You can imagine what people said. The white community called Harrison an Indian Giver. His own people called him a traitor." She paused, bit her upper lip. "They found him face down in a mud puddle. They called it suicide, said he was drunk, but he was in AA with me—was six months sober."

"So what happened? He was murdered?"

She shrugged. "He's an Indian. The police found what they expected to find—Damn, that car's moving—"

She was right: sixty in a thirty. "Why didn't Harrison just paint other paintings for the Community Center or Krasner?"

"You make it sound so easy." She shook her head gently, chin barely moving. "Those paintings represented his life's work—some took up to twenty-five years to get right."

Suddenly a pop pop, like Black Cat firecrackers, and the Catalina swerving randomly before bumping its driver's side wheel against the edge of a curb. The car launched, three, four feet in the air, turned sideways, then righted itself, the front end lifting before dropping and hitting the ground first, wheels busting, the front axle snapping and bits of chrome and glass filling the night with metal fireflies. The car pushed up divots of grass, before stopping short of a buzz of hedges.

The two of them scrambled from the crumpled car. He hit her with the .32 in his left hand. She dropped to her knees, blood dripping from her open mouth like small coins.

Cheryl. I'd seen her before. At Gus's. Back booth, Krasner mut-

tering, "you're the best piece of ass I've ever had."

I reached for the .45 in my glovebox and shouted at him to drop the fucking gun, now.

The .32 fell by his Italian shoes.

Just then the porch light of the high square box of a Victorian home lit up the yard and several people, a family and their guests, filled the spaces around us.

"Look at my car—" Krasner screamed. "Goddamn it. Look at it—"

Donna called for Cheryl, desperately searching all around. In the commotion of gunplay, and the harsh glow of the porch lights, Cheryl had run down the hill behind the home, losing herself in the dotted dominoes of birch trees.

THE COPS ARRIVED within seconds.

That's what they do for the rich.

I smoked three or four Luckies while Officer Mooney, a red head with a marine cut, chastised me for playing cowboy. He also gave Donna a hard time. A social worker, you know better. "Why didn't you call us, instead of sending a cab on a wild goose chase."

"Because I was there." I smiled, my lopsided grin. Donna knew exactly what I meant: you cops wouldn't have been there in seconds, not for her, not for a case involving people from the rez.

Afterward, I drove Donna back to the rez's Community Center. She wanted to walk and think. Her gray eyes held a generous light. "That cop was an asshole."

"Yeah."

"Thanks, for trying."

"Yeah—"

The silt lines of snow were now falling like a beaded curtain. Donna wasn't wearing a knit cap and I wanted to offer her mine, the one in the glovebox near my gun, but I was afraid of appearing patronizing or some damn thing.

She reached for the door handle. "What do I owe you for all your time? I know you shut off the meter—"

"Make it five."

"That doesn't seem fair—"

"Tuesdays are slow. Real slow."

Donna handed me a Lincoln and two ones, and climbed out, buttoning up her mackinaw. All of the homes around the Center were small boxes with tar paper roofs. Smoke from their chimneys filled the black sky with spots of bleach.

"You want to get a coffee or something?" I don't know why I said it, but I just did.

"I don't drink coffee—"

"Oh—"

"How about egg creams at Regehr's?"

"Sure. I'd like that," I said. "Orange?"

"Orange." She smiled. "You can reach me at the Center."

THE NEXT NINETY MINUTES were interminable: long silences between rinky-dink two-dollar fares. I had some French fries from Gus's all-night diner, a maple donut, and a pint of milk. I ate in my cab and watched the snow gently falling. I was next up on the board, and I couldn't afford to miss a call.

Maybe I drove Claude Harrison at one time or another. I couldn't really place him. I read about his death in the *Winsome Mercury*, but—

Compositional tension. This one fella went on and on about it in my hack. It was like last summer, maybe two summers ago, and he wore a Woody Guthrie T-shirt and faded jeans.

"People to the left or right of the frame, none of that classic Renaissance T shit. And the horizon line, high or low. Never in the middle."

He smoked skinny black cigars and had me drive him to the IGA for tomato juice, dry mustard, worcestershire sauce, and cayenne pepper. "Part of the cure." He laughed. I didn't get it.

Maybe, now, I *did* get it: that concoction was an alcohol substitute, maybe that *was* Claude Harrison.

I don't know.

AFTER DRIVING A YOUNG WOMAN back to Polis College from a Bible study group, I got a request call. Daws motel, a white cinder block affair with black shutters.

It was well past midnight. Two guys were waiting for me, outside room seven. They spoke Spanish and talked about Krasner having a pilot's license. There were all kinds of rumors that the lawyer flew drugs back and forth to Mexico. Between the burly fellas, held by the elbows, was Cheryl. She wore a short sky blue jacket and a coral-colored knit cap.

The jacket was unzipped. Underneath she wore a white diaphanous blouse, veiny, like the wings of a dragonfly.

They crowded in back.

The fellas had cameras around their necks and the one wearing a navy peacoat with army tiger-stripe pants carried a tripod.

They wanted to go to Krasner's. I recognized the Parkhill address.

I turned around in my seat and made direct contact with Cheryl's green eyes. They weren't murky then. "Do you want to go there?"

"It's my idea—"

The fella, who didn't know which branch of the service he favored, said that wasn't exactly true.

"The boss wants to see her and the boss gets what the boss wants."

Seems the gunshots and totaled Catalina were all forgiven.

"Milton promised me one of the paintings if—" Cheryl's voice vaguely wandered away.

WHEN YOU DRIVE A CAB for fifteen years you sure hear a lot of stories, gossip, bits of trivia, and hard-edged opinions. A few years back, a fella from the rez was in my hack, his black-brown eyes blurred by alcohol. "You know I read somewhere that so many white folks think they're one-eighth Cherokee. It's a joke, innit? You all have no idea what it means to be me. Shut the fuck up."

The man had a point.

I WAITED AND WAITED and waited. Twenty minutes. My deck of Luckies was down to two smokes.

The meter ticked.

Five, ten, fifteen minutes.

A bright splash of light. Another splash.

A bare hip, a breast, pressed into the lattice design of the shimmering window. Cheryl looked bored as Krasner kissed her.

A third splash. It was like walking on the face of the sun.

Five more minutes. I smoked my last Lucky. And then a scream. The girl—I grabbed my .45 and ran toward the columns, the door.

That's when I found Krasner spread across a white shag rug, a tomahawk splitting his face.

The back door was open, the screen flap-flapping.

The men were gone. Cheryl was on some kind of psychedelic elixir, the moths getting bigger and bigger—there was a spot of one on her left hand that she just couldn't remove the wings from.

Artifacts were everywhere: display cases full of arrowheads, tin stars from Arizona marshals, Colt Peacemakers, and large rocks with single dimples—probably milling stones; walls darkened by tomahawks, Winchester 73's, pelts, and dream catchers; and those paintings, Harrison's, mixed in with a batch of Frederic Remingtons.

And that young brave in that yellow-gray sea of grass implor-

ing me—

I moved closer, drawn in by his look and the shadows of little crosses from the fire filling the grass with the hard skull lines of Calvary.

In the corner, a small tight scrawl: Claude Strangeways. His artist's name: Strangeways, not Harrison.

Strangeways. Claude and Cheryl were related, maybe father and daughter. "No wonder you want the paintings," I muttered in her direction. "No wonder."

She clutched another moth and smothered it in her tight fist.

Last March, *The Train* with Burt Lancaster played at Winsome's Bijou Theatre. It centered around a group of resistance fighters whose mission was to seize a Nazi train full of French paintings the Nazi's had stolen. At the time, I thought the whole preserving culture angle was nuts. All those men dying for some goddamn paintings.

But now—

I removed all of Strangeways's works from their frames and gently rolled them up. The works of Remingtron I cut in two with a buck knife and threw on the fire. Chunky flames scratched and clawed, filling the air not with the paints' oils but the heavy smell of the canvases, and every now and then as each painting curled, nearing its end, a sharp afterglow fissured.

That was something. It warmed me, it felt good.

MINUTES LATER WE WERE out at the Community Center. Cheryl was conked in the backseat. She fought me when I tried to put her clothes back on, so I wrapped her in a thick tribal blanket that had been hanging on a bedroom wall. Eddie Sands, fashion consultant.

I felt shaky, cold. I turned on the high beams. Hammered the horn.

Again, again, again.

Eventually people came. I mean it was nearly two, two-thirty in the morning, but they came, skin glowing with waxy snow and yellow moonlight. There. I saw Donna in her red mackinaw and teachers, maybe, tribal leaders, husbands, wives, mothers.

I wished Claude Harrison could have seen all this. What his alter-ego Claude Strangeways might have painted in that moment: his people and me outside my cab, coming up for air, snow softly falling into the collar of my leather jacket, and his paintings rolled in my hand, a gift returned in the spirit of reconciliation for the living and the dead and all the ancestors yet to come.

About the Author

GRANT TRACEY is the author of the Hayden Fuller Mystery series, as well as many other crime noir and literary stories. He teaches film and creative writing at University of Northern Iowa and is a long-serving editor of *North American Review*. His previous Hayden Fuller novels are *Cheap Amusements*, *A Fourth Face*, and *Neon Kiss*, which are available as stand-alone books and in the collection *Five Hard Bites* along with the novella *Day of the Dragons* and the short story "Shot, Reverse Shot."

Grant's detective fiction has also been published in *Freedom Fiction Journal*, *Femmes Fatale Flashes*, *Groovy Gumshoes*, *Merry Creepsmas* (the Green Book), *The Museum of Americana: A Literary Review*, *Tough*, *Mag Pie* magazine, *Twelve Winters Journal*, and *Bang!: An Anthology of Modern Noir Fiction*. The chapbook *Winsome/Bend of the Sun* was published by Final Thursday Press. Moreover, Twelve Winters brought out *Final Stanzas*, a collection of literary short stories; and *Toronto, 1965: Cheap Amusements' Beat*, a memoir. He co-hosts the podcast *A Lesson before Writing* with Brady Harrison and Ted Morrissey.

In addition to writing, teaching and editing, Grant is active in community theater as both an actor and director. In 2025, he wrote and directed his first feature-length film, *By the Stars of Saint Matthew*. Having grown up in Toronto, Grant is an avid Maple Leafs fan.

Visit twelvewinters.com/Grant_Tracey for further information and links to Grant's work.